Alan Joh~~nso~~ ...~~oy~~ was published in 201~~5~~. ~~It~~ won the ~~Royal~~ Society of Literature Ondaatje Prize, and the Orwell Prize, Britain's top ~~p~~olitical writing award. His second volume of memoirs, *Please Mr Postman* (2014) won the National Book Club ~~a~~ward for Best Biography. The final book in his memoir ~~t~~rilogy, *The Long And Winding Road* (2016), won the ~~P~~arliamentary Book Award for Best Memoir.

Alan was a Labour MP for 20 years before retiring ahead of the 2017 general election. He served in five cabinet positions in the governments of Tony Blair and Gordon Brown including Education Secretary, Health Secretary and Home Secretary. He and his wife Carolyn live in East Yorkshire.

Praise for *The Late Train to Gipsy Hill*

'Fascinating and ingenious'
Melvyn Bragg

'A smart, captivating, modern but timeless thriller'
John Marrs

'Featuring espionage, the Russian Mafia and a gorgeous female on a train with a deadly secret, the tantalising plot has set Alan up for dominance of the bestseller charts for years to come'
Fiona Phillips

ALAN JOHNSON

THE LATE TRAIN TO GIPSY HILL

WILDFIRE

First published in 2021 by
WILDFIRE
an imprint of HEADLINE PUBLISHING GROUP

First published in paperback in 2022 by
WILDFIRE
an imprint of HEADLINE PUBLISHING GROUP

1

Cataloguing in Publication Data is available from the British Library

ISBN 978 1 4722 8614 7

Typeset in Sabon LT Pro by EM&EN
Printed and bound in Great Britain by Clays Ltd, Elcograf S.p.A.

Headline's policy is to use papers that are natural, renewable and recyclable
products and made from wood grown in well-managed forests and other
controlled sources. The logging and manufacturing processes are expected
to conform to the environmental regulations of the country of origin.

HEADLINE PUBLISHING GROUP
An Hachette UK Company
Carmelite House
50 Victoria Embankment
London EC4Y 0DZ

www.headline.co.uk
www.hachette.co.uk

To Peter Carlen,

a fabulous teacher who inspired me

to want to be a writer.

PRINCIPAL CHARACTERS

THE RUSSIANS

Denis Smolnikov – *film maker, friend of the President with close links to the Russian criminal network Krovnyye Bratya*

Igor Golovin – *human rights activist exiled in London*

Sergei Dzyuba – *dissident journalist exiled in Amsterdam*

Stanislav Miranchuk – *former KGB/FSB agent now active in Krovnyye Bratya*

Ivan Ilkun – *head of FSB in London*

Anton Sidrenko – *leader of Krovnyye Bratya*

Vladimir Granat – *property tycoon and senior figure in Krovnyye Bratya*

Dimitry Podkolzin – *former military, now Krovnyye Bratya's head of security*

Maria Paseka – *Anton Sidrenko's wife*

Andrey Morozov – *Krovnyye Bratya 'heavy'*

THE UKRAINIANS

Arina Kaplan – *waitress at the Strand Hotel*

Viktor Rubchenko – *Arina's friend*

Principal Characters

HOUSEMATES AT 27 MOUNT STREET
Gary Nelson
Jason Cowan-French
Melissa Thomas
Knuckles

POLICE OFFICERS
Detective Superintendent Louise Mangan
The Commissioner (unnamed)
Deputy Commissioner Karen Dale
Assistant Commissioner Brian Baker
Assistant Detective Superintendent Connor O'Farrell
Detective Constables Geoff Tonkin and Rashil Din
      (a.k.a. Torvill and Dean)

ALSO
Rachel Nelson – *Gary's mum*
Tobias Parnaby – *the dentist Rachel works for*
Duncan McDonald – *Gary's friend*
Marilyn Kelsey – *Gary's boss*
Jamil – *Gary's workmate*
Terry – *Gary's elderly neighbour*

1

Friday, 10 July

There is a cat in the Strand Hotel that is said to be fifty years old. It arrived in the Swinging Sixties when the hotel was at the epicentre of London's cultural renaissance, and was named Oskar after its German owner who managed the hotel at the time.

Rarely have the myths about the Strand matched reality but there is usually a sliver of accuracy. For instance, the Beatles are supposed to have stayed there in the 1960s whereas the truth is that Brian Epstein spent one night at the hotel in 1961, not long after he'd met the band and well before they were famous.

It is similarly claimed that Terence Stamp once had a suite of rooms where he'd partied with Julie Christie and Alan Bates. In fact, one of the cameramen working on the movie *Far From the Madding Crowd* had a room for a week during a break from filming in 1966.

As for Oskar, far from being fifty years old, he is simply the latest in a long line of hotel cats with identical colouring – pure white with a splash of tortoiseshell on head and back. Since that first cat arrived in the sixties, successive Oskars have sat sphinx-like in the hotel foyer or wandered through the bar, restaurant and reception rooms bearing witness to the comings and goings at this busy auberge.

The elegant, sixty-bedroom hotel in Pimlico trades upon this harmless folklore, even displaying a photograph of the feline methuselah in a brochure that repeats the inaccuracies that add such charm to its impeccable reputation.

But on Friday, 10 July 2015, murder would be committed at the Strand Hotel. For once, what would undoubtedly become part of the myth would be a reality, with the cat a passive observer.

On that fateful morning, Oskar wandered into one of the smaller reception rooms on the first floor which Denis Smolnikov, a Russian visitor who had long frequented the Strand, had booked for an hour from 11 a.m.

Mr Smolnikov, a barrel-chested man with a deep voice and imposing presence, was a famous producer of documentaries and claimed to have been commissioned by CNN to make a film about the suppression of political opposition in Russia. He was there to meet Igor Golovin, the well-known human rights activist who had been exiled in London ever since attracting the enmity of the Russian President a decade ago. The slight, cerebral Mr Golovin arrived at 10.45, bending down to stroke Oskar before vigorously shaking hands with his host.

Two other Russians arrived at the same time as Mr Smolnikov. The journalist Sergei Dzyuba had flown in from Amsterdam where he'd lived in exile since writing an article exposing the extent of Russian criminal activity in London. Known to both Golovin and Smolnikov, Dzyuba was principally responsible for brokering the meeting. His long, greasy hair fell almost to his shoulders and from beneath its dishevelled fringe his tired hazel eyes gazed around the room suspiciously. The other Russian was Stanislav Miranchuk, the film-maker's assistant. He wore black horn-rimmed glasses, had a small blue tattoo under his ear lobe and carried with him a discernible air of menace. This quartet chatted amicably, quaffing tea and scoffing pastries as they discussed the important issues of liberty and free speech that the documentary was going to explore.

Oskar sat under the trestle table, from where a young waitress was dispensing refreshments. She was a strikingly attractive girl with long, ash blonde locks bunched into a hairnet in accordance with the hotel's rules on hygiene. This accentuated her perfectly round grey eyes and high, pronounced cheekbones. Her accent suggested that she was possibly Russian, certainly Eastern European.

Oskar watched as Denis Smolnikov gave the waitress precise instructions as to how and when to serve the next round of hot drinks: which cups of tea or coffee were to be placed where. Indeed, Mr Smolnikov had spent so much time at the trestle table that an observer such as Oskar could be forgiven for thinking that he was one of the hotel staff.

The men were left in peace to conduct their business for half an hour until a commotion erupted. Several revellers decked in the colours of CSKA Moscow, the Russian football champions who were playing a friendly match at Chelsea that evening, burst into the room chanting their allegiance. They'd clearly started on the vodka early. Some carried open bottles of the stuff and were liberally pouring measures into the tea and coffee of their new-found friends. But Oskar noticed the bottles of water that they all seemed to have jammed into the back pockets of their jeans.

The men at the table raised their cups in salutation and there was laughter and good-natured banter as the football fans weaved around the reception room.

Oskar barely blinked. He saw a bearded man in the distinctive blazer of a Strand Hotel manager enter the room and leave again silently a few minutes later without appearing to have spoken to anybody. Smolnikov's assistant, Miranchuk, followed him out.

Oskar observed Denis Smolnikov giving the waitress final instructions, ensuring that she knew which cup of coffee to place before Igor Golovin, before being drawn into the melee caused by the chanting football fans. Smolnikov was a Director of CSKA Moscow and was due to attend the match that evening.

Oskar, watching carefully, was almost sure that the flustered waitress had put the cup meant for Golovin in Smolnikov's place.

It would take Denis Smolnikov six days to die from the 30.5 micrograms of polonium-210 he consumed at the Strand Hotel that morning.

2

Gary Nelson lay awake contemplating his uneventful life. He'd passed the point where sleep usually prevailed and begun his futile night-time pursuit of reflection. The streets of Crystal Palace had settled into silence as he stared at the ceiling, following the shapes projected by the headlights of an occasional passing car.

Gary was twenty-three and the most adventurous thing he'd ever done was leave the dull provinciality of Aylesbury and the council house he'd shared with his mother to strike out alone towards excitement and opportunity in the big city. That was three years ago and all that had materialised was monotony.

He understood his personal deficiencies all too well, but on restless nights like this he couldn't help analysing them. He was tall, but an inch or two shorter than he'd like to be; slim, but a few pounds heavier than he should be. His dark curly hair was okay (apart from having been cut too short by the Turkish barbers up on Westow Hill) and his round face with its green eyes and aquiline nose was pleasant enough for him to be described as 'good-looking'.

But it was character that troubled Gary more than looks. He considered himself to be a reasonable specimen of the human race; compassionate and even-tempered but with something missing. Something indefinable that he nevertheless sought to define in his sleepless introspection. There was a meekness, a propensity to always concede the point. Often described as being good-natured, he yearned to be bad-natured – just for a change. He'd never had much of an idea what he wanted to do with his life, only that he wanted to live it with gusto. The best way he could describe it to himself was that he wanted a big life and the one he was leading now, even after making the move to London, seemed very small.

As for his love life, it mainly consisted of a series of one-night stands; of first dates that rarely led to a second. Gary was a romantic without a romance; an adventurer more reticent than intrepid where women were concerned; a buccaneer who'd yet to find his way to the sea.

He shared this house at 27 Mount Street with three others. Jason Cowan-French was the eldest and the only one over thirty. He had the kind of self-confidence that always disconcerted Gary whenever he encountered it. Jason had apparently once served in the armed forces, but now worked in the City, earning more than enough, his housemates assumed, to live on his own in one of those soulless luxury apartments around Canary Wharf rather than share a house in this unfashionable part of south London beyond the reach of the underground.

Knuckles was the newest housemate. He'd signed all the paperwork as 'Mr I. Murray' but announced, 'They call me Knuckles' upon arrival, with no further elaboration. A stick-thin Ulsterman from Belfast, he was around the same age as Gary but with his prematurely thinning hair and the wire-framed glasses he wore, looked much older. Knuckles was currently working as a runner for a media company and described himself as an apprentice TV star.

Melissa Thomas was the youngest housemate. Blonde, petite and barely twenty-one, she'd come to London from South Wales and worked in advertising. Mel (as she liked to be called) read constantly, loved music and seemed unaware of Gary's silent admiration.

The four of them shared a house built when Joseph Paxton's magnificent glass construction was first attracting people and prosperity to what had until then been known as Penge Common. But now, like most of the elegant buildings in Crystal Palace, it had been divided into flats, although 27 Mount Street, unusually, had a large communal living room and kitchen. Jason, Knuckles and Melissa had rooms below this central feature, whilst Gary had to climb a narrow staircase to the room he was in now. It wasn't the best in the house, but it was the biggest and being high up suited him. He'd always been fascinated by the stars and was willing to sacrifice comfort to be closer to them.

Having lain awake since 11.30, Gary had already gone over every detail of the Tuesday evening he'd just spent with two of his housemates that had contributed to his restless mood. They'd devised the ritual of a once-a-week gathering to discuss domestic issues in reasonably pleasant surroundings. The original idea (Jason's) was that they'd go to a different pub every week, but for months now they had used the same one – the Dog and Pheasant on the corner of Anerley Road, where the beer was better than average and Knuckles could get the pickled eggs that he had a strange (and, to the others, incomprehensible) yearning for.

It was rare for all four of them to be present at these Tuesday gatherings, but Jason had drawn up a list of Standing Orders that included the requirement for any two housemates to attend for the meeting to be quorate. This week only Knuckles was absent, working late on a show called *Celebrity Stitch-Up* in which (he'd told his housemates) stars demonstrated their sewing and crocheting skills, competing for the title Knit of the Year.

Jason and Melissa were already settled in the saloon bar when Gary arrived, delayed by a faulty train outside Balham. He worked in the Accounts Payable department of a national newspaper. The office was in Covent Garden and Gary had to endure the misfortune of Southern Rail on a daily basis, whereas Melissa and Jason were both fortunate enough to travel to and from work in the City on the more modern and reliable London Overground.

Gary had applied for his job while still living at home in Aylesbury and always meant to get something else once he'd arrived but, with typical inertia, never had. That evening he'd felt the familiar pang of inferiority tinged with jealousy as he walked into the pub to find Jason and Melissa giggling together. He was peeved by the secret joke that they made no attempt to share. Then, as Gary settled opposite them with his pint of Fosters, Jason announced that the meeting had concluded.

'One decision has been made, which is that we install a sink tidy purchased from communal funds.'

'Two questions,' said Gary after taking his first gulp of lager. 'One, what the hell is a sink tidy, and two, which communal funds would those be?'

Jason explained how triangular plastic 'tidies' were once a feature of every respectable sink in the land and were essential for good hygiene and the future of the planet.

'As for communal funds, I should have said that another decision has been made in your absence; that each tenant be asked to pay a pound a week into a petty-cash fund for small necessities.'

Gary, already irritable, got into a silly argument about whether a decision on financial matters should require unanimity. This provoked a fierce response from Melissa.

'Oh, perhaps we should introduce a single transferable vote. It's only a frigging pound, Gary. For a sink tidy, for God's sake.'

Her mellifluous Welsh accent made the cursing seem more hostile than it was probably meant to be, and Gary was shamed into silence. The sink-tidy row set the pattern for the evening and, for that matter, so many other evenings at the Dog and Pheasant.

Tall, confident, double-barrelled Jason, broad of shoulder, relaxed of manner and revelling in a natural sense of authority, would poke fun at Melissa, causing

Gary to intervene on her behalf only to be shot down in flames by the woman he was desperate to impress.

On this occasion Jason had plucked the book that Melissa was reading from her handbag, announcing author and title loudly and disparagingly. 'A. S. Byatt, *A Whistling Woman*,' he pronounced slowly. 'Bet this is a page-turner.'

'Part of her Frederica Quartet and far too sensitive for you, Jason,' Melissa said, nonchalantly sipping her gin and tonic. 'I'd stick to the stuff you're bound to like – macho stuff like Hunter S. Thompson or the orcs and elves in Tolkien, presuming you've ever read a book, that is.'

'Nothing wrong with sensitivity anyway,' Gary interjected. 'I love Jane Austen.'

'I hate Jane Austen,' Melissa said, snatching the book back from Jason and heading off to the Ladies'. Gary had never actually read any Jane Austen but felt as wounded as if he had. Later on, just before closing time, the conversation turned to sport. Melissa was ridiculing Jason's devotion to rugby.

'Rugby players aren't as tough as they pretend to be anyway,' she said. 'I once went out with one who was such a hypochondriac he went to A & E because he thought he was peeing blood. It turned out he'd eaten some beetroot.'

'Couldn't have been much of a rugby player if he ate salad,' observed Jason. 'Anyway, you're Welsh. You're supposed to love rugby.'

'Licensed thuggery – I hate all sport . . .'

'Me too,' agreed Gary. 'Especially football.'

'. . . except football,' Melissa concluded her sentence.

After an awkward silence she said, 'Me and my dad were season-ticket holders at Swansea.'

Once again Gary's obsequious dissembling (far from disliking sport, he was passionate about cricket) had got him nowhere.

On the way back to Mount Street, Melissa put her arm through Jason's – two protagonists united by mutual respect. Gary mooched along beside them thinking of all the witty things he should have said over the course of the evening.

Now, two hours later, he could feel sleep descending at last. Another day lived without incident. All the excitement in life lies in the unseen future rather than the disappointing present? Who was it who said that? He couldn't remember. Perhaps it was an original thought. He fell asleep slowly reciting the words in his head, like a mantra.

3

Friday, 10 July

It may have only been a friendly match, but a decent crowd had arrived at Stamford Bridge to see it. The evening was balmy and the atmosphere benign. With nothing to play for but pride, there was no edge to the usual rivalry amongst supporters.

For Chelsea fans the terrible drought of the non-footballing weeks between May and August was almost over. Their team were league champions and this match was a tasty hors d'oeuvre for the feast of football to come.

Moscow's fanatical supporters relished the opportunity to see CSKA play against one of Europe's elite teams, whose owner, Roman Abramovich, had been associated with their club when they'd lifted the UEFA Cup in 2005. It was the tenth anniversary of that great victory, the finest in their long history.

The two sets of fans streamed along the Fulham Road, most in shorts and T-shirts as if heading for the beach. Older Chelsea fans could remember when the league season ended in April and didn't begin again until it was almost autumn; a time when many professional footballers were able to switch to cricket for the three months of summer.

As for the more mature amongst the CSKA supporters, there was nostalgia for the old days when their club was the official team of the Soviet Army.

But for them all, tonight was not about seasons past but the season to come; an opportunity to see new players who'd arrived in the close season and assess their team's chances of achieving even greater glory over the coming months.

Denis Smolnikov arrived in the Chairman's Suite at Stamford Bridge ten minutes before kick-off, sweat glazing his fleshy face, his full lips and clear blue eyes forming an apologetic expression. As a Director of CSKA Moscow he'd been invited to the dinner hosted by Abramovich for visiting VIPs which had just concluded in his absence.

Smolnikov was a popular man. His fame and charismatic personality quickly attracted an audience. Russian colleagues had been concerned by his late arrival, but he explained that in the course of a frantically busy day several meetings had overrun. He mentioned the CSKA fans who'd come to the Strand Hotel that morning and joked that they'd been responsible for his disrupted schedule.

Several attractive young women vied for his attention. Amongst the Russian women at the dinner there appeared to be none who failed to meet such a description. Smolnikov, the famous film-maker, was a man to be admired, and courted, and seen with. His fame had begun with a TV series following the lives of ten Russian children born in 1990. It had some of the highest viewing figures ever recorded and became a token of the new Russia emerging from the Soviet years. Everything he'd done since had enhanced his reputation and increased his influence.

The Russian ambassador pushed through the coterie to shake the hand of the latecomer. There had been pressure on Chelsea to cancel this match because of the political fallout from Russia's annexation of Crimea the previous year and the ambassador had worked hard to make sure it went ahead. His presence this evening was symbolic and Smolnikov paid him due deference.

The match was about to begin and as the assembled VIPs moved en bloc towards the cushioned seats of the Director's Box, Smolnikov hung back to talk to his assistant Stanislav Miranchuk, who'd been with him at the Strand Hotel that morning and who had been the most agitated about his boss's late arrival.

The two men moved to a far corner of the suite to converse in Russian, away from the staff who were busily preparing the room for the next bout of hospitality at half-time.

Miranchuk removed his horn-rimmed glasses and as he polished the lenses with his CSKA scarf said, 'What happened?'

'I'm not feeling a hundred per cent, but never mind that, where did you get to this morning? You left the Strand without telling me.'

'I saw something. A guy with a beard came into the room in a Strand blazer; someone I've never seen at the Strand before. I followed him out of the room and saw him take off his jacket and leave the hotel, which made me even more suspicious.'

'Who was it?' asked Smolnikov.

'I don't know, but I got Morozov to follow him. Now we know where he lives and will soon be paying him a visit.'

There was a roar from the Moscow fans as their team forced a corner.

'Was everything administered properly this morning?' Smolnikov asked.

'Yes, that bastard will feel the first pangs in a day or so. Just a little nausea at first and perhaps the beginning of a headache. Nothing much. He'll put it down to travel sickness. It's good that he'll be well out of the country before experiencing the effects. We don't want to spoil our patch.'

'No,' Smolnikov agreed, 'or burden the NHS.'

Laughing, the two men sat on a couple of stray chairs, lighting cigarettes (in contravention of the No Smoking signs) and stretching their legs.

Miranchuk said, 'Sometimes I think we can do anything we like in London. It is ours – we own it.'

'Careful, my friend,' Smolnikov responded, sitting up straight and grabbing a saucer to use as an ashtray. 'I'm not sure the President is entirely happy with our activities.'

'But that doesn't stop him using us when he wants to. Anyway, you're his buddy, so what's the worry?'

'Our President is ruthless,' Smolnikov said. 'Doesn't matter if you're friend or foe or even family. If he sees you as a threat . . .'

'But why would he see us as a threat?' Miranchuk protested.

The two men reflected for a moment, blowing smoke rings.

'He didn't authorise what we did today. Today we deal with our enemy, an enemy of Krovnyye Bratya,' Smolnikov said, referring to the biggest and most vicious arm of Russian organised crime operating in the UK. Also known by its abbreviation as KB, it had been formed by the *siloviki*, a clan of former KGB men, to be a kind of organised-crime component of the Russian state, but had begun to exercise greater independence after the KGB had been renamed (but hardly reformed) as the FSB when the Soviet Union collapsed. Miranchuk worked for Krovnyye Bratya and Denis Smolnikov had formed a close association.

'But you're right. He has no reason to see us as a threat,' Smolnikov continued. 'We supplement his power – we don't challenge it.'

'And we have links to the police here that our FSB friends will find very useful,' Miranchuk added.

'That's right. While it's unwise to embarrass the President, causing him a little consternation once in a while shouldn't cause us any problems. Well done today.' Smolnikov placed a hand on his colleague's shoulder. 'And now I must join Mr Abramovich in his private box. One of his lackeys told me he was expecting me there, and Roman is not a man to be kept waiting.'

*

As Miranchuk was finishing his cigarette after Smolnikov's departure, another man slipped quietly into the chair beside him. It was the slim, impeccably tailored figure of Ivan Ilkun.

'Ivan, I thought you'd be here somewhere. You should have come over to meet Denis. I could have introduced you,' Miranchuk said, shaking hands with his new companion.

'I am just a humble agent of my country, not worthy of the attention of such a famous man,' Ilkun said, brushing a stray piece of ash from the lapel of his dark blue suit.

He was a handsome man, square jawed with a high forehead and deep-set eyes. The two men were almost exact contemporaries and had known each other since their army days. But whereas Stanislav Miranchuk had then laboured in the lower orders of the security services, Ilkun had risen to the rank of colonel in the foreign intelligence division of the FSB. He'd recently taken on a looser, more unspecified role that had brought him to London at the turn of the year. Having met up for a beer at Easter, this was the second time the two men had come into contact on their new territory.

'In any case,' Ilkun continued, 'I do know Denis. We worked together about ten years ago but he's probably forgotten me by now. And I didn't want to interrupt what was obviously a deep and meaningful conversation. What are you two up to?'

'Oh, this and that. Nothing that should trouble you FSB boys.'

'Krovnyye Bratya is beginning to trouble us just a little, my friend,' said Ilkun. 'We must not be distracted from our work in Ukraine.'

'Of course. Do you think we don't know how important the Crimea thing is?'

'I'm sure you do know, but Crimea is just the start. Eventually the entire country must once more be under our control. Which is why we can't afford any unintended consequences from your activities.'

Miranchuk smiled. 'But Ivan,' he said, 'you know that I am only a lowly foot soldier. If you want to convey a message to Krovnyye Bratya why don't you speak with Sidrenko.'

'I know that Anton Sidrenko is your leader,' Ilkun said, 'but I also know that you and Smolnikov were up to something this morning at the Strand Hotel that nobody told us about. Sergei Dzyuba was there and what you don't know is that Mr Dzyuba is now doing some important work for us in relation to Ukraine.'

Miranchuk was alarmed by this information but maintained a serene smile. 'Smolnikov has been given a commission by CNN to make a film,' he said, 'that's all the meeting was about. The President knows the value of these films; they give Denis the credibility he needs for his other activities, including in Ukraine. Activities that help the President. For all I know, Smolnikov informed him personally. They used to be judo partners, you know.'

'Ah,' exclaimed Ilkun, 'the depth of meaning behind those three small words "used to be".' Reaching in his pocket for a pen he scribbled a mobile number on a stray napkin and handed it to Miranchuk.

'You gave me your contact details when we had that drink,' Miranchuk protested.

'Those were the office numbers I give to acquaintances. This is the special number I give to friends. I can be contacted on that number or you can always find me at the cathedral.'

'I'd forgotten about your Christianity,' Miranchuk said, transferring the number from the napkin to his iPhone.

'In the days we worked together, religious belief was still treated with suspicion, but now the Orthodox Church is a crucial part of the new Russia. Once the President revealed how he himself had been secretly baptised in the Soviet era, those who'd previously suppressed religion became sudden converts. I have always been devout. It's not too late for you, my friend – come along to our church in Knightsbridge. It would be good for your soul.'

'My soul is just fine, but thanks for the invitation.'

Ilkun pulled his chair closer. Lowering his voice to a murmur, he said, 'Listen, Stanislav, I know the meeting this morning wasn't just to arrange a film. Things are changing. Under Yeltsin we swallowed so much freedom it almost poisoned us. The President has reasserted the power of the state, but his mission is not yet complete. Krovnyye Bratya is not playing a good game and you should be thinking about transferring to a different team.'

Their conversation was interrupted by another, louder roar from the terraces.

'We certainly need to play our game better than The Horses,' Miranchuk said, referring to the nickname of CSKA and the fact that they'd just gone a goal down.

The FSB man slipped away as silently as he'd arrived. When Miranchuk joined Smolnikov at half-time he asked the film-maker how he was feeling.

'Not great,' Smolnikov replied. 'But don't worry, I'll survive.'

4

Two days earlier – Wednesday, 8 July

An African sun had already burnt away the mist as Gary left for work the morning after his restless night of contemplation. Outside the house opposite, on a folding canvas chair, sat Terry.

Having lived his entire eighty-six years in that house, Terry was a piece of living local history. He once told Gary how he remembered sitting on his father's shoulders watching the great fire that destroyed the actual Crystal Palace in 1936. From a vantage point at the top of Westow Road, he'd watched the 990,000 square feet of cast iron, glass and timber collapse as one of the greatest fires ever seen in London blazed so fiercely that it could be seen, it was said, across eight English counties.

Eventually Terry inherited the rent book when his parents passed away; he'd married from the house and fathered a child there, subsequently downsizing to one floor to manage alone after his son left home and his wife had died. In fine weather Terry liked to sit outside from early morning until sunset, the only interruption being for an hour or so when his designated carer, a jovial, tubby lady called Grace, came to cook and clean for him.

Gary always enjoyed chatting with Terry. Intrigued by a man who'd lived for almost nine decades in the house he was born in, he was also impressed by Terry's full head of grey hair brushed back on both sides of its high parting. Beneath the fringe, a pair of watery blue eyes had long ceased to be in proper working order.

The reason those eyes looked so kindly upon Gary was because of an act of charity mingled with deceit that had taken place a few months earlier. It was an incident that Gary wasn't proud of.

One Saturday morning he'd returned from his usual weekend run to find Terry in a state of anguish, beckoning to him from across the road. The electricity in Terry's kitchen had failed, leaving him unable to enjoy the tea and toast that he made for himself first thing every day. Grace was on holiday and the replacement carer didn't come until much later at weekends. Terry's son lived too far away to be of any help. Would Gary come in and take a look at the problem?

Gary agreed but only because he couldn't think of a plausible excuse not to. Raised by a single mother, he hadn't acquired any of the manly skills that he presumed were passed from father to son. He knew nothing about electricity and was barely capable of changing a light bulb.

Terry led Gary up the stairs to the kitchen of his first-floor domain, where a teabag in a cup and an untoasted slice of Hovis sat forlornly on the side. As Terry explained the importance of his morning routine and how much that slice of bread, properly toasted and buttered, would contribute to his happiness, Gary resolved to pull the cooker away from the wall and remove the casing from the grill in order to gaze inside meaningfully so that at least Terry would see him going through the motions before admitting defeat.

A screwdriver was produced, but as Gary squeezed himself behind the cooker he glanced at the double socket into which the cooker and the electric kettle were plugged. It was switched off. Somebody, probably the replacement carer, had been over-meticulous in their work.

For reasons that he found hard to justify to himself, Gary, having discerned the cause of the problem, carried on regardless, unscrewing the outer casing of the grill while Terry stood with him in the kitchen wittering on about the importance of breakfast to an old man's constitution. Gary grew into his impromptu performance, issuing the occasional tut and sigh as he pretended to adjust the wires at the back of the grill and then fiddle with the base of the kettle before surreptitiously turning the electricity back on.

As the grill heated up and the water began to bubble, Gary told Terry that he shouldn't have any more trouble with these newly fixed appliances. The old man's admiration poured out, nearly as warm as the water that was soon to emerge from the boiling kettle.

Gary didn't entirely escape retribution for this duplicity. It subsequently caused embarrassment at work after Terry had himself shown a capacity for deviousness by tricking Gary into giving him the contact details for his workplace ('Just in case anything happens in the street that I need to let you know about') and then writing a letter to The Manager, extolling the virtues of 'this fine young man'. Gary, Terry's letter went on to say, had come to the aid of his elderly neighbour by using 'his exceptional skills as an electrician without seeking any financial reward'.

The letter in Terry's spidery but legible handwriting was reproduced in the company's monthly staff newsletter, and subsequently Gary's workmates referred to him with affectionate sarcasm as 'Sparks'.

Terry's cheery greeting on this fine July morning put a spring in Gary's step as he walked towards Crystal Palace station to face the misery of his daily commute. He often thought that if insurrection were ever to break out in England it would begin in those old carriages, packed to the gunwales and untroubled by air-conditioning. It would come after the fourth announcement of a delay to the service, the people lifting their eyes from their newspapers and phones to strike a blow against oppression. It would be a classless struggle; after all, the First-Class carriages had long been surrendered to the proles as there was no practical method of segregation on this travelling shrine to wretchedness. But these dark thoughts, which had entertained Gary through many a difficult journey into London, had recently been replaced by far more pleasant ruminations.

For the past three weeks Gary had been sure to secure a seat in the third carriage from the front as the train arrived almost empty from Sutton to half-fill at the Palace before heading towards the packing stations of Gipsy Hill, Streatham and Balham. He made his way to this carriage because, in a window seat, was a young woman of about Gary's age who had become the object of his mute but profound affection.

He'd even begun, almost subconsciously, to dress more smartly. Having gone to work in whatever old T-shirt first came to hand as he groped in the wardrobe, he now found himself wearing the polo shirts usually reserved for evening wear. Today, for instance, he was flaunting a pale blue Ben Sherman and the beige skinny jeans that his mother had bought him for his birthday. And he shaved more carefully, spending time in front of the bathroom mirror – time that would have been spent sleeping before this transformation.

But none of this helped him overcome a basic problem. Gary would not have described himself as shy, but when in close proximity to a woman he found attractive, a debilitating diffidence descended. Sometimes, as with Melissa, he said the wrong thing – more often he struggled to say anything at all.

This inability to engage with women he fancied was undoubtedly a major reason for his discontent. In all of his twenty-three years Gary had only had one serious relationship. That was with Emily Swanson in the sixth form and she had dumped him for Duncan McDonald, his best friend. It wasn't so much that Gary was unlucky in love as that he was untested, untried, lacking in experience.

The girl in the window seat of the third carriage had become another object of his immense, untethered adoration. Her long ash-blonde hair, grey eyes, high cheekbones and shapely legs, bare beneath her summer dress, would have attracted the attention of any young heterosexual, but what transfixed Gary wasn't her beauty so much as the ritual way she enhanced it: applying her make-up in the same way every morning in full public view.

It seemed to Gary to be such an intimate activity that it should surely be confined to the bedroom. His romantic nature refused to accept that the pressures of modern life meant that women simply didn't have the time to complete this essential toilette before leaving home. She wasn't the first woman he'd observed putting on lipstick or powdering her nose in public, of course she wasn't. It was just that he'd never seen the full process carried out in such a methodical, meticulous way; and never by a girl as fascinating as the one who had by now begun her performance as Gary settled into his ringside seat on the other side of the aisle.

Some preliminary work had obviously been done before the train arrived at Crystal Palace, a little like the grouting and washing-down with sugar water that decorators engage in before painting a room. Now, at this stage, a leather pouch had been pulled from her handbag, out of which came a succession of tiny pots and tubes, creams and lotions, perfumes and powders.

The carriage of commuters, expanding with every stop, was her audience as she used her right hand with great dexterity to handle the various tools at her disposal, applying foundation and brushing blusher onto her fine cheekbones.

The eye shadow required a particularly delicate application and was followed by a black pencil that was used to underline those lovely grey eyes. Still apparently oblivious to Gary and his fellow travellers, she then swapped the hand mirror for her phone (in selfie mode) for the final stages.

After brushing her hair and as the train slowed on its approach to Clapham Junction, she would paint some cherry-red lipstick onto her pouting lips while gazing at her reflection on the phone. For Gary, this was always the highlight of the show, like the climax to a grand opera.

This precise routine never varied. After her lipstick finale the girl would quickly pack all of the implements back into the leather pouch and smooth down her dress before the train arrived at Clapham Junction, where she'd disembark along with most of the carriage, leaving Gary, ignored and unnoticed, to carry on to Victoria.

Gary had no idea that this woman was about to change his life by beginning a process that would come close to ending it.

5

That weekend was to be spent back in Aylesbury. In Gary's current disconsolate mood going on one of these regular monthly visits to see his mother felt like a regression, as if he'd made the wrong move in a board game and was having to return to the start as punishment.

If he had something compelling to do in London the visit could have been postponed. Alternatively, he could have arrived in style, with a new girlfriend to introduce; his housemate Melissa, perhaps, or the mystery blonde from the train.

Something unusual had occurred when he had seen her on his Friday morning commute. He'd been watching the make-up process closely as always, careful to disguise his observation by having a copy of the *Metro* open in front of him. Gary didn't want the girl to think he was some kind of stalker. His was a fascination rather than an obsession; an entirely healthy attraction. Many long and happy liaisons had begun on a train. Why shouldn't this be another one?

There was something different about Friday. Such was Gary's knowledge of the girl's make-up routine that he'd noticed a significant omission. On that Friday morning there was no lipstick.

At the point where it was usually applied, just as the train slowed on its approach to Clapham Junction, looking into her camera reflection, she'd brushed mascara onto her naturally long eyelashes. Gary wanted to raise an objection – like an umpire at a tennis match indicating a faulty serve. This was the time for lipstick not mascara. But those pouting lips had arrived naked into Clapham Junction where, as always, the girl 'de-trained' (as they liked to say on Southern) without even the slightest glance in his direction. Such a small and insignificant change in the morning routine shouldn't have mattered; but to Gary it did.

A day later and the Saturday-morning weather matched his mood – dull and grey – as he travelled to the Mandeville Estate in Aylesbury. Knuckles had offered to give him a lift, having taken possession of a luxury rented car in which to run actors to and from the film set at Pinewood Studios.

'But Pinewood's nowhere near Aylesbury,' Gary pointed out.

'But they're both in Buckinghamshire. Surely the county can't be that feckin' big.'

Knuckles, who only had a tenuous grasp of England's geography, badly wanted to show off his Jaguar XJ (as well as his highly developed driving skills) to his non-driving housemate.

Gary liked Knuckles (just as he fancied Melissa and distrusted Jason). A man rarely stumped for something to say, Knuckles never revealed much about himself, but he'd been a source of cheerful encouragement ever since moving into 27 Mount Street shortly after Gary had.

As they'd eaten their microwaved meals on Friday evening with the house to themselves (Melissa had gone home to Swansea for the weekend and Jason was elsewhere), Gary proceeded to tell Knuckles about his fascination with the girl on the train, seeking advice on how to engage her in conversation.

'Sure, the only thing you need to do is stand up when she stands up and shuffle off the train with her,' Knuckles suggested.

'But Clapham Junction's not my stop.'

'What the hell has that got to do with it, you feckin' idiot. Make it your stop. Embrace that stop. Own that stop. If you're trapped in the crush with her, you'll have the opportunity to begin a conversation. What is wrong with you? When you die do you want the inscription on your headstone to read "He only ever got off at the right stop"?'

'I bet Jason would know what to do,' Gary said dejectedly.

'Get a grip here, will you? You're better looking than Jason, better company than Jason. All he has that you lack is confidence. It shows, it's palpable – your feckin' timidity is emblazoned across your forehead. I've told you what to do. You don't need Jason's bloody advice.'

'Is that what you'd do?' asked Gary.

'Me? I'd be interested in the make-up for sure, but not the girl.'

There was an awkward silence as Gary realised that his enigmatic housemate had revealed something important about himself.

Gary arrived at the house in Aylesbury at the usual Saturday time, sat in his usual chair at the kitchen table and ate the two slices of buttered toast that his mother had prepared – as usual.

Rachel Nelson, Gary's mother, stood over him as he munched away. She was a slim, elegant forty-one-year-old who had dedicated most of the last twenty-three years to her only child. She'd fallen pregnant just after her eighteenth birthday, the outcome of a clammy one-night stand on a sultry summer's evening in 1992. She'd gone to a dance at Aylesbury College with a girlfriend and met a tall lad with dark, curly hair and a lop-sided grin who danced well and made her laugh with his impersonations of John Major and Sean Connery. They drank too much and, in the college grounds, 'over embraced' (to quote the expression her mother had used to explain Rachel's pregnancy to her father). Rachel knew only three things about Gary's father – that his name was Daniel, he'd been training to be a police officer and he lived in London. Her parents wanted to track him down, but Rachel felt this would only complicate the situation.

She desperately wanted to keep the baby for reasons she found impossible to articulate and she wasn't sure that the father would feel the same way. A child should be a cause for unbridled joy not suspicious resentment.

Besides, the detection work involved in tracking down Daniel would be laborious, and she simply didn't have the motivation. Rachel was entirely happy with the consequences of her actions but felt that Daniel should be allowed to carry on with his life as if nothing had happened. He hadn't forced himself upon her and she may well have indicated, in her alcohol-induced gregariousness, that she'd 'taken precautions' – which she had, having been on the pill since she was sixteen. The problem was that since breaking up with her first steady boyfriend she'd been less meticulous about taking it. She hadn't even arranged to meet Daniel again although he had asked for her phone number, which she'd scrawled on the back of a cloakroom ticket. He never rang.

Rachel named the baby Gary, after Gary Barlow, her favourite member of Take That. She'd even toyed with the idea of calling him Gary Jason Howard Mark Robert Nelson, such was her devotion to Britain's favourite boy band, but her parents convinced her it was too great a burden to place upon a child.

Instead she named him Gary Daniel Nelson, feeling that it was only right to commemorate the father in this way; and there was no doubt he was the father. Although she'd lost her virginity to Mr Steady Boyfriend, she'd not had sex with anyone else until that night. Indeed, her self-imposed chastity may have been a partial explanation for what happened; that and the heat, and the handsome man she was with, and the cool grass, and hearing 'Could It Be Magic' wafting across the playing fields from the college disco.

At first, she'd told Gary that his father had gone missing shortly after the birth, but eventually, when she thought he was old enough to understand, she told him the truth. It was an awkward conversation conducted in her blue Ford Fiesta as the two of them drove to Swanage to join her parents, who'd rented a holiday cottage for a week.

She remembered the occasion vividly. They'd listened to a documentary on the car radio about missing persons, and eleven-year-old Gary had suggested contacting the charity mentioned in order to try to track down his father.

It was the perfect opportunity to reveal the truth. Having conducted the conversation in her head many times, she was able to explain what had happened with reasonable fluency. Sitting beside one another in the car staring straight ahead through the windscreen seemed to help, producing the required level of intimacy without the need to look each other in the eye.

To hear that your father was not only unaware that he was your father but ignorant of your very existence must have been a shock. But Rachel never ceased to be amazed at the quiet fortitude of her son. For her, the years spent in exclusive control of Gary's parenting had been completely fulfilling. She hadn't pursued her childhood ambition to be a nurse, but she had found work as an assistant in a dental practice which, along with her parents' financial contribution, provided a reasonable standard of living.

As for men, she'd had the occasional boyfriend through Gary's childhood but shunned any serious relationship. She wasn't prepared to share her parental responsibilities and worried that the arrival of a father-figure, let alone a stepfather, would destroy the special bond between mother and son.

Looking at Gary on this Saturday morning, while he scoffed toast at the kitchen table, she swelled with maternal pride. He had her green eyes, but the dark, curly hair, full lips, broad shoulders, long legs and Roman nose were his father's, and the combination was a good one. She knew that her son wanted more from life: that he'd left school with three A Levels (two Cs and a B), determined not to go to university but unsure what he wanted to do; that he'd moved to the capital a few years before because 'London was where things happened' but that he was still waiting for whatever 'things happened' to happen to him.

As soon as he was beyond her parental responsibility, she'd dabbled in online dating and had met a divorced plumber called Will who'd stayed the odd night but never on the weekends when Gary was home. She still found it difficult to share her life with anyone but her son, whose company she so enjoyed. This afternoon he would mooch around watching cricket on television and this evening help her cook dinner. They'd watch a film together before Gary went off to his bedroom, preserved exactly as it was three years ago when he left, with posters depicting the planetary system, Arcade Fire,

Laura Marling and *Close Encounters of the Third Kind*, his favourite film.

This house on the Mandeville Estate was the council house Rachel had grown up in. Her parents had bought it from the council in the 1980s. After her father's premature death from a heart attack while cycling home from work not long after that Swanage holiday, her mother had met a man from Aston Clinton, just up the road, remarried and moved into her new husband's home, leaving Rachel to continue Gary's upbringing in a duet rather than a trio.

The fact that her son returned home regularly reassured Rachel that the bond remained strong and that things had worked out well despite the strong sense of guilt that assailed her occasionally over her son's fatherless state.

Gary mentioned that he'd be meeting his old school friend, Duncan McDonald in the local pub on Sunday lunchtime and that they'd probably get a table in the carvery.

'Best book it now,' Rachel said distractedly. 'It's Father's Day tomorrow and they're bound to be busy.'

It was then that Gary said something that made Rachel, who'd been fussing around the kitchen sink, come to a complete standstill.

'If only I had a dad to have lunch with.'

He was perusing the cricket scores in the sports section of the Saturday paper and hadn't even looked up while uttering these words that so shocked his mother.

Rachel responded as calmly as she could, 'You've never said anything like that before.'

'I was joking, Mum,' he said, and, as if just noticing the effect, 'I was being funny – lunch with a stranger would be more entertaining than with old Dunc.'

'Oh, I see,' Rachel said. 'Maybe you should just crash another table pretending to be some celebrating father's long-lost son and leave Duncan on his own.'

They both laughed, but there was no laughter in Rachel's eyes.

6

Soho on a Saturday evening in summer is no place for the faint-hearted. Its narrow pavements spill over with organised groups of Japanese tourists, meandering families from various American cities and clusters of youngsters on weekend breaks from Amsterdam or Berlin. The indigenous tribes are also out in force, the restaurants full of pre-theatre diners, the pubs with stag- and hen-night parties.

Through this throng walked Stanislav Miranchuk, surveying the revelry through his black horn-rimmed glasses, a disdainful look on his granite-like features. Cutting into an alley off Old Compton Street, he tapped a code into the device positioned beside a steel-plated door and entered the quiet confines of a private club.

Two guards at the entrance embraced him affection-ately but asked for his phone – and his gun. Miranchuk surrendered both and was allowed to mount the unlit staircase. He entered a suite of rooms where about sixty people were mingling happily, the men dressed in suits and ties despite the heat and lack of air-conditioning, the women tottering on high heels, their abundant jewellery reflecting the dull orange glow of the tasteful lighting.

There was a fully equipped bar and a Dave Brubeck record played softly beneath the muffled conversation.

Miranchuk, a frequent visitor, recognised most of those in attendance, but nothing registered except the person he'd come to see. In the corner stood a tall, slender man, with the solemn expression and gaunt figure of a fasting monk. Anton Sidrenko was the leader of London's most notorious Russian gangster mob, the Krovnyye Bratya. They shook hands before Sidrenko led the way into a back room where they were joined by his two most senior associates.

'How is he?' Sidrenko asked in Russian as the two men settled on the comfortable upholstery. The other men continued to stand.

'Not good,' replied Miranchuk.

'Then we must get him back to Moscow where he can be looked after properly.'

'He's too sick to travel. He was okay yesterday evening at the football, just a little queasy. But he got worse through the night and went to St Thomas' Hospital at midday. They admitted him straight away and he called me to go over. He will get good treatment there. It's one of the best hospitals in England.'

'So, what do the doctors think is wrong with him?' Sidrenko spoke slowly. One of his associates had offered round a pack of Russian cigarettes and he was savouring his first drag.

Miranchuk spent ten seconds staring at the floor before saying, 'You're not going to like this, but the hospital thinks he's been poisoned. They've called in the police.'

An almost perceptible frisson broke across the room. Sidrenko uttered some Russian expletives as he rose to his feet and began to pace the floor.

'I want you to tell me everything that happened yesterday at the Strand Hotel,' he demanded.

Miranchuk went through the events of Friday morning in detail.

'So, we successfully administered the treatment?' Sidrenko asked when he'd finished.

'Yes,' said Miranchuk. 'Denis Smolnikov was happy that our mission had been completed. He was looking forward to going back to work on his documentary.'

'When this news gets out, we will have FSB on our backs,' Sidrenko remarked, referring to the Russian federal security service. 'The President knew nothing of this operation.'

Miranchuk didn't say he was aware of this following his conversation with Ivan Ilkun at Stamford Bridge. He thought it politic not to mention that exchange. Instead he said, 'The hospital told me that, because St Thomas' is close to Parliament and Whitehall there are always reporters sniffing around. They say within an hour of Smolnikov being admitted, the Sunday papers were making enquiries.'

'And what did the hospital say?' asked Sidrenko.

'They referred them to the Metropolitan Police.'

'Can't we get our man in blue on to this?' asked Vladimir Granat, Sidrenko's most senior lieutenant. 'We need to know what the police are doing. Hopefully they will not go public yet.'

'I think they will,' said the other lieutenant, Dmitry Podkolzin, a big man with the physique of a weightlifter. 'If the Sunday papers know about Smolnikov being in hospital the Met is bound to say something. The only point to saying nothing is if it kills the story. Denis being a prominent film-maker and friend of the President, this would be unlikely. The police will conclude that they may as well try to keep some control by giving a quote.'

Sidrenko continued to pace up and down, his long legs covering the limited floor space in a few strides.

'Igor Golovin and Sergei Dzyuba were the only other people at that meeting apart from you and Denis,' he said, as much to himself as Miranchuk. 'It's unlikely that those two would be involved in anything like this. They don't deal in that kind of shit, and anyway, if they are frightened for their own safety, why jeopardise it further?'

Returning to the armchair he said, 'But there were also our friends from CSKA.'

'All of whom were recruited by me, for a purpose,' said Miranchuk.

'Which just leaves the waitress and that bearded guy who you spotted coming in to help her. Remind me why he aroused your suspicion.'

'Because I know that hotel. We use it all the time. I'd never seen that guy working there before. I followed him back to reception just to have a chat and suss him out. To my surprise, he took off his jacket and walked straight out.'

'You followed him?' asked Granat.

'I didn't want to leave Denis for too long, so I got Morozov, who'd been keeping watch outside, to follow him.'

'And then?' Sidrenko asked.

'Well, we have an address. We know where he lives.'

'Okay, we need to talk to him and that waitress. Hopefully Smolnikov will recover, but we need to know what happened here.' Sidrenko leaned across to touch Miranchuk's knee. 'And I want you to personally oversee this. Nothing heavy. I don't want you to attract unwelcome attention.'

'The waitress is a very attractive girl,' said Miranchuk, his mood lightened by having offloaded the bad news. 'I wouldn't mind questioning her myself,' he leered.

Sidrenko gripped Miranchuk's shoulder tightly.

'If you want glamorous pussy there's plenty available back there,' he said, pointing to the next room. 'Help yourself but don't lay a finger on that girl. She's just a kid, trying to earn a living. We only need her help to understand what happened.'

He unfurled himself from the low armchair and straightened his tie.

'Now come and relax with me. That's what this place is for. Maria is with me, come and have a drink with us.'

Maria Paseka was Sidrenko's wife, the First Lady of Krovnyye Bratya. They had been together since meeting at university in St Petersburg. Anton Sidrenko had gone on to pursue a career in business while Maria, who, like him, had studied law, became a leading advocate in the Russian courts. She had kept her name after they'd married. The couple were now in their mid-forties with two grown-up kids. Sidrenko divided his time between Moscow and London while Maria lived almost exclusively in England, at their palatial flat in Knightsbridge or their house on the Surrey Downs.

Sidrenko guided his subordinate to the table where Maria Paseka sat talking quietly with some female friends. The club had filled with new arrivals – Russian emigrés close to Krovnyye Bratya, some visiting politicians from St Petersburg who were on the payroll, and English associates who helped run KB's network of money laundering, prostitution, people trafficking, drug dealing and extortion.

Maria Paseka stood to embrace Miranchuk as he joined the table, taking the seat between her and Sidrenko.

'How lovely to see you, Stanislav,' she said, turning her full attention away from her friends and towards the new arrival. Petite, with dark eyes and small features, her long dark hair was pulled away from her forehead by an expensive-looking designer Alice band.

'Has Denis come with you?'

Miranchuk gave a brief explanation of what had happened to the film-maker, but was interrupted by the waiter bringing a round of drinks and Sidrenko insisting that they stopped talking shop.

'This is a man in need of respite,' he told his wife. 'I brought him over here to relax and enjoy himself.'

The jazz had given way to rock and the floor of the biggest room had been cleared for dancing. Maria's friends insisted that she should join them on the dance floor. The two men remained watching through the doorway, Sidrenko continuing to chain smoke while Miranchuk sipped his vodka martini, deep in thought. The dancing grew wilder; early-evening cocktails had been followed by huge bottles of expensive champagne, cigarettes by crystal meth and other assorted drugs.

After ten minutes of silent contemplation, Sidrenko leaned towards his guest. 'I always get the feeling that you are repelled by this decadence,' he said.

Miranchuk sipped his drink but said nothing.

'We Russians are divided between the advanced and the primitive. All nations are the same, but few have been denied and suppressed for so long, forced to accept the crude and rudimentary. Those days are over. Refinement and wealth are in the ascendancy, but the barbaric is still there not far beneath the surface. We are regaining our pride. In the same way that our President takes back Crimea, so Krovnyye Bratya extends the empire of Mother Russia. We all have our roles to play.'

Granat was passing by, taking some drinks to another table.

'And this man has perhaps the most important role of all,' said Sidrenko, turning in his seat to pat a friendly hand on his colleague's arm.

Granat laughed. 'Only because I pay for the drinks,' he said.

The two men had worked together in London for

twenty years, building a criminal network that augmented Granat's legitimate business interests: legitimate in so far as he bought and sold properties; illegitimate in its clandestine offshoot which was money laundering.

Amongst the Russian criminal fraternity, London had become known as the world's laundromat, washing billions of pounds of dirty cash every year. Granat had the perfect vehicle through which to pass money syphoned off from the gold rush of Russia's newly privatised utilities. The money was invested in office developments, luxury apartments and the acquisition of houses for rent. Grant Properties was the Anglicised name of the company he'd created when he came to England in the Yeltsin era. While others had faltered when the Russian presidency changed hands, Granat had increased his fortune. Yeltsin's 'anything goes' approach had changed to a more disciplined regime in which Sidrenko and Granat thrived. Granat always ensured that the required commission went back to the Russian state. A small, overweight man with thinning milk-white hair, the property tycoon was as usual entertaining a cohort of young women to whose company he now returned.

The music had quietened, Foo Fighters having given way to a slow ballad. Maria Paseka returned to the table flushed and slightly dishevelled from the dancing. She held out her hand to Sidrenko, imploring him to dance.

'No way,' he said. 'Take Stanislav.'

As they moved sensuously together on the dance floor, Maria stood on tiptoe to whisper in Miranchuk's ear. 'It's been too long, my love.'

Miranchuk gripped her waist tightly in response, carefully manoeuvring them further from Sidrenko's eyeline.

'He goes to Moscow tomorrow for a week,' she continued. 'Come to the flat and let me see what I can do with whatever that is that's pressing so insistently into my groin.'

7

Duncan McDonald had resumed best-friend status following the ruptured relationship caused in the sixth form of Mandeville Comprehensive when he'd stolen Gary's girlfriend. In truth Gary had never harboured much of a grudge anyway, having quickly come to the realisation that Emily Swanson was much more mature than he was, with an air of what Gary took to be sophistication; something he'd read about but never encountered before.

It wasn't as if Duncan had set out to steal Emily away. After a year of 'going out' with Gary, Emily had simply transferred her affections to another classmate. It was as simple as that. A changing preference, like suddenly switching from McFly to The Kooks or from Bin Weevils to Minecraft – a question of progression. One night at a party that Emily had arrived at with Gary, she left with Duncan. Rather than being triumphal, there had been an apologetic look on Duncan's face as he passed Gary in the hallway on his way out, hand-in-hand with Emily. Gary thought that she could at least have had the decency to look shamefaced, but her demeanour as she sauntered past suggested it was all highly amusing.

Gary was forlorn for weeks, but the new relationship didn't last long, ending when Emily won a place at East Anglia University, leaving Aylesbury for good. The last anyone heard was that she was engaged to a racehorse owner in Newmarket.

Duncan was sipping a pint of London Pride and reading *The Sunday Times* when Gary arrived at the pub carrying his overnight bag, ready to catch the train back to London afterwards.

'I don't know why you waste your money buying a Sunday paper. You can read everything on your phone,' said Gary as he settled opposite his friend, having already taken a gulp of lager on his way from the bar. Duncan had texted him to say that the carvery was full and that he wasn't hungry anyway. Gary threw three bags of compensatory cheese and onion crisps and a packet of dry roasted peanuts onto the table.

'Analysis, my friend, analysis. An app can only skim the surface, this newspaper gives me a deeper understanding of the events that shape our lives and is way more satisfying. Think of your app as a bag of crisps, whereas this,' he said without looking up, 'is a three-course meal in the carvery. How's it going?'

'Oh fine, everything's going fine. What are you so engrossed in?'

'This Russian stuff. They say the guy who was poisoned is a suspected FSB agent.'

'Ah, that would be the Finnish State Ballet,' said Gary through a mouthful of crisps.

Duncan rolled his eyes. 'The FSB is the successor organisation to the KGB, and the significance of this news is that the assumption that the target was one of the many Russian dissidents who now live in our fair country was wrong. The FSB would appear to be the poisoned rather than the poisoner.'

'How fascinating,' Gary said sarcastically.

'If you're not careful you'll end up like Gordon Bates.'

'That's cruel.' Gary was already chuckling before they said together, 'The boy who thought that the Gaza Strip was the football kit that Paul Gascoigne wore in the 1990 World Cup.'

Gary said, 'Didn't we also convince him that granola was the country where they made the breakfast cereal?' provoking renewed merriment.

Duncan wanted to turn to a more serious subject. Folding away his newspaper he asked, 'So what's happening on the girlfriend front, my city-dwelling buddy?'

'Not much. My boss at work is fit but at least ten years older than me and way out of my league.'

'What about your flatmate?'

Gary slaked off another mouthful of beer before moving his chair away from the table and stretching his legs.

'You mean Melissa – I do not fancy her, I like her. Our relationship is based on intellect rather than lust.'

'Right, drawn a blank there as well then, eh?'

Duncan worked for Bucks County Council in Environmental Protection and was content in his work and his life. After Emily there had been a succession of girl-friends before he met the woman he was now living with. They were expecting their first child. Duncan's was a settled, satisfied existence. He had no ambition to move away from Aylesbury – unless it was to Wendover or Buckingham, moving into a bigger, better house as his career progressed and his salary increased.

The two friends liked to discuss many things – cricket, music, saving the planet – but Duncan had become increasingly aware of Gary's loneliness and always tried to steer the conversation towards more intimate matters. Knowing that his friend was a single child from a one-parent family whose only close relationship had been with his mother, Duncan believed that if only he could find the right girl Gary's life would be transformed. It was as simple as that. Their regular Sunday reunions in the pub had become more interrogational as Duncan sought to encourage and cajole his friend into overcoming a natural shyness and infuriating lethargy.

It wasn't as if his friend was plug-ugly. Throughout their schooldays together, or at least since the opposite sex had assumed a greater importance, Gary had been the fancied as much as the fancier. Duncan remembered Shirita Khan from Form 5Y telling him how she felt that the only way she'd ever get to go out with Gary was through an arranged marriage, and Denise Mackie putting it around that Gary must be gay, which made him the coolest kid in the fifth year for a while. Duncan himself had sometimes wondered whether he really knew about his friend's sexuality – until Emily Swanson came along and seduced them both.

That rupture in their relationship had long been repaired and now Duncan was determined to help Gary find serenity. He was convinced that all his friend lacked was what Mr Price, their head teacher at school, used to refer to as 'gumption'. Few of the pupils had any idea what Mr Price meant. It was even said that Gordon Bates had gone to the local hardware store and asked for a tin of it. Duncan just knew that Gary didn't have any and that it was his duty as official best friend to compensate for this deficiency from his own surplus supply.

Eventually, over their second pint, Gary told Duncan about the girl he watched every morning applying her make-up on the train; how beautiful she was, how her inscrutability excited and fascinated him in equal measure. As with Knuckles on Friday evening, Gary was keen to get some practical advice. How could he begin a conversation? How to break the ice? As Gary drifted back from the reverie he'd slipped into while describing the methodical way that her make-up was applied, he saw that Duncan was giving him a look of disdainful incredulity.

'This isn't difficult, my friend. Even Gordon Bates would know what to do in this situation,' Duncan said forcefully. 'Next time just bloody sit next to her.'

8

There was an unseasonable chill in the air as Gary made his way to work on Monday morning. It hadn't prevented Terry from occupying his customary position on the canvas chair in front of the two stone steps leading up to his front door. He wore an old donkey jacket as a concession to the weather. The usual pleasantries were exchanged before Gary strolled off towards the station.

Having been mulling over Duncan's advice all the way back from Aylesbury the previous day and amalgamating it with what Knuckles had said on Friday, Gary was determined that this was the day for action. He would sit next to the girl after boarding the train at Crystal Palace and get off with her at Clapham Junction to continue what he was sure would, by then, be a deep and meaningful conversation. He'd put on his best Nike trainers and a brand-new Vivienne Westwood shirt beneath a light hooded anorak. Rain was forecast.

But when the 8.30 train pulled into Crystal Palace and Gary entered the usual carriage three from the front, it was empty. For the first time since his infatuation had begun, the girl wasn't in the window seat, catching the light to better apply her make-up. Such was Gary's disappointment he even checked the other carriages, moving swiftly between the interlinking doors to try to complete his search before the train filled up at Gipsy Hill. There was no sign of her.

His foray had left him seatless, the hordes having boarded like an invading army just as he finished his search in the final carriage. Despite her apparent absence, he kept to his plan of disembarking at Clapham Junction, standing by the staircase to scrutinise the passengers who'd got off with him in case she'd escaped his notice.

Catching the next train twenty minutes later to complete his journey to Victoria, a disconsolate mood descended. It was Monday morning, the weather was poor, the woman who lightened his life was missing and now he would be late for work.

At Victoria, Gary joined the usual throng of commuters waiting to pass through the bottleneck at the top of the descent into the underground. It was, as always, a silent congestion that gradually dispersed onto the platforms below.

He took the Victoria Line train to Green Park, changing onto the Piccadilly Line for the three stops to Covent Garden, where a bearded busker seemed to have a permanent pitch. His repertoire consisted of a single song – 'Where Do You Go to My Lovely' – sung to the accompaniment of an out-of-tune guitar. Gary trudged along cursing Peter Sarstedt but nevertheless dropping some small change into the busker's upturned flat cap. He always donated to musicians more out of respect for their calling than the competence of the performance.

In this he'd been heavily influenced by his mother, who donated to whatever cause presented itself. He was convinced, growing up, that half the print run of *The Big Issue* found its way into his house every month, so often did his mother bring duplicates of the same copy home.

The Accounts Payable – AP – department of the major national newspaper where Gary worked was an open-plan office in a building off Long Acre. His twenty or so fellow workers were in their twenties or thirties and had come to London from around the world. There were Moroccans, Koreans, Nigerians, twin brothers from Senegal. In all the time he'd worked there Gary was only aware of one colleague who'd moved to a role elsewhere in the newspaper group. Every other departure had been to another employer, usually after about eighteen months of this remorselessly mundane occupation.

It was principally inertia that tied Gary to his workstation. As a result, he'd become the most senior operative – not that this carried any kind of enhanced status. The majority of employees were part-time, combining work with study. For them this was a staging post – for Gary it felt increasingly like a terminus.

Jamil, who sat next to him in the far corner of the office, was from Egypt and studying medicine at UCL. He and Gary had formed a strong bond. They looked after one another's interests.

'Hey, Sparks,' Jamil said by way of greeting. 'Get busy – The Ice Queen is on your case.' This was a reference to their boss, Ms Kelsey, who was only tenuously connected to Gary's work area, descending periodically from the plush offices upstairs to offer what she considered to be words of encouragement and even inspiration. Few in her team were encouraged and none were inspired.

Marilyn Kelsey was the woman who Gary had admitted fancying in his Sunday-lunchtime Aylesbury interrogation by Duncan. She was also the 'Manager' who'd received Terry's letter. It was Ms Kelsey who had decided to highlight this paean of praise to Gary's electrical skills in the company newsletter.

A tall, graceful, red-headed Australian in her mid-thirties with an impeccable dress sense, Gary had carried a torch for her ever since coming to work here three years before. The swish of her skirt as she passed his desk, the delicate scent of her perfume, the elongated elegance of her demeanour beguiled him. The rumour was that she'd come to England to marry a City stockbroker but that they'd split up and she now lived alone.

Every Monday morning, first thing, Ice Queen Kelsey would give a five-minute team talk to Accounts Payable, focusing on the week ahead. This invariably ended with a meaningless homily such as 'You can only achieve what you aspire to', or 'Getting to the top requires a climber not a ladder'. In one of these team talks a while ago she'd finished by saying, 'Always remember, you can't cook a turkey in a fridge', a statement so completely meaningless that, combined with the half-smile that flitted across her porcelain face, it had led Gary to suspect that she was engaged in deliberate, self-aware parody. Far from attempting to be motivational, Ms Kelsey was simply taking the piss. Her whole management style was a form of mockery and the joke was actually on the team not their leader.

Gary didn't tell anybody about his suspicion, not even Jamil. He considered it to be an intimate secret – something that only he knew about his boss and that bound them closer. He was in on the secret and liked to think she knew that he knew.

Now, on this Monday morning, he'd missed the team talk and his absence had been noticed. Unlike the rest of them in Accounts Payable, Gary was permanent rather than temporary. For those like him, classified as 'staff', arriving even a few minutes late was frowned upon. Twenty minutes was a serious transgression.

His phone rang almost as soon as he sat down. It was The Ice Queen.

'Gary, how good of you to join us. Can you pop up to my office during your lunchbreak? I need to have a word and I think this should be in break time rather than work time, don't you?'

'Sure, Ms Kelsey. I'll come straight up at one o'clock.'

'As I've told you before, please refer to me as Marilyn. Formalities are for weddings and funerals.'

Gary had half an hour for lunch from one to half past. It never varied and neither did the lunch itself – a cheese and ham panini from the café across the road. Today he'd have to go hungry. Gary felt it was a small price to pay for an audience with The Ice Queen.

It was five to one when he arrived for his appointment. Ms Kelsey was behind her desk gazing intently at her computer screen as Gary knocked and entered, having taken the lift to the unfamiliar opulence of the Executive Floor.

'Ah, Gary,' she exclaimed warmly, moving through the Laura Ashley furnishings in her substantial office to guide him in. They chatted idly for a few minutes with Gary expecting the tone to change when Ms Kelsey got on to the subject of his late attendance, but to his amazement the subject was never raised. Instead he was praised for his role in successfully dealing with an increase in the '2% Net 30' arrangements under which the company deducted 2 per cent from the invoice if the recipient insisted that payment be made within thirty days.

There were technical issues with the software that Gary had helped to overcome. While they were talking these through, one of Ms Kelsey's many assistants came in with coffee, a couple of ham sandwiches and a packet of hand-cooked crisps. 'I didn't want you to go unnourished,' Ms Kelsey explained as she re-crossed her legs, having got up to help arrange the little feast that now lay on the table between them. Gary couldn't suppress a look of surprise, which Ms Kelsey mistook for concern.

'You're not a bloody vegan, are you?' she exclaimed, making it sound like a condemnation. Gary, having assured her that, far from being a vegan, a couple of chicken legs wouldn't have gone amiss, settled back to luxuriate in the moment. Marilyn Kelsey's grey pleated skirt had lifted slightly as she sat back down, exposing a tantalising few inches of creamy thigh which Gary was trying to identify as bare or clad. A seduction scene had begun to play in his imagination as Ms Kelsey brought their technical discussion to a close, the last of the crisps disappearing into her perfectly proportioned mouth.

'Time to get back to work,' she was saying. 'We won't get off the island if we never set sail.'

She stood up, carefully brushing crumbs from her skirt. Gary was heading for the door when she glided across to cut off his retreat.

'I wonder if you could do me an enormous favour,' she asked, placing a hand on Gary's shoulder. 'I'm having some problems with the electrics in my house. The kitchen lights over the work surfaces are buggered and every time the vacuum cleaner is plugged in half the fuses blow. Thanks to your appreciative neighbour we all know what an expert you are on all things electric.'

She paused, pushing a card with an address in Fulham into Gary's hand.

'I'd be so grateful if you could pop round some time to take a look at it for me. Can we fix something up – soon?'

9

Monday, 13 July

'Suction please, Rachel – I said suction, please.' Mr Parnaby was displaying faint signs of irritation with his assistant. Rachel Nelson was distracted. It was Monday morning and she couldn't stop thinking about her son's opaque reference to Father's Day two days before.

'Sorry, Mr Parnaby.' She inserted the long thin snout of the suction machine into the patient's mouth, allowing Mr Parnaby, the dentist who had employed her for twenty years, to resume his task of drilling and filling.

Despite all their years together, Rachel had never addressed her boss informally. His full name, Tobias Cornelius Parnaby, was proudly displayed all around the surgery on various certificates of qualification. But to Rachel he was 'Mr Parnaby' in front of patients and 'Mr Parnaby' in the little pantry at the back of the surgery where they had sat together through the years, mugs of tea in hand, talking over their problems – or, to be more accurate, Rachel's problems for which the kindly dentist had always been as willing a receptacle as the little spittoon next to the dentist's chair.

Throughout the twenty years they had worked together Parnaby had been able to contrast his own comfortable, settled existence with the travails of Rachel, a single mother if not exactly by choice at the beginning, with increasing resolution as the years passed.

Mr Parnaby had never supplied a shoulder to cry on, because Rachel never cried, but he had listened as his assistant recounted her determination to preserve the cocoon of devotion she'd spun around her son against any intrusion from the various men who'd hoped to be her suitor.

A small man with a neatly trimmed goatee beard and soft brown eyes under unkempt eyebrows, Tobias Parnaby was old enough to be contemplating retirement.

He smiled to himself as he recalled some of the scrapes that Gary had got into as related by Rachel through the years, over tea and biscuits in that snug back room.

There was the time when Gary was first fixated by cricket and had been taken by his late grandfather to watch a county match at Buckingham. A batsman hit a six right into the stand where Gary was sitting, encouraging the then nine-year-old to attempt a catch. He'd caught the ball but fell backwards over a row of seats, fracturing his elbow. The day ended with Gary and Granddad enduring a six-hour wait in A & E.

Then there was the story that Rachel had related about Gary being attacked by some boys on the Mandeville Estate as he walked home from school. Gary had arrived indoors with a black eye, claiming to have had an accident in the school gym. Half an hour later Rachel answered a knock on the door to find an irate father of a boy from the estate demanding that 'the man of the house' come out to face him.

The man's son, one of the attackers, had come off particularly badly as Gary fought them off. Another gang member had followed Gary home and reported his address to the seething, thickset plaintiff who now sought redress on Rachel's doorstep. Given his demand and the fact that he lived on the other side of the estate, Rachel quickly calculated that he had no idea about her personal circumstances.

She told the man, calmly and politely, that her husband was away at the moment 'in Hereford, training with his unit', but if Mr Angry would care to leave his contact details, she was sure he'd be in touch as soon as he returned. The man had stood for a moment in quiet contemplation before doing an about-turn and walking off. After Rachel shut the door, she and Gary, leaning against it shoulder to shoulder, collapsed giggling to the floor.

Mr Parnaby remembered how shocked Rachel had been by the latent aggression her son displayed in that incident and how Mr Parnaby had sought to reassure her that it was nothing to worry about; that Gary was just a strong lad who could look after himself and his reluctance to tell his mother about the cause of his injury was something to be commended rather than condemned.

He also remembered Rachel recounting the difficult conversation in her car when she'd told Gary the truth about his father; how she'd been vigilant afterwards for any sign that her son had been affected, but none had emerged, which made her all the more worried that Gary was suppressing emotions that would be better released.

Rachel was grateful for Mr Parnaby's gentle imperturbability, while for his part Mr Parnaby regarded his diligent assistant as heroic in her quiet dedication to her son. The father of two boys, Tobias didn't exactly think of Rachel as the daughter he never had but he did regard her as his closest female friend; a status which Mrs Parnaby resented without Tobias ever seeming to notice.

As they sat in the pantry later that morning, dunking digestives into cups of PG Tips, Rachel told her employer about Saturday's conversation.

'He's never seemed at all curious about his father, let alone resentful that he didn't have one. I thought he'd accepted the situation and now I worry that he hasn't. That he's harbouring a deep desire to meet his dad.'

'Hardly a deep desire, Rachel. Surely a mild curiosity at the most,' Tobias said, wiping crumbs from his lips and lifting his mug for another mouthful of tea.

Rachel looked distractedly past him, as if trying to discern a pattern on the painted green wall.

'I've been so selfish,' she said softly. 'I wanted Gary all to myself and made a virtue out of it by telling myself that I was protecting his father from the burden of responsibility, that it was best for him and for Gary, while knowing full well that it was only really best for me.'

After ten seconds of silence, Mr Parnaby put his mug down and shifted position so that he was directly facing his assistant.

'Why don't you find Gary's father?' he asked, looking into Rachel's eyes. She gave an involuntary jolt as if she'd been tasered. Parnaby continued, 'All your reasons for not finding him are time-expired. It's not as if he'd be asked to take on responsibilities that he resented or that he'd complicate Gary's upbringing. Your son is now fully up-brung. And whether or not Gary *wants* to know, surely he *ought* to know.'

'But where would I begin? How can I track him down?'

'There are detective agencies. I'll pay – my bonus to you for twenty years' service.'

'No,' Rachel said firmly. 'First of all, I'm not accepting any money from you for what is my responsibility, and secondly, I don't want anyone else involved.'

'Then let's do the detective work ourselves. I'm sure we can find him.'

'But after all this time?' she said. 'Surely it will make things worse – he'll be married and have children of his own.'

'Rachel, he *has* a child of his own, he's called Gary.'

'I know, but what would I say?'

'That, my dear, is a second-order question,' the dentist said. 'First, if you agree, we try to find him. Once we've done that, then you can think about what to say.'

Rachel silently nodded her assent, staring into the bottom of her cup as if the tea leaves could reveal what lay ahead.

It was cold in Amsterdam. An unseasonal chill seemed to rise from the River Amstel and envelop the city in late-afternoon gloom as Sergei Dzyuba struggled to cover the four hundred metres between his apartment and the clinic on Czar Peerstraat.

He'd lived in the Netherlands for two years since leaving London following his exposé of Russian organised crime that was published in the *Sunday Telegraph*. As well as identifying the scale of the problem, he'd named the leaders of the largest and most vicious gang, Krovnyye Bratya, and been forced to flee in fear of his life.

Dzyuba was in his early thirties, of average height with the long, lank hair of a heavy-metal rock star. His wife and child had gone back to Russia rather than be exiled in Amsterdam, but their safety remained a cause for concern. A series of articles that Dzyuba had written when the President was first elected had marked him out as a dissenter and the family had originally moved to London precisely because of the enmity he'd attracted from Moscow. Dzyuba had managed the dual distinction of becoming an enemy of the state and of a Russian criminal gang, although in reality everyone knew the two were linked as closely as conjoined twins.

His perilous situation had eased dramatically over the past month or so. His wife was from Crimea and had instilled in her husband a fierce sense of injustice about the decision of the USSR sixty years ago to make a gift of Crimea to Ukraine. Dzyuba had written an article for *Newsweek* explaining the historic inequity and supporting the President's initiative to restore Crimea to what he'd described as 'its rightful place'.

While he hadn't written the article to curry favour with the administration, that had been the effect. There was a thaw in relations. Dzyuba had been contacted by the Russian embassy in the Netherlands. Suddenly he was no longer *persona non grata*: cordial relations with his homeland were re-established and by the beginning of July he'd accepted a request to coordinate a meeting in London between his friend (and former fellow dissident), Igor Golovin, and Denis Smolnikov, the acclaimed Russian film producer.

It had taken an effort for Dzyuba to be convinced that he could travel to London in safety, but in the end the embassy had provided him with a letter from the President guaranteeing safe conduct. Arrangements were now being made for him to rejoin his family in St Petersburg and take up a salaried position with the Ministry of Information, writing propaganda in support of the annexation of Crimea.

He'd been reflecting on these positive developments that morning as he completed his final session with the two Metropolitan Police detectives who'd travelled over to interview him about the poisoning of Denis Smolnikov. His gentle interrogation had ended with Dzyuba agreeing to go back to London to testify if necessary. That was five hours ago. By now the detectives would be well on their way back to London. He'd been feeling okay, putting the mild stomach cramps and slight headache he'd been suffering down to the symptoms of the IBS that he'd had on and off for years. This appointment to see his doctor had only been made to get one of his regular prescriptions.

Now as he inched his way towards the clinic, he was barely able to stay upright, so severe had the pain in his stomach become. A tingling had developed in his palms and the soles of his feet that he remembered from somewhere as being associated with certain types of poison. As he crossed a bridge he was forced to stop and vomit into the canal below. How could he have been poisoned? Despite the letter from the President, Dzyuba had stuck to the self-preservation techniques that had kept him alive through the period when he'd been most at risk. He'd eaten nothing at the Strand Hotel and drunk only from the previously unopened plastic bottle of mineral water that he'd brought with him to the hotel. The arrival of a bunch of CSKA supporters splashing vodka around hadn't tempted him to abandon his well-developed routine. Their invitations to imbibe had been politely declined.

The Met officers had told him that Smolnikov had likely consumed a poisoned coffee that was meant for somebody else. They'd also said that the film-maker had accused him of being the poisoner – an accusation that even the police considered fanciful. Why would he turn from journalism to assassination to murder one of the President's friends, just as the President was allowing him to return to some kind of normal existence?

By the time he arrived at the clinic Sergei Dzyuba was barely conscious, finding it as difficult to think as to walk. The nurse on reception took one glance at the man entering her clinic before ordering an ambulance. The intrepid journalist was soon on his way to intensive care.

10

There was a full attendance at the housemates' Tuesday get-together the following evening. Gary had gone straight to the Dog and Pheasant from work. He was disconcerted. Instead of telling Ms Kelsey the truth about his lack of even a rudimentary understanding of electronics, he'd reaffirmed his commitment to pay her a visit on a date to be arranged over the next few weeks.

Gary was aware that this was likely to end in humiliation or maybe even death by electrocution, but the excitement of visiting The Ice Queen sent a current surging through him equal to anything produced by the National Grid.

The visit had been mentioned in the one interaction he'd had with his boss that day. 'Don't forget your tool kit,' she'd trilled suggestively as they ended their brief encounter in the corridor. The thrill of anticipation had not only brightened his day, it had diverted his thoughts away from the girl who'd been missing from the train again that morning. Gary assumed she was on holiday and resigned himself to a temporary suspension of his morning treat.

He was the first to get to the pub and was cradling his pint while gazing into the middle distance, imagining how a visit to Ms Kelsey's house in Fulham might develop, when Melissa arrived.

'Don't tell me,' she said, plonking her handbag on the seat opposite. 'You've taken up transcendental meditation.'

Melissa found her purse and went to the bar, following the protocol that each housemate would purchase their own drink. Returning with a gin and tonic she collapsed into the chair opposite, shaking out her extravagant mane of blonde hair and then blowing at a stray piece of fringe that had fallen across her eyes, a gesture performed so often it should have been annoying, but one that Gary found endearing.

She had a copy of the *Evening Standard* poking out of her bag, its front-page headline screaming 'RUSSIAN ROULETTE' above a story about suspicion for the Russian poisoning falling upon a gambling syndicate run by 'Novy Ruskies on the make in London's West End'.

'I'd be happy to leave them to murder each other but the trouble with the stuff these bloody Russians use is that it could end up poisoning half of London – this polanian stuff.'

'Polonium,' Gary corrected her.

'Smart arse,' Melissa spat back.

Jason and Knuckles arrived together and once they'd purchased their drinks the weekly meeting got underway and was finished in half an hour. The main item of business was the damp patch in the communal living room, about which Jason had been delegated to make representation to their landlord, Mr Grant.

'Just be careful you don't eat or drink anything while you're with him,' suggested Knuckles.

'Why?' asked Melissa.

'Because, as I discovered today, Mr Grant is actually an ex-pat Russian whose real name is Vladimir Granat.'

'Who told you that?' demanded Jason.

'It just so happens that the job I'm working on at the moment is a documentary exposé about the property market in London and the way it's being dominated by foreign investment,' Knuckles explained. 'Our landlord has one of the biggest property portfolios and, as the programme will reveal, may well be a bigger gangster than Rachman ever was.'

'It's just as well that I'll only be meeting the managing agents,' Jason said. 'From what I hear, nobody actually gets to speak to Grant himself.'

'Sure, he'll have no interest in this little backwater of his empire. He owns half of feckin' Knightsbridge,' said Knuckles.

'You're bound to get on with him, Jason,' observed Gary, 'what with you both being representatives of the nouveau riche.'

'That's French, not Russian,' said Melissa.

'In a perfect world,' Knuckles ruminated, 'the French would cook, the Germans would manage our money and the Russians would protect our property.'

'And deal with damp patches,' added Jason.

'Seriously though, it is a bit worrying that he's linked with organised crime. Do you think he's mafia?' Gary asked reflectively of no one in particular.

'Did you never watch *The Sopranos*?' asked Melissa. 'We've got nothing to worry about. The Mafia never defecate on their own doorstep.'

'That's the New York mafia,' Gary retorted.

'New Jersey, actually,' Melissa shot back.

'Our damp patch seems to have turned into a criminal conspiracy,' said Jason.

'Yeah,' said Melissa. 'Stop being ridiculous, Gary. Anyway, why can't one of you men fix the problem without involving our landlord?'

'Guess that none of us has the required skills,' said Jason. 'But don't you have some kind of building trade, Knuckles?'

'I have indeed, but as an electrician.'

'An electrician?' said Gary. 'You're an electrician?'

'Fully trained at Bombardier in the fair city of Belfast,' Knuckles declared proudly.

Gary processed this information while the others chatted away about this and that. Jason was first to leave, saying that he had to meet a business associate for dinner at the Queens Hotel. Melissa stayed, keen to know more about the documentary Knuckles was working on and the exploits of Mr Grant, their landlord.

'Look, I'm just the runner, but I keep my ears and eyes open. This Grant, Granat fella, he's dangerous and I shouldn't have been shooting my mouth off about him.'

'Don't worry, we won't tell anybody,' said Melissa light-heartedly.

'Oh, I know I can trust youse two, but I wouldn't trust Jason as far as I can throw the dodgy bastard.'

Gary deliberately slowed his beer intake to ensure that he and Knuckles were the last to leave.

After Melissa had gone and they were settled over a final pint (with a pickled egg for Knuckles), conversation turned to how Gary had fared with the girl on the train and whether he'd taken the sage advice offered in their last tête-à-tête. Gary explained how events had conspired against him, but went on to tell his friend about his flirtation with Marilyn Kelsey.

'Jesus, Gary, it's one woman after another with you. And how can I help with this one?'

Gary leaned forward conspiratorially to explain the plan that he'd only just conceived.

11

Wednesday, 15 July

Wednesday at work passed so slowly and uneventfully that Gary found it difficult to stay awake. He was feeling the effects of the previous evening's alcohol intake. The bad weather had continued, and it was the wettest day of the summer so far. Forced to wear his hooded anorak again, Gary had walked to the station watching the rain bounce up off the pavement like thousands of tiny fountains. Perversely his crapulous state enhanced his determination to go drinking again after work.

Jamil happened to be on a late shift that ended at 6 p.m., so the two workmates walked through the evening downpour for a drink together. Teetotal Jamil placed a lime and soda opposite Gary's pint of lager and talked about the situation back in Egypt in response to Gary's concerns about Jamil's family.

'My father is a surgeon in Cairo. He knew Mubarak was corrupt, but my family never supported the so-called Arab Spring. It was a concoction of the Western media. My father predicted that it would end in a move away from the modern, secular state that the majority of Egyptians want to live in. I don't agree with him, but I never trusted Morsi or the Muslim Brotherhood. So, like most of my countrymen I am conflicted. I don't want to swap one dictatorship for another but at least the army brings stability.'

'Will you go back when you've qualified?' Gary asked.

'My father wants me to but I'm keen to defy him and by the time I qualify he'll be much too old to tell me what to do. We all have battles with our fathers, no?'

Gary nodded, unwilling to get into a discussion on a subject he knew nothing about and more interested in talking about Ms Kelsey.

'You know what I've noticed?' said Jamil. 'That woman always glances over to where we work whenever she graces our floor with her presence.'

Gary gave a 'so what?' kind of shrug.

'Granted she may find my dark Arab eyes beguiling, but I think she's looking at you.'

Gary told Jamil about his Monday-lunchtime meeting with The Ice Queen, how he had foolishly agreed to be her repairman and the truth about his falsely acquired reputation as an electrician.

'So, put her off. Don't visit. She'll soon give up and get someone qualified.'

Gary took the address card that Ms Kelsey had given him out of his wallet, perusing it as he said, 'But wouldn't it be great to see The Ice Queen in her palace; to talk to her away from work; get to know her better; impress her?'

'Well, you'd better be sure to seduce her before the house blows up,' said Jamil.

'Fortunately, one of my housemates is an electrician. My plan is to tell Ms Kelsey that I'm busy in the evenings but can't risk leaving her in danger so I'm sending someone who has worked with me on this kind of job just to make sure everything is safe. He can do what needs to be done during the week and I'll carry out a final check at the weekend whenever she's around.'

'But she may decide that if the thing's fixed, she won't need you to pay a visit.'

'My housemate will tell her that it's essential that I give it the once over – some kind of trade regulation. Besides, if she does as you suggest I'll know she's not using this as a ploy to get to know me better – and you and I both suspect that she is.'

'Sounds a bit convoluted to me,' said Jamil. 'It's not like you to live so dangerously.'

After a few more rounds they left, though Gary had barely got through the door before remembering that he'd left Ms Kelsey's address card on the pub table, returning seconds later to tuck it safely into the pocket of his anorak.

He didn't get to Victoria station until well after the main rush-hour crowd had dispersed. Settling into his seat on the 20.56 he turned to the sports app on his phone for the latest cricket scores before gazing idly out of the window.

As the train pulled into Clapham Junction, Gary spotted her – the girl whose make-up routine had obsessed him for the past few weeks, standing on the platform with a knot of passengers ready to board the train several carriages down from where he sat. She'd been missing from his train again that morning and as he'd never seen her on his homeward journey, Gary's natural assumption, now seemingly confirmed, was that their finishing times didn't coincide.

There she was, the subject of his infatuation, carrying an umbrella, her lovely blonde hair pulled back into a ponytail, and wearing a long thin cotton skirt. Inspired by his conversations with Knuckles and Duncan at the weekend (and the three pints of lager he'd consumed with Jamil), Gary determined to walk back through the carriages in the hope of sitting next to her and starting a conversation.

Leaving his seat, he passed through the connecting doors to find her carriage while thinking frantically about his opening line.

'Do you know where the toilet is?' popped into his head, having worked its way up from his bladder, but he decided it wouldn't make the most favourable impression. He was mulling over an elaborate ruse that involved him pretending to have found a lipstick on the train and wondering if it was hers when he went through yet another connecting door to suddenly find himself in her presence. She was by the window halfway down the carriage, facing him in a nest of four seats. There was nobody next to her or immediately opposite.

He caught her eye and smiled like an idiot as he walked towards her. To his amazement, as he was carefully constructing an opening line in his mind, she greeted him.

'Tom,' she said warmly, reaching out her hand and beckoning him to occupy the seat beside her.

'Clare,' he replied, slightly disconcerted but cottoning on to what he thought was a bit of alcohol-induced play-acting.

'How lovely to see you,' she continued in an Eastern European accent as thick as the air in the carriage.

'Clare' stroked his arm as he settled beside her, chatting like old friends as she reached in her handbag and brought out the leather make-up pouch that Gary was so familiar with. He played along, smiling and nodding, too relieved at his good fortune to question whether his attractive new friend was suffering some kind of heat stroke.

The inane chatter continued as she released Gary's arm to dextrously wield the mascara brush with one hand and hold up a little silver hand-mirror in the other. The brush was brandished with practised speed and when the mascara had been applied, she pulled Gary's hood almost over his eyes and playfully held the mirror up as if urging him to check his reflection. The two words that Gary saw written on the surface with the mascara brush were faint but distinct: 'HELP ME', they said.

The long day had yet to give way to dusk. The rain had eased. Some lights were going on in the houses beside the track, revealing the evening routines of the occupants for a fleeting moment as the train rattled towards Crystal Palace and beyond. Gary hadn't noticed the other commuters in the quarter-full carriage. Now he scrutinised them, aware that the danger posed to his new friend must be close. Why else would she communicate like that? He saw a cluster of tired passengers, travelling too early to be on their way home after a night out and too late to be working reasonable hours.

Some of the women had kicked off their shoes and all the men in suits had loosened their ties. They looked crumpled by a combination of hot weather, rain and the normal pressures of commuting in and out of London. None looked more dishevelled than the two men who sat facing them on the other side of the aisle immersed in their phones. Gary noticed that the bespectacled one with close-cropped hair and a blue tattoo on his neck was constantly looking their way, taking his horn-rimmed glasses off to polish them on his untucked shirt every so often.

'Tom' and 'Clare' continued their pretence of being two old friends who'd bumped into each other by chance. Gary even took Marilyn Kelsey's address card from his pocket to use as a prop in this theatrical performance, pointing to it as if to convey a piece of important information while muttering softly, 'The two guys across the aisle?'

She nodded her assent, chuckling merrily as if responding to a bit of playful flirtation. Gary was impressed by her acting ability but most of all he was enthralled by her gentle touch, the dulcet accent, the smooth elegance of her neck as her head was thrown back in mock laughter. But, transfixed as he was, Gary was thinking hard – planning their escape.

Moving even closer, he whispered, 'We're getting off at the next stop, follow me.'

The train was approaching Gipsy Hill where it emptied in the evenings in the same way that it filled in the mornings. A queue of commuters formed at the carriage doors as the train pulled in. Gary leapt up, pulling his companion to her feet.

'Let's get over to the Gipsy Tavern before I die of thirst,' he said loudly. They were out and up the stairs before the two men in the opposite aisle had stirred into action. Gary guessed that he had a ten-second advantage and he calculated that their pursuers would think they were going out through the ticket barriers and across to the fine old pub that was practically opposite the station entrance. But instead, as they turned right at the top of the stairs towards the barriers and out of sight of their pursuers, who were still puffing their way up the steps, he led 'Clare' across the bridge and down onto the opposite platform where a Victoria-bound train was just pulling in.

They jumped aboard. Gary stood by the carriage doors to make sure they weren't followed onto the train, which was soon on its way back to London. Sitting in the otherwise empty carriage, Gary felt that it might be time for his exciting new friend to explain exactly what was going on.

12

There was live music at the Gipsy Hill Tavern every Wednesday evening and a raucous rendition of 'Whiskey in the Jar' by an Irish folk trio drifted through its open doors as Stanislav Miranchuk approached. He crossed the main threshold while Morozov, his colleague, entered through the door at the back.

The beer garden was empty apart from a dismal group of smokers huddled in the drizzle. If 'Tom' and 'Clare' were here, they'd be inside.

'Whiskey in the Jar' had given way to 'Dirty Old Town' by the time the two men had completed a reconnaissance, working their way in from the two entrances and meeting in the middle of the bar having scanned the faces of the seventy or so customers enjoying liquid relief on a muggy night.

Morozov had already put out a call for backup and was confident that within minutes fellow Krovnyye Bratya associates would be patrolling the surrounding streets using the photograph that he'd taken surreptitiously on the train to identify the young couple they were pursuing.

The barman was asking what they wanted to drink and Miranchuk decided that as they were here, they may as well order something. He was tired and thirsty. Running around the streets outside like a headless chicken had no appeal for him, and in any case, he needed time to think. They took two pints of cold Guinness to a table as far away from the band as they could get.

Miranchuk knew he'd messed up. Losing the girl would be regarded as a serious failure. Anton Sidrenko had been clear in his telephone call from Moscow that morning.

'The police will take the waitress to the Strand Hotel for a re-enactment. At around 8 p.m. she'll leave alone, the police having told her she could go home to be contacted again in the morning.

'She is being delivered into our hands. All you need to do is make sure she gets back to her flat in Sutton. That's where you'll seize her – you understand? Discreetly, with no fuss. We have arranged a safe house and all the measures are in place to take her to Moscow if necessary.'

At the end of the call Sidrenko had again emphasised that the girl was not to be harmed.

'Be gentle. You do know how to be gentle, don't you, Stanislav?'

Miranchuk wasn't renowned for gentility. He had a powerful physique and was proud of his fighting ability. He enjoyed violence; had done ever since he was a kid in one of the toughest districts of Moscow. That was where he acquired the small blue tattoo under his right earlobe, the mark of the teenage pack he once ran with.

Raised in care, joining the army at eighteen had disciplined his brutishness. It was as a soldier that his enjoyment of conflict was given purpose and structure. His natural intelligence, untapped at school, was nurtured. From the military he followed the well-trodden path into what was then still the KGB, where he learned to speak English and was sent to work at the Russian embassies in Washington and then London.

Miranchuk had been involved in the elimination of many enemies of the Russian Federation, extinguished many lives.

There was a fine line between doing it for the State as a soldier or an officer of the KGB/FSB and doing it for an organisation like Krovnyye Bratya, to which he'd been recruited personally by Anton Sidrenko. Previously he'd taken orders from military high command. Now he took orders from Sidrenko, Vladimir Granat and Dmitry Podkolzin; a different kind of high command.

The three organisations – military, secret service and Krovnyye Bratya – were interconnected. He had now dedicated himself to the latter, but to all intents and purposes life went on as before.

He was still registered as a diplomat at the Russian embassy, his (enhanced) salary was still paid into his bank account every month and Miranchuk continued to occupy the grace-and-favour flat in Kings Cross that had come with the embassy posting.

Now he was forced to reflect on the first serious setback of his entire military career (he still thought of himself as working for the military).

He'd accompanied Denis Smolnikov on a mission, as he'd done many times before. He liked being with Smolnikov, the well-respected documentary director lauded across the world as a champion of the oppressed but who was, in reality, a friend of the oppressors.

Now Smolnikov was in intensive care fighting for his life. It had happened on Miranchuk's watch. And the waitress had vanished, slipped away, once again on Miranchuk's watch.

If only his instructions had not been so placid, he thought. This girl must have served the poisoned coffee to Smolnikov, albeit inadvertently. Why all the tenderness? He could have plucked her off the street as easily as pulling petals from a flower. Didn't Sidrenko appreciate that they could act with impunity?

There was no need for this excessive caution, particularly now they had a senior Met police officer on their payroll. With a little force the waitress could be safely under their control rather than lost to the night.

He'd given much thought to the approach that Ivan Ilkun had made at the football match. His old FSB comrade had offered an escape route from Krovnyye Bratya that he may well need and that became more attractive the more he thought about it. If the President no longer supported the activities of KB, the safest place to be was back in the FSB.

As he and Morozov sipped their drinks in silence, Miranchuk tried to turn his mind to more pleasant things.

He'd spent the night with Maria Paseka. Indeed, when Sidrenko rang that morning he'd still been with her in the hotel room. During the six months of this affair they'd always used hotels because he was sure that his flat was bugged by the embassy.

Leaning back against the pillows on the dishevelled bed, he'd watched Maria getting dressed while her husband issued instructions to him down the line from Moscow. Miranchuk enjoyed the sensation of power over his boss that this gave him. He knew he'd strayed into dangerous territory, but Maria Paseka was a risk worth taking.

Ten years his senior, she had a depth and vitality missing from the younger women he usually pursued. They talked a lot between sessions of frantic love-making; about their lives, their beliefs, about Russia. Maria had been a student when the Soviet Union collapsed and remembered the sense of release.

'You were too young to know what communism was like,' she'd said to him last night. 'We used to ask what the difference was between capitalism and communism.'

'And what was the answer?' asked Miranchuk, fully aware of the old joke but keen to hear his lover deliver the punch line.

'Under capitalism man exploits man, whereas under communism it's the other way around.'

'And have your hopes been fulfilled?' he'd asked, pulling Maria closer to him as they lay across the enormous bed.

She'd answered by pointing out that she wouldn't have been allowed to leave Russia under the old regime, let alone live in London.

'Now,' she'd said, 'we live under capitalism but it's KGB capitalism. Oh, I know that you were a KGB officer, as was the President, and that the organisation had to change because of its reputation, but the only difference between FSB and KGB are two initials. Now its influence is more powerful than ever and I'm still not sure if that's a good thing.'

Miranchuk told her that from his perspective they were restoring the dignity of Russia after the humiliation of the Yeltsin years. The FSB had been a good training ground but Krovnyye Bratya was different. It wasn't under state control. He related what Smolnikov had told him the other night, that they supplemented the power of the Kremlin rather than challenging it.

They talked well into the night. Miranchuk had been the instigator of this liaison, but Maria had entered into it enthusiastically and now seemed addicted to the intrigue. Did she fully appreciate the extent of Sidrenko's delinquent activity? Miranchuk often wondered this to himself. She sometimes spoke as if her husband was the CEO of a car-manufacturing company or the head of some kind of international charity rather than leading one of the most powerful Russian criminal networks in Europe.

Miranchuk loved being with Maria and felt no need to remove her rose-tinted spectacles. He perceived a deep well of sadness beneath that confident exterior and would have liked to have the time to plumb its depths. But he sensed that she would eventually tire of these erotic interludes and move on, perhaps to another lover.

There would be no scenes, no amateur dramatics. Neither of them had ever suggested that this was anything more than a temporary attachment. He found it difficult to admit to himself that his affection for Maria was more profound than for any other woman he'd been with. Miranchuk knew such an attachment would be a weakness – and he despised weakness.

By now the folk trio were singing 'Danny Boy' as their set came to an end. Morozov was lumbering back in from the beer garden where he'd gone to take a call.

'No sign of them,' he said in Russian. 'We're watching the girl's flat in Sutton and some of our best guys have done a sweep down to Dulwich and up towards Crystal Palace.'

'Okay,' said Miranchuk. 'God knows who that guy with her is. An old boyfriend, a flatmate, he could even be an FSB agent.'

'What?' Morozov said incredulously.

'I'm serious. Look, the FSB knew nothing about the Strand Hotel business. This will cause them great embarrassment – they'll be furious about being left in the dark.'

'Didn't Smolnikov tell them? Or Sidrenko?'

'No,' Miranchuk replied emphatically. 'If you think the answer will be negative it's best not to ask. Besides, Sidrenko thinks we're past the stage of having to seek permission every time we want to take someone out.'

'Fine, but why would they send in an FSB agent?'

'Because of what happened to Smolnikov,' said Miranchuk. 'They'll want to talk to the waitress as much as we do.'

'But she knew the guy on the train,' Morozov said. 'She greeted him when he came into the carriage.'

'That's true. But I can't believe it was a chance encounter. If it was, why aren't they here? That guy suggested they have a drink at the Gipsy Tavern, so if they're not here it suggests it was a deliberate ploy to get her away from us. If not the FSB, then who? We have to find out who that guy is.'

Miranchuk concluded the conversation by lifting his glass for a final mouthful of stout.

'Oh, I nearly forgot,' said Morozov, reaching into his pocket. 'He dropped the card they were looking at on the train. I picked it up as we got off.'

He handed the card to Miranchuk, who studied Marilyn Kelsey's home address.

'Good work, my friend,' Miranchuk said, taking off his horn-rimmed glasses to polish them. 'Perhaps somebody should pay this lady a call.'

13

In a small room off a long corridor in New Scotland Yard, several people were in conference. Detective Superintendent Louise Mangan was giving an update on what had been a case of attempted murder. A tall woman with shoulder-length chestnut-brown hair, Mangan's tired eyes surveyed the room as she explained that the word 'attempted' could now be discarded.

'The man provisionally identified as Denis Smolnikov died in St Thomas' Hospital at 03.00 hours this morning. He had been in this country for ten days on one of his regular visits, during which he always used the Strand Hotel as the base for his meetings with various associates. It was at such a meeting last Friday that Smolnikov was poisoned with the deadly isotope polonium-210.

'The Security Service has long suspected Smolnikov to be associated with Russian organised crime as well as having links with the FSB. A good friend of the President – they go back years, having worked together in the old KGB – he uses his reputation as a documentary producer to gain access to people and places useful to his spying activities. On Friday he was meeting the Russian human rights activist Igor Golovin, who may well have been the intended victim.'

ALAN JOHNSON

'Is Golovin cooperating fully with us?' asked Deputy Commissioner Karen Dale, the senior Met officer for whose benefit this briefing had been arranged.

'I spoke to him yesterday,' said another conference participant, Mangan's Assistant Detective Superintendent Connor O'Farrell, a thin, dark-haired man with sharp features and a pallid complexion. 'He's shocked, scared and convinced that some diplomatic strings will be pulled to get him extradited to Russia to stand trial. I'm not sure if he realises that this is now a murder enquiry with him as a suspect.'

'But do we think he was involved in the poisoning?' asked Assistant Commissioner Brian Baker, the fourth person at the gathering.

'No,' said Louise Mangan emphatically. 'There were no substantial traces of polonium on him, no more than would be expected given that he was sitting next to Smolnikov. The experts tell us that polonium-210 drifts around in a kind of miasma so he was bound to have some of it on him, but if he'd administered it himself it would have been far more evident. Besides, why should he place himself in further jeopardy by murdering someone who he genuinely believed had come to talk to him about making a film?'

'Wasn't he suspicious about the invitation?' Assistant Commissioner Baker asked incredulously.

'No, because Smolnikov really is a Russian film producer. The spooks say that an essential part of his cover is that he has made documentaries critical of the Russian authorities – over Chernobyl, for instance. He did actually have a CNN commission for the film he was talking to Golovin about.'

'But surely he will have known about Smolnikov's activities – even the Sunday papers were reporting that he was an FSB agent.'

'That's because we briefed them,' O'Farrell interjected. 'We didn't want the public to believe that an innocent man had been poisoned in a London hotel.'

'The Russians went absolutely ballistic when they read those allegations in *The Sunday Times*,' Deputy Commissioner Dale said, 'which is why the Foreign Secretary as well as the Home Secretary is taking such a close interest in all this. The Russians have already demanded that Smolnikov's body be flown back to Moscow. The Commissioner needs to be absolutely sure that we're pursuing the right line.'

'Let me reassure you, Karen,' said Mangan, who had known the Deputy Commissioner for many years but never grown to like her. 'We are confident that Golovin was more likely to have been the intended victim than the assailant. Igor Golovin is a mild-mannered academic. There is nothing in his background to suggest that he'd even shout at somebody let alone try to murder them. Nothing leads us to doubt our original suspicion that the poisoned coffee was given to the wrong man.'

'By this waitress woman?' Baker asked.

'Yes, by Arina Kaplin.'

'And what do we know about her besides the fact that she's vanished?'

'She's a twenty-four-year-old Ukrainian national,' Mangan continued, 'who has worked at the Strand for just over a year.'

'We strongly suspect that she's here illegally,' added O'Farrell as he walked to the water cooler to top up his paper beaker.

The heat was intense after the previous day's rain.

'Visa overstayer?' asked the Assistant Commissioner.

'We don't think so. More likely smuggled in by people traffickers. We can't find any trace of a visa being issued in her name, and while she claimed to have a passport at home I doubt if we'll find one.'

'Have we searched her flat?'

'Doing it now,' said O'Farrell.

'Bit late,' observed Baker.

'But she's not a suspect and never has been,' Louise Mangan responded. 'The only reason we're searching her flat is because she's disappeared.'

'You mean you lost her,' Baker said.

Detective Superintendent Louise Mangan saw the need to be frank about the disappearance of Arina Kaplin.

'Having questioned her for two days with full cooperation we made it clear to her that while she wasn't a suspect, she had probably inadvertently been responsible for Smolnikov drinking the poisoned coffee. It was therefore in her own interests to remain under our protection. While the poisoning happened last Friday, it was midday Saturday before Smolnikov went to St Thomas' and the poisoning was traced back to the Strand Hotel. The waitress, Arina, was picked up on Sunday and was with us until the reconstruction of the crime scene carried out at the Strand yesterday.'

'But wasn't she still in your protection when she vanished last night?'

'No,' said O'Farrell. 'If she'd been under our protection, we'd have taken her back to her flat in a car, not on a bloody train. After the re-enactment she slipped out of the hotel and we presume headed home. She didn't tell anyone she was leaving and as she wasn't handcuffed or under arrest, we could have done nothing about it even if she had.'

Louise Mangan flashed a hostile glare at her subordinate before stating firmly, 'I do think we had a duty of care towards that girl and, given that she's an important witness, we should have kept a closer eye on her.'

'Okay, okay, let's get back to the timeline of last Friday. From what we've gleaned from the recently departed Mr Smolnikov, from Golovin and from the girl, what do we think happened at the hotel?' Deputy Commissioner Karen Dale was reasserting her authority. Louise Mangan handed over a single sheet of foolscap with the bare details that she now proceeded to expand upon.

'Igor Golovin entered the Strand Hotel at 10.45 on Friday, 10 July. He met three Russian men: Denis Smolnikov, the film-maker; Sergei Dzyuba, the journalist; and one other, introduced as Stanislav Miranchuk, an assistant to Smolnikov. Golovin describes him as being well-built with short blond hair, thick black, horn-rimmed spectacles and with a tattoo on his neck.

'Golovin and Dzyuba are always careful about who they meet. Both realise that they could be targeted by the Russian authorities. Indeed, Dzyuba now lives in Amsterdam precisely because he feels safer there than in London. You may remember, he wrote that article about Russian criminality being so prevalent here that London has become known as Moscow-by-the-Thames.'

'And he actually named some of the gang leaders in the article, which is why he had to move to the Netherlands,' interjected Baker.

Mangan resumed her narrative by moving on to the next bullet point.

'At about half past eleven a bunch of five or six rowdy Russian football supporters came into the hotel and went straight to the meeting room, where they were apparently dispensing vodka into everyone's cups.'

'So that's where the polonium came from?' asked Baker.

'Possibly, but we can't trace any of those involved, let alone their vodka bottles. There were around a thousand CSKA Moscow fans in London for Friday night's match and almost all were on their way back to Russia by the time Smolnikov went to the hospital. Incidentally, he's a CSKA director and was at the match. While he was compos mentis he told us that nothing happened at Stamford Bridge and neither did he drink any of the vodka that the fans were distributing at the Strand. He claimed to us that his coffee was poisoned by Dzyuba, but he was hardly going to admit to trying to murder Golovin, was he?'

'And where is Mr Dzyuba?' asked Deputy Commissioner Dale.

'He's back in Amsterdam, where two of my men interviewed him over the weekend,' said O'Farrell. 'They came back on Monday and say the guy couldn't have been more helpful. He backs up Golovin's view that the premise for the meeting at the Strand was genuine and says he noticed nothing suspicious. There is no motive for him to poison Smolnikov but we've applied for a European Arrest Warrant to bring him back here if we need to, although he seems perfectly willing to return of his own accord. We got a call from the Dutch police this morning to tell us that he's fallen ill. Not sure what the problem is; our guys say he was perfectly fit when they left on Monday.'

Louise Mangan carried on. 'It was the waitress, Arina Kaplin, who told us how particular Smolnikov was about the pot of coffee that was to be served to Golovin. He put her under so much pressure and harassed her so much that she feels he was instrumental in any mistake she may have made.'

'Why didn't Smolnikov distribute the bloody coffee himself?' asked Karen Dale.

'Well, it was the waitress's job,' continued Mangan.

'It would have probably aroused suspicion for him to wait at table. The problem for us is that we can find no trace of the poison anywhere but in the cup that Smolnikov drank from. Given the nature of the stuff, we'd expect to find traces of polonium all over the place as it was shifted around. Usually we'd be able to trace a poison like this back to its source, but we can't and that's a mystery. How did it just materialise in Smolnikov's coffee?'

'How do we even know that he was poisoned at the Strand?' Baker asked.

'Because,' said O'Farrell, 'apart from the clinician's report about how long it had been in his system corresponding with his visit to the Strand, as Louise said, we know because of the polonium traces on the cup he drank from. The one that we think was meant for Golovin.'

'Do you have CCTV footage?' asked Baker.

'There is a camera in the room, but it appears not to have been working that morning,' replied Mangan. 'Smolnikov probably disabled it.'

'I suppose it's convenient for us politically as well as professionally to ensure that the late Mr Smolnikov takes the rap for his own murder,' mused Assistant Commissioner Baker. 'But that will only happen if we ensure that our sole objective witness, Miss Kaplin, is available to give evidence. Which is why it was so careless of you to lose her. Have we any clues as to where she's gone?'

'If she was heading back to her flat, she never got there,' reported O'Farrell.

'We're currently inspecting CCTV footage from the trains she is most likely to have travelled on.'

'There's one other thing you should know,' said Louise Mangan. 'The other Russian at the meeting, the man known as Stanislav Miranchuk . . .'

'Yes,' said Deputy Commissioner Dale. 'The one who was Smolnikov's assistant.'

'Yes, the guy with the tattoo – we strongly suspect that he's a major player in Krovnyye Bratya. As you know, they are the dominant Russian criminal network in this country. Smolnikov was up to his neck in their activities.'

'Which makes it even more imperative to find the girl,' said Dale. 'The likelihood is KB will also be after her, so it's a matter of who finds her first. She's unlikely to survive an encounter with those vicious bastards. Make sure you stay in touch with the right people.'

Louise Mangan knew this was a reference to the security service, who were keen to take a more prominent role.

Karen Dale had one more thing to say. 'As you know, we haven't publicised the fact that Smolnikov is now dead. The Foreign Office is keen not to damage relations with Russia further by announcing his demise before family members have been informed, and they're all in Moscow. It's therefore unlikely to hit the headlines until tomorrow at the earliest.'

The meeting concluded, but just as the participants were about to leave, one of Mangan's subordinates poked her head around the door.

'Sorry to interrupt,' she said, 'but I thought you should know this straight away. We've found some CCTV footage of the missing girl on a train from Clapham Junction last night.'

14

Thursday, 16 July

Gary was prodded awake by the woman who had first introduced herself to him the previous evening as 'Clare'.

It was the morning after the adventure on the train, and in the course of a long conversation that had begun as their train pulled away from Gipsy Hill station, continuing as they walked through the streets of London SW1 scoffing pizza and ending at the Premier Inn, Victoria, he'd learned that 'Clare' was Arina. She now knew that 'Tom' was Gary and had given him a much better understanding of the danger she was in.

They had checked into this twin-bedded room as Mr and Mrs Nelson using Gary's debit card. Sleeping in separate beds they'd exchanged only the slightest intimacy when Arina kissed Gary's cheek before the lights went out, thanking him for his help.

Now as she bent over him the next morning fully dressed and ready to leave, his first inclination was to embrace her. But Arina was distant and business-like.

'I just want to say thank you and goodbye,' she said as he rolled onto his back. 'I never forget your kindness, but I go now.'

'Where will you go – to the police?'

'No, not the police. I tell you last night, police will hand me over to Russians.'

It was true that they'd rehearsed these arguments the night before. Gary had made the mistake of first thinking Arina was Polish, then Russian. ('Not Polski, not Ruskie – I'm from Ukraine.')

She told him how she'd entered the country illegally ('I have to find good work – everything in Ukraine is depression'), smuggled with nine others in the back of a truck carrying agricultural equipment; that she'd told the police she had a visa but they would soon discover this was untrue.

She'd recounted how a dodgy employment agency had found her the job at the Strand Hotel as a waitress and general dogsbody; how the pay was poor but that it provided her with enough to live on and was far more than she would receive in Kiev; how she wanted to be an actress and had studied drama at college in Ukraine.

Gary had offered congratulations upon her performance when he'd stumbled into her carriage the previous evening.

'You even had me thinking we must be old friends rather than complete strangers.'

'But you did know me. You watched me closely every morning when I put on make-up.'

Gary had said that as far as he was aware, she'd never paid him the slightest attention on those morning train journeys; never so much as glanced in his direction.

'You don't understand women,' Arina had chuckled.

'Of course I notice you. A woman always notice when attractive young man is paying her attention.'

But the bulk of their long conversation had consisted of Arina giving her escort a description of what had happened at the Strand Hotel the previous Friday morning; how she was detailed to serve refreshments in the reception room hired by Mr Smolnikov, who everybody at the hotel knew well because he was such a frequent visitor. She told Gary about Smolnikov's interest in the distribution of teas and coffees, about the friendly invasion of CSKA Moscow fans (that she herself supported Dynamo Kiev, a far superior team); how the police had arrived at her flat on Sunday and the way in which they treated her, just a waitress trying to earn a living, as if she was some kind of criminal.

When Gary asked why she'd left police protection, Arina said a police officer had told her to go. The Russians may well have been tipped off because they were outside, and she recognised one of them as being with Mr Smolnikov at the Strand Hotel on Friday.

'Those men were waiting. They follow me on bus to Charing Cross – I can tell they are Russians – I know they want to do me harm. They say little, but I know. They are in same carriage from Charing Cross to Clapham Junction, get off with me there to change trains, stand near me on platform, watching, watching all the time. You saw them sitting near me, that they follow when we get off.'

Arina was desperate for Gary to believe that she wasn't imagining all this, whereas Gary, smitten by the pleading look in those beautiful grey eyes and charmed by her delicate vulnerability, would have believed her if she'd claimed she'd been followed by Martians.

'But Arina, this isn't Moscow,' he'd tried to argue, 'it's London. Our police are different. There is no corruption here. You mustn't be afraid to go to them.'

Arina had looked at him with affection.

'Sweet Gary, so naive about these things. Listen, a Russian is poisoned by another Russian. What if he dies? I am important witness. I am also an illegal. The man who is poisoned is very important, personal friend of Russian president, as he never stop boasting to us at the Strand. Russian authorities want to talk to me in Moscow.'

'Yes, but the police won't let them because the poisoning was in London.'

'Why your police want to be bothered with this? Russians poison each other – they don't poison English person; it's Russian problem, let them sort it out. This waitress girl is illegal. Why should we protect her? Let Russians have her.'

Gary had made no progress in changing Arina's mind the previous evening and it was clear that he wouldn't succeed this morning as she was about to leave.

'Where will you go now?' he asked.

'I have one Ukraine friend, a man who was smuggled in with me. We stay in touch. I know he can get me home to Kiev. He say it many times – if ever I need to go back home, go to him. Even with no passport, he tell me he can do it.'

'You have his address?'

'Yes, Viktor has flat in Battersea. I should have gone straight to him yesterday instead of trying to collect my things.'

Gary started to feel the first twinges of jealousy as he wondered about the nature of her friendship with this 'Viktor' person, but he forced his mind to more practical matters. 'You certainly can't go to your flat now. Those goons on the train will have it staked out,' he said, impressing himself by his ability to slip so easily into what he presumed to be the lingua franca of the criminal underworld.

'Don't worry, I won't. I go instead to see Viktor.'

She stood up to leave. Gary, still lying bare-chested in bed, grabbed her arm.

'I'm coming with you,' he announced.

An hour later Gary and Arina were on their way to 28 Kennedy Mansions. They stopped for coffee at a Costa on the corner of Battersea Park Road, taking a seat outside, from where Gary reported sick for work by texting Jamil and asking him to pass on the message to Ms Kelsey.

Jamil texted back to ask what the ailment was. 'Tell her I've got Russian flu,' Gary replied.

He smiled to himself, biting into an almond croissant, the sun on his face and a sense of well-being in his soul. He was enjoying this.

Arina sat beside him engrossed in her phone, legs elegantly crossed, blonde hair falling across her face, looking lovelier than ever to her rescuer. She wore the same long, light summer skirt from the previous day but had somehow conjured up a skimpy sky-blue top exposing an expanse of cleavage to the sun. Her make-up had, as usual, been expertly applied; on this occasion in the hotel bathroom rather than on the train from Crystal Palace.

Gary knew that they were in danger but found it difficult to even comprehend the concept. Arina's friend would take over as her protector and get her safely back to Ukraine, leaving Gary to go back to his mundane routine, but only temporarily. He would stay in touch with Arina; fly to Kiev to meet her, go travelling, perhaps to Spain or Greece; spend time in America; emigrate to Australia – all these options seemed to Gary to be entirely plausible as he sat daydreaming in the sunshine.

'I try to contact Viktor to tell him we're coming, but he doesn't respond.'

'He might still be asleep,' suggested Gary, checking his watch. It was still only 8.35.

'He would usually be awake by now.'

Arina's response made Gary wonder again if she and Viktor were more than just friends. He heard his thoughts being articulated even as they formulated.

'Are you and Viktor an item?' he asked.

'An item?' asked Arina, genuinely perplexed.

'You know – are you lovers?'

'That is none of your business.'

Arina's grey eyes flared.

There was a moment of resentful silence until Gary said, 'Well, you have just spent the night as my wife. I felt entitled to ask.'

Her glare softened and they both laughed.

'No, Gary, we are not and were not lovers. Me and Viktor have never been the item, as you say.'

They decided to go to Viktor's flat despite the lack of response to Arina's calls and texts.

It was in a four-storey block that would have been stylish in the 1930s when it was built but had aged badly. There was a controlled entrance, the code for which Arina tapped in, reigniting Gary's suspicions about her relationship with Viktor.

Arina, sensing this, said, 'I never been here but Viktor gave me the code in case I have to.'

'And do you have a key to the flat?' asked Gary as they climbed three flights of stairs towards number 28.

'No, I don't,' Arina answered, but as they reached the fourth floor, they saw that no key was necessary. The door was slightly ajar as if the occupant had just stepped outside to collect something off the doormat.

Arina nudged it open, calling Viktor's name as she crossed the threshold. Gary had felt the atmosphere chill when they'd entered the block. A construction of its time, the interior was all cold tiles and iron bannisters. Summer heat had never pervaded the cool enclave of that stairwell.

Now he felt a deeper chill, like moving from a fridge to a freezer; a definite sense of presentiment.

A radio was playing in one of the rooms as they tentatively entered the hallway. Incongruously, the cheery voice of Chris Evans was easing the nation into the day ahead.

Gary went into the bedroom. It was empty, the bed not slept in. There was a row of suits and jackets on an open rail inside the door and a wardrobe that Gary opened as if expecting Viktor to be hiding there. A clock by the bed ticked so loudly it competed with Chris Evans blaring out of a different room.

Suddenly the noise from the radio stopped so abruptly it caused Gary to rush out of the bedroom towards the small kitchenette, where he found Arina, her hand still on the radio she'd just turned off. There was no scream, no cry of anguish, only a stunned silence as Arina stared at the man tied to the kitchen chair with his throat cut. On a piece of white gauze taped across his mouth were the words 'Krovnyye Bratya'.

15

Gary had only seen one other dead body. He'd gone with his mother and grandmother to the undertakers to say a final farewell to his granddad before the coffin lid was secured for the funeral.

That had been a peaceful encounter with death. He remembered a waxy facial pallor being the only indication that Granddad wasn't simply having a snooze after his Sunday roast.

In contrast, the sight of Viktor induced a cold terror that began in Gary's bowels, froze his blood and kept him rooted to the spot. He felt the urge to scream but it became trapped deep inside him, emerging eventually as a gasp.

He felt Arina's hand as she placed it gently on his shoulder. Having gained Gary's attention, she pointed silently towards the one door they hadn't looked behind. It led off the kitchenette, probably into a utility room.

Gary was shocked to see that Arina had a large carving knife in her hand that she'd removed noiselessly from a set attached to a magnetic strip along the kitchen shelf.

He hadn't contemplated the possibility that Viktor's killer might still be in the flat, but Arina had and was beckoning Gary towards the closed door.

The bedroom clock continued to tick loudly. A broad beam of sunlight had angled its way through a high window like a yellow ribbon pinned along the murky green wall.

Arina gestured for Gary to pull the door open while she stood poised with the knife, ready for whatever emerged. She silently mouthed a count of three, whereupon Gary pushed down on the handle and pulled back the door.

A red plastic-handled mop fell out, clattering noisily on the tiled kitchen floor. Having satisfied themselves that there was nothing more in the utility room, they left the flat but only after Arina had returned the knife to its rightful place, wiping the handle and any other surfaces she'd touched.

The front door had a substantial silver knob that Gary pulled behind them, leaving the door slightly open, just as it was when they arrived.

They were soon on the main road. Arina had to put out a restraining hand to prevent her companion from breaking into a run. Gary wanted to get as far away from the horror of that flat as he could. He allowed himself to be guided towards a bus stop where a Number 44 had just pulled up. It was almost empty but only when they were seated on the very back seat of the upper deck did they feel able to talk.

Gary implored Arina to go with him to report this to the police. Smolnikov may have been poisoned, but so far as they knew he was still alive. Viktor most certainly wasn't. They had discovered a murder. They had to report it.

Arina listened as she gazed out of the window. There was a ten-second silence before she said, 'If we go to police I will either end up like poor Viktor or be imprisoned in Russia – one thing or other. That tape across Viktor's mouth, it said Krovnyye Bratya, which in Russian is Blood Brothers. God know who they are but if they kill Viktor, they could kill me. But you, Gary, should never have become mixed up in this. You are a sweet boy and I am grateful for all you do, but now I let you go. If you want to report to police, of course you should, but I need time to find somewhere safe to hide for day or two. I only ask that you don't report until this evening.'

She paused before continuing. 'Thank you for helping me, Gary, but it's best if you get off at next stop and go back to normal life.'

Gary weighed up his options. His enjoyment of this adventure had evaporated with the discovery of Viktor's body. He could walk away now without anybody but Arina knowing of his involvement. Her Russian pursuers had seen him on the train, but his hood was up and anyway they could have no idea who he was beyond Arina's reference to him as 'Tom'. One anonymous call to the police to report the murder and he would have done his duty as a citizen.

Set against that, Viktor's murder clearly suggested that Arina was in even greater danger than he'd realised. Her fears about being handed over to the Russians couldn't be easily dismissed. How could he abandon her now?

She could as well lay low with him at 27 Mount Street as anywhere else.

The bus stopped, but Gary didn't get off.

Detective Superintendent Louise Mangan was examining the still photographs from the CCTV footage that she'd watched four times already. She was with a dozen or so officers who were part of the expanding team dealing with the Smolnikov case.

'So,' she said to Assistant Detective Superintendent O'Farrell, 'we know that the blonde is definitely our waitress, that Miranchuk is in that carriage and that he and his pal follow her off the train at Gipsy Hill. We have absolutely no idea who the man in the hooded top is or where they went next.'

'You know my view,' answered O'Farrell. 'It's difficult to see him clearly. The hood hides his face and it's a poor image anyway, but I think that the guy getting off the train with her was the one responsible for luring her away from us at the Strand Hotel yesterday. As for where they went, they certainly didn't go through the ticket barriers at Gipsy Hill.'

'Show me the barrier footage again,' Mangan ordered.

The CCTV images from the station forecourt clearly showed Miranchuk, the tattooed Russian, going through the ticket barrier at 21.36 looking anxiously around, followed by his companion, but with no sign of the waitress or the young man who'd stepped off the train with her.

Mangan spoke again. 'So, she leaves the train well before Sutton, where she lives, and then vanishes with somebody we know nothing about. Have we checked that they didn't go through those barriers much later?'

'Yes,' said one of the CCTV technicians, 'we studied the footage right up until the station closed, but the thing about Gipsy Hill is that if you cross the bridge to the London-bound platform, there's an exit with no barriers.'

'In that case, the lad with our waitress must know the area. If he was one of the Russians, why would he have led her away from them? To me it looks more like a chance encounter than a planned escape.'

It was a statement rather than a question, and was aimed at her subordinate, who despite his supposed expertise in Russian gang culture, had failed to protect their star witness properly and had spent much of the last half hour suggesting that the man she'd stepped off the train with might have facilitated her disappearance.

Connor O'Farrell said nothing, allowing the implied criticism to remain unchallenged as he professed close interest in the rest of the CCTV stills.

'Right,' said Mangan, 'we concentrate our attention on the Gipsy Hill area. Do what you can to enhance the image of that young man so we can check it against criminal records. Distribute anything we've got and get the spooks involved. We have to find our waitress, which means we need to identify this man.'

'They make a lovely couple,' observed one of the coppers.

'They won't look so lovely if Krovnyye Bratya gets hold of them before we do,' said the Detective Chief Superintendent.

When she got back to her office a call came through from Assistant Commissioner Baker to tell her that the Government was insisting that news of Smolnikov's death could not be withheld any longer. A press release was being prepared, embargoed until 9 p.m.

Louise Mangan knew that this would detract from her efforts to make progress. She and her colleagues were bound to be distracted by the intensification of media interest.

The Russians would say that the poison was administered by a waitress who the Metropolitan Police had allowed to wander off. The problem was that the accusation was entirely reasonable, and while the truth was probably that Smolnikov had somehow managed to poison himself, the disappeared waitress was the only person who could offer any kind of testimony.

Hopefully Miranchuk and his thugs hadn't caught up yet with Arina Kaplin, but they probably knew more about her whereabouts than the Met did.

And now there was the emergence of this friend of Ms Kaplin who O'Farrell thought was some kind of accomplice. Mangan didn't buy the theory, nor did she trust the man expounding it.

Louise Mangan was a forty-five-year-old, divorced mother of two who was used to working under pressure – had always claimed to thrive on it. Her entire working life had been spent in the police force; she'd married a copper – divorced a copper. She had little doubt that their shared occupation had contributed to the break-up. More specifically, she had found it difficult to cope with his resentment when she was promoted, and he wasn't.

She remembered how, when she and a select group of senior colleagues had been invited to dine with the Commissioner one evening soon after her promotion, her husband, who was supposed to be looking after the kids while she was out, announced late in the day that he had to cover for an officer who was off sick. It was too late to arrange an alternative babysitter and she'd had to pull out of the dinner.

Louise was convinced that he'd feigned the staffing emergency and she'd used her authority to check if her husband had been telling the truth. He had, and she felt terrible for doubting him; it was a betrayal that felt as stark as if she'd slept with another man.

Yet his resentment about her promotion was palpable. It emanated from him like radio waves from a transmitter. In the end, divorce became inevitable but they remained on friendly terms. He'd met a girl from Exeter and transferred to Devon and Cornwall Police. Far enough away to ensure their paths never crossed but not too far for their two daughters to go to see him.

The only relationship she had these days was the one she had with work, which became more and more intense as the years went by.

Now she was leading a case that was becoming increasingly difficult.

It would be so much simpler if that waitress was still in custody or, heaven forbid for the girl, even if she'd been successfully abducted by those Russian gangsters. At least then they'd have something to focus on. The intrusion of this third party, whoever he was, had added further complexity to an already convoluted situation.

The phone rang. Brian Baker was on the line.

'I just wanted you to know that the Commissioner is taking a keen interest in this,' he said. 'He thinks it wouldn't be the end of the world if that girl was found by the Russian authorities rather than by us.'

'Which Russian authorities?' she asked. 'The FSB or Krovnyye Bratya?'

'I'm not sure there's any real difference, is there?'

'Only that KB are likely to kill her here and the FSB more likely to take her back to Moscow first.'

'Let's not be too emotional about this, Louise. As O'Farrell says, Krovnyye Bratya are unlikely to want to kill her, and it's far more likely they will be working with the FSB on this and both will want to question rather than kill her.'

'So, you want us to wash our hands of this and leave the poor girl to her fate?' Mangan could feel her anger rising worryingly close to the surface.

'First of all, Louise, I'm conveying the thoughts of the Commissioner . . .'

'Heavily influenced by Karen Dale,' Mangan interrupted.

'The thoughts of the Commissioner,' Baker continued, 'who is about to have a pile of ordure descend upon him and who feels that this waitress is Russia's problem rather than ours. Think about it, Louise; we now have a murder case on our hands involving a Russian friend of the President. No Brits are involved. There are Russian dissidents, Russian gangsters and a Ukrainian waitress who had no right to be in this country in the first place.'

There was silence.

'Tell me something, Brian,' said Mangan eventually. 'Did we collude with the Russians to hand that girl over yesterday? Is that why she walked straight into their hands outside the Strand Hotel?'

'There's no collusion with anybody, Louise. I'm just passing on the Commissioner's thoughts. You're in charge of this case and you know you'll always have my support.'

Assistant Commissioner Brian Baker had indeed provided encouragement and reassurance throughout her time in New Scotland Yard, and Mangan regretted her aggressive tone.

'I'm sorry to be so tetchy, Brian. Not everyone on the team is as supportive as you, but I'm determined that it should be the Metropolitan Police who finds this girl. She's our responsibility and I have no intention of subcontracting this to a bunch of Russian thugs.'

The conversation kept replaying in Detective Superintendent Mangan's head long after she put the phone down.

16

And so it was agreed, on the top deck of a bus they hadn't planned to board, travelling to a destination as yet unknown: Arina and Gary decided to stay together.

The horror of what they'd just seen seemed to draw them closer. There was a new level of intimacy in the way they talked to one another; the casual gestures, a hand being placed gently on an arm or a shoulder, the way they held each other's gaze, listened sympathetically to each other's point of view.

Arina tried once more to convince Gary that she could manage alone.

'I go to Ukraine embassy,' she whispered, the bus having acquired a few more passengers as it trundled through Battersea in the comparative calm that followed the rush-hour storm. 'They will help me.'

'Wouldn't they be obliged to hand you over to the police? Waitresses can hardly claim diplomatic immunity.'

'Ukraine and Russia are enemies, almost at war – I am Ukraine citizen. Embassy will help, I am sure.'

Gary googled the Ukrainian embassy on his phone.

'It's in Holland Park. Do you want to go there now?'

'No, not now. Krovnyye Bratya know I am Ukrainian. The embassy is obvious place for me to go.'

'Are you saying it's not an option?' Gary asked.

'It is only option,' Arina said. 'But not yet. First, I need to change way I look – then time to think.'

An hour later, Gary was waiting for Arina to finish the shopping that his fast-depleting funds were financing. Arina told him that her debit card could be used to track her movements and asked if Gary could be her provider for the time being.

'I will repay you fully – I promise.'

They were in Croydon on their way to 27 Mount Street, Gary having worked out a circuitous route to Crystal Palace that avoided Gipsy Hill (which they both agreed was somewhere else that was likely to be under surveillance).

When the shopping was over, they carried two carrier bags onto a Number 410 bus. By now it was early afternoon and whilst Gary was confident that none of his housemates would be at home, it was no surprise to find his elderly neighbour keeping watch as usual. Terry's watery eyes mistook Arina for Melissa, whose name he shouted across the street in response to Gary's waved greeting.

'Who is Melissa?' Arina asked as the front door closed behind them.

'One of my housemates,' Gary explained, amused by Terry's mistake. 'You are a bit similar, I guess – she has long blonde hair as well.'

'So, this Melissa, she is your girlfriend? She and you are the item?'

'No,' Gary laughed as they climbed the stairs. 'We barely tolerate one another. She hates me.'

'I don't think anyone could hate you, Gary,' Arina said as they entered the big communal room on the second floor.

She dropped her carrier bags to the floor, turned to face him and, for a fleeting moment, Gary felt inclined to hold Arina in his arms; to pull her close as if the physical contact would dispel the awful image of Viktor; as if by embracing they could escape from the terrible danger they were in.

But at that precise moment Jason emerged from the kitchen.

'Don't mind me,' he said, sensing that his appearance had been an unwelcome shock. 'I just live here.' He held out his hand to Arina.

'Oh, this is Jason,' Gary recovered quickly from his nonplussed state. 'Jason, this is . . .' There was a pause.

'Lilia,' said Arina. 'Lilia Zinchenko.'

'Lovely to meet you, Lilia – good to know that Gary's got himself a girlfriend at last.'

Gary felt himself blush as he told Jason that 'Lilia' would be staying for a couple of days.

'Well, as you know, house rules state clearly that we all have to be given 24-hours' notice before anyone stays over, but as you've never done this before we can doubtless make an exception for the lovely Lilia.'

Jason explained that he was packing his bags for a work trip to Zurich. He was about to head for Gatwick and would be away until next Wednesday.

They spent an awkward half hour forcing out small talk before the taxi arrived, and Jason went on his way, kissing Lilia farewell as if they were already old friends.

'Don't you two do anything I wouldn't do.'

'Which leaves lots of scope,' Gary muttered along to the punchline of one of Jason's overused bon mots.

'He's a knobhead,' Gary apologised to Arina after Jason's departure. She'd begun to unpack the stuff purchased that afternoon.

'I thought he was charming.'

'Did you need to change your name for him?' Gary asked, slightly miffed by this response.

'Of course.' Arina looked incredulously at her companion. 'The police look for me. Gangsters look for me. My name is bound to be in media eventually. I need to change name and I need to change way I look. Jason has my new name but not my new appearance – unfortunately. But if he's abroad for a week it doesn't matter. By time he gets back I'll be long gone.'

Gary listened to her as he made coffee for them to drink with the tuna and sweetcorn sandwiches they'd bought in Croydon.

If only they'd arrived a little later, he mused. Jason would not have seen Arina, but at least he had gone now, and Gary only had to cope with Melissa and Knuckles during Arina's short stay.

As they consumed their late lunch at the kitchen table,

they reluctantly broached the subject of what they'd seen that morning. Arina told Gary that Krovnyye Bratya must be the name of a criminal gang who Viktor had crossed. Working at the Strand she'd heard references to the fearsome reputation of London-based Russian criminals.

'Poor Viktor,' Arina said sadly. 'I suspect they hurt him before they kill him.'

'Do you think they were trying to find out if he knew where you were?' Gary asked.

'I don't know. Perhaps. But Krovnyye Bratya is probably involved in people smuggling and Viktor was as well. He wasn't gangster so far as I know. He had nothing about me. I take his mobile phone to destroy in case information there is useful to police.'

'I'm surprised his murderers didn't take it. Wouldn't it have your mobile number, given that you rang him?'

'I only ring him this morning from café. Russians were gone by then. But is curious that they left it.'

'Where is it now?'

'It's in River Thames, with mine.'

'What? You've got rid of your phone as well?'

'Yes, in case they use to track.'

'I didn't see you get rid of anything.'

'You, Gary, are very observant when girl puts on make-up on train, but not so observant when we got off the bus and walk over Battersea Bridge.'

This girl is full of surprises, Gary thought admiringly.

Arina went into the bathroom of 27 Mount Street at 3 p.m. and emerged an hour later to startle Gary, who for a second or two thought a stranger had wandered into the house.

Arina's lovely blonde hair was gone, cut with the scissors and clippers she'd purchased in Croydon, the debris carefully swept up and placed in the carrier bag that had contained the shopping.

Gary was amazed how short it was; and dyed so black – crow black. The effect was as if her bare skull had been painted.

'You like?'

Gary's face registered shock more than admiration.

Arina, standing in his white towelling robe, looked stunning, but nothing like the woman he'd walked in with.

'Now I am Lilia Zinchenko, not Arina Kaplin.'

Later, after she had applied make-up with more mascara and a paler tint to her face, the difference was even more pronounced.

Arina insisted on looking her best for the arrival of Melissa and Knuckles and was wearing one of the sunfrocks she'd purchased. She also insisted on preparing a three-course Ukrainian meal for four, including borscht and chicken Kiev. They devised a subterfuge as they walked round Sainsbury's buying the ingredients. They would say that they knew each other from work and had dated a couple of times. Lilia had been forced to temporarily vacate her flat because a serious water leak had flooded the kitchen.

Gary's housemates arrived shortly after each other at around 6 p.m. and, once they had got over their surprise at having a temporary housemate, the evening went well. Lilia lavished charm on Melissa, telling her how much she liked her hair and that Wales was her favourite part of Britain. Having discovered later that she hadn't even been there, Gary could only wonder once more at his companion's acting ability.

Melissa reserved all her malevolence for him.

'Why didn't you tell us she was coming to stay? You know the house rules,' she hissed as Lilia disappeared into the kitchen between courses.

'Something came up,' pleaded Gary.

'I bet it did,' she responded.

As for Knuckles, he was just grateful for such a wonderful meal. He'd usually be microwaving some noodles.

There was a point in the evening when Gary, sipping another glass of sauvignon blanc and watching Arina weave her magic on Melissa and Knuckles, experienced a huge sense of pride, as if this beautiful woman really was his girlfriend, and had passed some kind of test designed to see if she could get on with his friends.

A crepuscular light fell across her face as she talked about how difficult it was to deal with Gary's shyness and how she'd had to coax him gently towards asking her out. This fiction was relayed with total fluency, as if she believed it herself. Gary had agreed to say as little as possible and to refer to Lilia as 'babe' to avoid any careless reference to her real name. He was happy to comply. Gary liked being Lilia's boyfriend. It mattered not if this woman's hair was long and blonde or black and cropped, he felt as if, for the first time in his life, he was seeing beyond superficiality and beginning to discover what it meant to truly care for somebody. But he was aware of something else – in this relationship he was very much the junior partner. Reflecting on that morning's events in Viktor's flat, he was in awe of Arina's calmness and presence of mind.

Gary and Knuckles washed up, leaving the two women chatting amicably over coffee at the communal table that had rarely entertained such a lavish meal. Gary refuted Knuckles' suggestion that this must be the girl he'd been so infatuated with as she applied her make-up on the train; the girl he'd spoken of in such glowing terms just under a week ago. Knuckles was keen to know if his advice about how to begin a conversation with her had been taken. Gary laughed, reminding Knuckles that the woman he'd seen on the train was a blonde. He told his friend that Lilia was a very different woman and said this convincingly because, in essence, she was.

Later, the four of them sat on the two large, battered sofas positioned around the TV in the lounge.

Knuckles had been showing off to Lilia, talking ebulliently about the TV production he was working on which involved a famous comedienne and a former Catholic bishop touring Dartmoor on a tandem, when Melissa suddenly shushed him into silence, insisting that they watch the ten o'clock news to hear the latest on the Russian poisoning that everyone was talking about.

It was the top story: the death of Denis Smolnikov, the diplomatic fallout and the efforts of the Metropolitan Police to find those responsible.

At the end of the report a grainy CCTV picture was shown of two people who the police wanted to interview, waiting to step off a train at Gipsy Hill station.

They were believed to still be in that area of south-east London.

'Oh, that's just down the road,' exclaimed Melissa. 'How exciting!'

Much to Gary and Arina's relief, neither of their dinner companions seemed to have the slightest notion that the man and woman in the grainy photograph were watching the television with them.

17

Friday, 17 July

Gary's room was not the most attractive, but it was the biggest of the four in 27 Mount Street. Big enough to accommodate a double bed with plenty of room left over for the pinewood desk, two-seater settee, chest of drawers and built-in wardrobe. Pinned to the wall were a chart setting out the fixtures for the cricket world cup and a Renoir reproduction.

As the highest room in the house, the tip of the London Eye could just be seen from its single sash window. This window could only be opened a few inches. On warm nights such as this, Gary always resolved to get it fixed, but never had.

When he followed Arina into the room half an hour after she'd gone to bed, the heat hung undisturbed by the slithers of breeze coming spasmodically through the narrow gap.

Melissa had left the communal lounge first and Gary had remained chatting to Knuckles after Arina had followed her out. The Irishman told Gary how much he liked Lilia and for a moment Gary was tempted to confide in his friend, to tell the truth about Arina and the perilous position they were in. What harm would it do?

Knuckles could at least supply a sympathetic shoulder. But he checked himself. Who was it who said it wasn't him who couldn't keep secrets, it was the people he told them to? Oscar Wilde? Arina had warned him not to confide in his housemates under any circumstances. His lips must remain sealed.

Arina was lying on the left side of the bed, the side closest to the window, gazing into the clear night sky when Gary came into the room. The bedside lamp cast an orange glint just powerful enough to read by.

'I'll sleep on the settee,' he said.

'No, I will not let you. If anyone sleeps on chair it will be me. But I have arranged bed.'

Looking closer, in the dim light Gary saw that she had placed three cushions from the settee down the centre of the bed to form a border.

'I like you, Gary, but I don't want to complicate things by turning our story into real life.'

'That's fine by me. I never had the slightest intention of trying anything on.'

He removed his jeans and placed them neatly in the wardrobe.

'You're not my type anyway – I like blondes.'

They talked quietly about the CCTV footage on the TV news and how thankful they were that Gary had his hood up and that the quality was so poor. Also, that Arina had rid herself of her most distinctive feature. She had been named in the TV report, but Gary wasn't. He remained Mr Anonymous, which meant they would be able to stay here for a day or two, planning and preparing their trip to the Ukrainian embassy. Gary would go into work the next day as normal in order not to arouse suspicion there.

He'd retrieved an old mobile and put it on charge for Arina so they could stay in touch. Setting the alarm on his own phone, he turned out the light and settled down to sleep.

The curtains were left open and Arina continued to gaze out. 'Such bright stars tonight,' she murmured wistfully.

'That's Orion,' Gary said, resting on one elbow and pointing into the night sky. 'In Greek mythology it's a hunter, in Indian a dancer, in Chinese a deer. I think the Greeks got it right; you can see the hunter's belt, formed by the three brightest stars – Zeta, Epsilon and Delta.'

'You are a, oh, what is it in English?' Arina asked. 'We say Astroloh in Ukraine.'

'Not quite an astrologer,' Gary replied. 'I have no interest in horoscopes. I'm more of an astronomer, I suppose. The stars have always fascinated me. Those three hunter stars are eight hundred light years away and one hundred thousand times more luminous than the sun.'

'Ah, but will the hunter protect us? We, the hunted.'

'I don't believe in mythology,' Gary said. 'We have to protect ourselves.'

'I feel safe with you,' Arina said, her hand reaching for Gary's across the cushions.

'I suppose you would, given that you've built a soft-furnishings version of the Berlin Wall.'

But Gary's tease was wasted. Arina had already fallen asleep.

Arina was still asleep the next morning at 7.30 as Gary crept silently out of the bedroom so as not to disturb her.

Melissa and Knuckles were wandering around the kitchen as usual in nightwear and dressing gowns, making toast and pouring cereal.

'Is your pretty friend using the bathroom?' Melissa asked.

'She's still asleep.'

'Tired her out, did you?' his housemate said as she pushed past Gary, carrying her washbag and make-up case.

'You know, I do think our Mel is jealous,' Knuckles said when she'd gone.

'Nah. She's just annoyed with me for breaking one of Jason's precious rules. I don't know if you've noticed, but she's been annoyed with me ever since I moved in.'

Knuckles was to spend his working day at the ITV studios on the South Bank and they agreed to travel up to town together.

When Gary went back into his room to say farewell to Arina, she was still asleep, face down, cuddling a pillow. After throwing on a pair of faded blue jeans and a short-sleeved checked shirt he left a note on her bedside – 'Gone to work' – and crept out again.

Melissa had a head start on her two housemates. She had an earlier train to catch and trilled a cheery farewell as she descended the stairs to the front door.

A few minutes later, when they heard the scream through the open kitchen window that faced out onto the road, Gary and Knuckles knew instinctively that it was her. They raced down the stairs together.

Terry was opposite, out of his chair and shouting, 'They've taken her,' pointing towards the junction with Westow Hill. A blue Nissan Micra was attempting to pull out into the traffic halted by the lights at the major junction with Crystal Palace Parade.

The two friends ran towards the car. They could see Melissa in the back struggling with one of the car's three other occupants. Gary and Knuckles reached the junction just as the Micra was about to pull away, a lull in the traffic having created a space.

Knuckles pulled at the locked back door and as the car began to go forward, Gary flung himself across the windscreen, clinging on to the driver's-side wing mirror while placing a foot against the mirror on the passenger side for purchase.

He found himself staring into the startled eyes of the large barrel-shaped driver who was cursing him in Russian. Another, thinner man was in the front passenger seat with one other comrade trying to restrain a kicking, screaming Melissa in the back.

The car accelerated and then braked hard in an attempt to dislodge Gary from the bonnet, but the car's room for manoeuvre was restricted by the density of the rush-hour traffic as well as the inability of the driver to see past the man stretched across his windscreen. The

Nissan crashed into a bus that was at the tail end of the queue of traffic. The three abductors burst out of the car and found themselves outnumbered as four guys rushed out of the Turkish barber's, shouting to Gary, 'Hey, you want some help?'

Gary was pleased he used that barber's so often and tipped so generously.

To his amazement, Knuckles had already delivered a stomach punch to the driver and a left hook to the thinner guy in the front passenger seat. But the man who emerged from the back still holding Melissa had a gun, which he fired into the air.

Gary, Knuckles and the barber's shop quartet froze. The gunman pushed Melissa away, firing into the air once more as he and his cohorts ran off into a side street. Nobody felt inclined to follow them.

Melissa was sobbing as Knuckles stroked her hair in an effort to calm her down. He manoeuvred her towards a chair that one of the Turks had placed in the shade while another came out of the barber's with a glass of water and handed it to Knuckles.

'You gave those villains a right pasting,' said Gary.

'Now you know why they call me Knuckles,' his friend said enigmatically.

One of the bystanders announced that the police were on their way. Others patted Knuckles on the back saying how he deserved a medal for his bravery.

In all the furore and chaos, Gary slipped away.

He was sure the abductors were Russians and that

they'd grabbed Melissa thinking she was Arina. Somehow, they had discovered she was at 27 Mount Street. He had to get Arina away from there fast.

Gary sprinted the two hundred yards back to the house. Terry appeared to have left his sentry post opposite, probably to get a better view of the action further down the road.

As he burst into the communal area and on up the stairs to his room, Gary was shouting Arina's name. But nobody answered. The house was empty. She had gone.

18

Arina Kaplin walked past the front door of the block of flats in Sutton where she'd lived since arriving in England. Her step was unhurried, her brain alert. She looked gamine, her cropped black hair complemented by a white T-shirt, beige jeans and navy-blue sneakers.

On her shoulder was the knapsack she'd taken from 27 Mount Street. It contained only her purse, make-up bag, the mobile phone that Gary had given her and the new clothes she'd purchased the previous day.

Hearing Melissa's scream, she'd rushed to the bedroom window in time to see the blue Micra screeching to a halt further along Mount Street with Gary and Knuckles in pursuit. Her refuge had been discovered.

Dressing quickly, she'd left via the back door, running through some dishevelled gardens and scaling a couple of crumbling walls to reach the road.

Arina's first instinct was to get away as quickly as possible. Her second was to use this opportunity to collect what she needed from her flat. If Krovnyye Bratya believed she'd been discovered at 27 Mount Street they were unlikely to be maintaining the same level of scrutiny in Sutton.

As for the police, her assumption was that, while they would have searched her flat, they wouldn't have the resources to put it under 24-hour surveillance. Neither was it likely they would have found what she now needed to retrieve. In any case, although she knew that coming here may be a serious miscalculation, there was no better option. It was a risk worth taking.

During her casual reconnoitre, Arina couldn't see anyone observing from parked cars. Neither could she see anything suspicious in the vicinity.

A young mother was bouncing a baby buggy down the steps of a house opposite; a bearded priest was waiting at a bus stop; a Parcelforce van pulled up to make a delivery and two women were delivering advertising leaflets.

Some ugly dark clouds blocked the sun, threatening rain, but the sticky July heat persisted.

Arina cut off to the right and circled the back streets, approaching her block from the opposite direction. The Parcelforce driver had just gained entry over the intercom and was manoeuvring an awkward package through the front door when Arina intervened to help him.

'Thanks, love,' the driver said as she held the door open and pointed him towards the lift before walking down the ground-floor corridor to her flat at the far end. Assuming that some kind of device would have been fitted to the front door by one set of pursuers or other in order to alert them to when it was opened, she turned the key knowing she wouldn't have long.

Picking up a claw hammer from the kitchen drawer she moved quickly into the bathroom using the claw end to remove the casement under the radiator. Dislodging the false bottom, Arina reached for the pressure point that released a second artificial base allowing her to reach into the hollow interior. From there she extracted three items wrapped in black cloth, placing each of them carefully into her knapsack.

Having checked that the coast was clear by looking through the spyhole, she stepped out of her front door five minutes after entering it.

Suddenly the Parcelforce man was rushing towards her down the passage. He carried no parcels. Arina let herself back into the flat but wasn't quick enough to prevent her pursuer from jamming his boot in the door. He was a big man and Arina knew she didn't have the strength to hold him at bay. Stepping back from the threshold, just as the man went to cross it, she kicked violently at the door and it hit him squarely on the forehead.

He swore and bent over, clutching his face, but stayed planted in the doorway, blocking Arina's escape. She ran back into the flat. An eerie silence descended, broken only by the suppressed curses of the delivery driver as he shook off his temporary indisposition.

Then he spoke into the silence. 'Let's not get silly,' he said in a gruff south London accent. 'You won't be able to open any of the windows, we've seen to that. I won't hurt you. My instructions are to take you alive. I know that you've just been caught up in all this.'

He spoke while moving slowly into the flat. 'We could be friends. You're a cracker, if I may be bold enough to say. We could have some fun if you want. That might even convince me to let you go.'

There was a brief silence until, entering the bedroom, he said, 'Just fink of yourself as a parcel I'm supposed to deliver in good condition. Nobody said I couldn't unwrap it first.'

It was then that Arina struck from behind, smashing the claw hammer into the back of the man's head. He fell, unconscious. Arina took his keys, left the flat and drove away in the Parcelforce van.

Gary was considering alternatives, trying to decide what to do next. His initial fear was that Arina had been abducted, but there was no sign of a forced entry let alone any struggle inside the house. The bed had even been made, which didn't suggest she'd been dragged from it.

She'd taken at least some of her clothes and, that most prized possession, her leather make-up bag, so had probably heard the commotion and decided to flee while she still could.

His thoughts turned to the morning's events. The attempted kidnap of Melissa suggested a case of mistaken identity. But how did they alight upon 27 Mount Street? Had they been followed back yesterday when Arina still possessed those long blonde tresses? That seemed the most likely explanation.

Now that they'd been discovered, they had to get out – Arina obviously already had.

The police would soon make the link between the Russian poisoning and the attempted kidnap of Melissa, who was probably being questioned at Gipsy Hill police station at that very moment. When she told them that she shared a house with the guy who'd clung to the windscreen they would come to question him. Why not just use this opportunity to tell the police everything? He would probably never hear from Arina again and would be more helpful to her by admitting everything than by refusing to.

He heard a key being turned in the front door. For a moment Gary froze until he heard the cheery voice of Knuckles calling up the stairs.

'Gary, are you there?'

Ten minutes later the two friends sat in the kitchen drinking tea.

Knuckles explained his theory that Melissa had been abducted by a gang who toured the streets looking for vulnerable women who they could sell into prostitution.

'I saw a documentary about it a while back. The Romanian and Bulgarian mafia are all over south London. It's getting like the Wild West out there.'

Gary asked if the police officers who'd arrived on the scene had been enquiring about him.

'Listen, so far as I know, the only reason the police want to talk to you is to put you forward for a feckin' commendation. But I pleaded ignorance about you. Sure, I could see you didn't want to be involved and I honestly don't think Melissa noticed that it was you who flung yourself across the windscreen, such was the state the poor girl was in. The Turkish guys might tell the police about you, but they only know you're Gary, they don't know where you live.'

Knuckles had given 27 Mount Street as his own address and been told that he'd be contacted to give a statement.

'Who knows? Perhaps one of the bastards I hit will put in a claim against me for assault. Stranger things have happened,' he reflected.

They both agreed that Melissa would now be safe under police protection.

'Why don't you get yourself off to work?' Knuckles asked. 'I presume Lilia has already gone in?'

Gary said that yes, she had and yes, he would. During the course of the conversation he'd suddenly realised where Arina would be. She would head for the Ukrainian embassy. He also knew that he must go there too; that he couldn't let things end like this; that he had to see Arina again – even if it was for the last time – to say goodbye.

If she was already inside the embassy, he'd ask to see her. They would say their farewells and he'd go off to work, to pick up the threads of the life he'd been leading before Arina had burst into it.

To have any chance of seeing her he had to leave now.

Knuckles grabbed his arm as he rose from the table.

'Are we still on for that visit to see your boss?'

Gary hadn't had time to think about Marilyn Kelsey or the plan he'd hatched to visit her with his electrician housemate. It seemed part of a different life, one he'd left behind, but one he'd shortly be going back to.

'Yes,' Gary shouted over his shoulder as he raced down the stairs, 'I'll sort something out with her.'

He wondered where he'd put that address card, the one that Ms Kelsey had handed him at the door of her office. No problem, he could ask her for another one. But as he closed the door of 27 Mount Street and took a back-street route to Crystal Palace station avoiding Westow Hill, he remembered when he'd last seen it – on that fateful train journey when he and Arina were pretending to be old friends and he was using Marilyn Kelsey's card as a prop.

Did he put it back in his pocket or had he left it on the train?

If he'd dropped it on the train, there was every chance that their Russian pursuers would have picked it up.

There was no time to think about that now. He had to get to the Ukrainian embassy to see the woman he'd begun to care for deeply. All other considerations would have to wait.

19

The decision had been made in an instant and Arina couldn't quite believe her good fortune as she drove towards Holland Park.

The familiar red van provided anonymity on the road and unquestioned access to any destination. She'd punched 'Embassy of Ukraine' into the van's satnav and was now well on her way to W11 3SJ. The Parcelforce van had obviously been stolen and sooner or later the fate of her assailant, presumably a local recruit to Krovnyye Bratya, would be discovered. But that was unlikely to be in the fifty minutes that this journey was due to take. Before leaving the flat she had destroyed the two-way radio that had been clipped to her attacker's uniform jacket, smashing it to bits with the claw hammer. She hoped they had no other means of tracking the vehicle.

In her knapsack were the things she'd needed to retrieve. Arina was pleased with how well they had been hidden; well enough to remain undetected through the rigorous search that she was sure her flat would have been subjected to.

Once safely inside the embassy she would ring Gary on the ancient mobile to assure him that she was safe, enquire about Melissa – and then bid farewell. It would be difficult to say goodbye, but she couldn't allow her actions to be hindered by sentiment.

She'd grabbed a Parcelforce baseball cap that had been hanging from a hook behind the driver's seat. It was too big for her, but she could see perfectly well from beneath its peak and the additional layer of disguise was useful.

Having never driven in England before, let alone London, navigating on the 'wrong' side of the road was a challenge, but the traffic moving so sedately along the congested A24 made it easier to adapt. By the time she reached Kensington High Street, Arina felt entirely proficient.

A few minutes later she steered the van into Holland Park Road and pulled into a vacant parking space marked For Resident's Only. The expensive houses that lined both sides of this exclusive street were bathed in tranquillity. A couple of young nannies pushed their prams towards the park, chatting merrily to one another as their charges slept. A cloudy sky seemed to trap the heat at ground level. There wasn't even the minutest breath of breeze. Apart from a couple of expensive cars that cruised by, the road was quiet.

The Embassy of Ukraine was no more or less grand than its neighbouring houses. What marked it out, apart from the blue and yellow national flag fluttering from a long pole, was the grid painted onto the road in front forbidding any parking.

Arina waited and watched for ten minutes before slowly driving up and down the street as if searching for an address. She was actually scrutinising parked cars to see if anybody was waiting and watching. They were all unoccupied. There was a cream Ford Transit with an empty cabin. She wondered if it contained any unseen observers in the body of the vehicle, but it was at least two hundred yards from the embassy and Arina felt secure in her disguise.

She parked the Parcelforce van on the grid in front of the embassy, pulled her cap even further down, got out of the van and pressed the bell on the outer security gates, carrying a few parcels taken at random from the van.

A woman's voice answered. 'Yes?' she said coldly.

'I have parcels for you,' Arina replied.

'Okay, someone will be down, but you should not park on the grid – you know for future,' the woman scolded in her heavy Ukrainian accent. 'I tell you Post Office people before, so please be aware – for future.'

For future, Arina thought. At least now I have such a thing. She had rehearsed the speech she would make in her native language once inside. The gate would soon be opened. She would be safe.

Gary came out of Holland Park station and checked the map on his phone. It had been a trek from Crystal Palace, culminating in a six-station ride along the Central Line. There was every chance that Arina would have got to the embassy before him, in which case he would make a plea for admission so that he could say farewell.

If she hadn't arrived yet, he planned to wait, either observing the embassy from a safe distance or perhaps being allowed to enter and wait inside.

He'd worked up a story about being engaged to a Ukrainian girl who was travelling to the embassy separately so that they could apply for a visa for him to visit the country for their wedding.

As he turned into Holland Park Road, he saw the blue and yellow flag, which immediately identified the embassy.

A Parcelforce van was outside. He watched the driver carrying parcels to the gate. There was something about the way she held herself, the tilt of her head, the way she moved. Then she glanced down the street towards him.

It was Arina – despite the peaked cap pulled low over her lovely eyes, Gary could see that the Parcelforce driver was Arina. Unable to contain his joy, he began to run towards her.

'Arina, Arina,' he cried.

Suddenly, a cream Ford Transit was in the road screeching to a halt alongside Gary. Three men burst out of the rear.

The gates of the embassy began to close again. The official who'd come to collect the parcels noticed the commotion and beckoned Arina to bring them through.

'Quickly,' he said. 'Come through or you have to stay outside.'

But Arina didn't go through. Dropping the parcels on the pavement, she turned away from the embassy gates and jumped back into the van. Reaching into her knapsack she unfurled the black cloth to release one of the objects retrieved from her flat. It was a Glock 22 handgun.

By now one of the men from the Transit van had caught up with Gary, bringing a massive hand down on his shoulder. Arina fired her first shot and the hand released its grip as a bullet shattered the man's knee. The other two pursuers stopped dead. A second shot disabled the Transit by bursting a front tyre.

The Parcelforce van was already moving as Gary jumped through its open side door. Arina quickly accelerated away from the Embassy of Ukraine and the safety that she'd come so close to securing across its threshold.

'Are you okay?' she shouted to Gary as she drove onto the main road.

'Yes,' he replied, still catching his breath. 'I think you just saved my life.'

'That makes us even. Perhaps you could be having think about what we do now.'

20

The Parcelforce van sped north up Ladbroke Grove towards Harrow Road, although its two occupants had no idea where they were going. Neither of them had any real knowledge of London's geography. Arina followed whatever route kept them moving at a reasonable pace, loath to turn off into any side streets where they could become trapped more easily.

This vehicle was coming to the end of its usefulness. The shots she'd fired in Holland Park Road would unleash an even more intensive search and she had to get as far away as possible from the incident. Gary lay amongst the scattered parcels, petrified by his brush with mortality and trying to make sense of what had just happened.

The sliding door behind the passenger seat was open and from his position in the body of the vehicle he could see Arina's profile: jaw set determinedly, scrutinising the road from beneath the peak of the baseball cap that was still pulled low across her forehead.

After ten minutes of silence Gary said, 'Look, Arina, I know I messed up back there and that you'd be safe in your embassy if I hadn't blundered along.'

Arina ignored him. A few minutes further on he asked, 'Why don't you drop me off here and go back?'

'To be captured by Russian gangsters?' Arina responded sharply.

'They won't be hanging around once the police arrive.'

'Then police will be hanging around – either way I am captured. Why you not think about something useful like where we go now?'

Gary had lots of questions, such as where did she get the van? And, more importantly, the gun? And how was a waitress able to use it so effectively? But he decided the atmosphere wasn't conducive to an interrogation.

'Back to Mount Street?' he suggested.

Gary told Arina how he and Knuckles had rescued Melissa and about the gunshots fired on Westow Hill.

'Knuckles didn't give the police any information about me, and Melissa was too terrified to notice anything. The Turkish guys just know me as Gary but have no idea where I live. So, as far as the police are concerned, I was just a passer-by who got involved and then walked away.'

'But Melissa will come back to your house, yes?'

'Eventually. First, she'll go wherever people go when they're under police protection while they try to figure out who tried to abduct her and why. Then she'll probably go and stay with her parents in Swansea for a while to recover.'

'Police know Knuckles is witness?'

'Yes, but he's not going to say anything about me – you can trust Knuckles.'

'But Gary,' Arina shouted through the partition, her voice rising above the throb of the traffic, 'the police will be coming to Mount Street to talk to him and they are likely to have more men in your area, particularly when they make link between Russians who try to take Melissa and what happened at Strand Hotel.'

'Okay,' said Gary, 'you're right. We can't go back to Mount Street.'

They lapsed into silence again until Gary had a better idea. After crossing the Harrow Road, they abandoned the Parcelforce van, leaving it neatly parked in a residential back street. Arina left the cap in the van, taking only her backpack, which contained the items she'd retrieved from her flat, including the gun. Gary used his mobile phone to guide them to Queens Park station, from where they set off – for Aylesbury.

Rachel Nelson was finishing work when she received a text message from her son.

> On my way to see you with a girl. Be great if you could put us up for a week or so. Xx

Gary's visits usually operated with an almost regimental precision. He arrived home on Saturday at a specific time and left the following day; they were monthly, not weekly, and he came and left alone.

Why was he heading homewards now? On a Friday? With a girl? He had never brought a girlfriend back from London. Never.

She'd mentioned the text to Tobias Parnaby as they tidied up the dentist's surgery after the morning appointments. His raised eyebrow was followed by some words of wisdom.

'Young men do strange things, Rachel, my dear, and the deeper the involvement of a young woman, the stranger they get.'

'But he was over at the weekend and never mentioned a girlfriend.'

'As the great bard said, "Love goes by haps; some cupid kills with arrows, some with traps." Doesn't matter if it's an arrow or a trap, it's always sudden.'

'Sometimes,' Rachel said as she wiped a work surface with an antiseptic disposable cloth, 'I don't understand a word you say.'

'What I'm saying is that he didn't mention the girl last weekend because they may have only just met. Have you never heard the term "whirlwind romance"?' Parnaby asked.

Driving home, having finished her morning's work, Rachel felt a thrill of anticipation. It had been a long time since she'd been able to put one of Gary's girls under close observation. She loved having her son home and the presence of a girlfriend made her relish the prospect even more.

Gary's only liaison that could justify the term 'serious' had been with Emily Swanson when he was still a schoolboy. There was the odd occasion after that when he'd brought a girl home for the evening but never since he went to London and never overnight, let alone for a week.

Rachel remembered Emily's visits and some of the other girls who came to tea. She was always fascinated to watch the interaction, noting her son's little acts of tenderness with maternal pride; the way he'd try to put his guest at ease; the strange way his personality altered when there was a girl to impress. It wasn't prurience so far as she was concerned, only a natural desire to see how the boy she'd raised reacted to another woman who, like his mother, had an emotional attachment. Rachel had no intention of hovering over the young lovers all week, but she would certainly spend at least one night putting them under close observation.

Mr Parnaby's theory of a sudden fixation wasn't one that Rachel shared. She imagined the girl as an unobtrusive creature who'd existed quietly in the background of her son's life for a while before he'd realised how much she meant to him. While Rachel remained curious about the rapidity of its emergence, she was certain about the benefits of this romance for Gary – and if it was good for Gary, it was good for her.

But there was another dimension to Rachel's benign temperament; she had discovered the name of Gary's father.

Tobias Parnaby, who as a magistrate and Deputy Lord Lieutenant of Buckinghamshire knew everyone worth knowing, had accessed the archive of Aylesbury College. He'd invented a story about his dental nurse (Rachel) going to the dance at the college in 1992 with a friend who'd met her future husband there. The couple had since emigrated to Australia and, for their twentieth wedding anniversary, his dental nurse wanted to incorporate details of the dance where they'd met, such as posters, invitations, etc., in a montage she planned to send to mark the occasion. Rachel could only marvel at her employer's creative mendacity.

Having been given the date of the dance, the college had found a file in the archive and agreed to let Rachel examine it on condition it never left the premises. On the previous afternoon she'd been left alone with the manila folder and a cup of tea in the office of one of the college's officials. Amongst reams of administrative bumf, she'd found a letter from the Police College at Hendon with the names of thirty trainees. As part of their eighteen-week programme they would be temporarily in the vicinity doing some work with Thames Valley Police and 'would love to be invited to the disco/dance'. Somebody at Aylesbury College must have heard about their secondment and written to Hendon for permission to approach them.

Rachel turned a page to find the list of names. There was only one Daniel. She let out a suppressed gasp as, alone in the small room, holding a cup of tea as yet unsipped and with the contents of the manila folder spread across the Formica table, she read the full name of the man she'd made love with on that balmy evening so long ago. The man who'd fathered her child was Daniel Henry Collins of the Metropolitan Police Force.

Rachel carefully removed a poster for the dance to photocopy in order to validate the yarn that Tobias had spun. Aware that if she asked for a copy of the names there'd probably be some data protection nonsense to contend with and convinced it would serve no useful purpose by remaining on the file, she also slipped the list into her handbag. Tobias Parnaby was now using his extensive network of contacts to find out if Daniel Collins remained a serving officer in the Met.

Rachel wondered if she should tell Gary. Parking her car on the driveway of her house, she concluded that it would be best to say nothing at this stage.

What if Daniel Henry Collins couldn't be traced or refused to have any contact with his son? The arrival of Gary with a girlfriend on his arm was excitement enough for now. Her son had spent twenty-three years knowing nothing about his father. Rachel felt he could wait a little longer.

21

On a dismal, muggy Saturday morning, at a stylish Regency house on a quiet street in Pimlico, Louise Mangan was to attend a one-to-one with her ultimate boss, the Commissioner of the Police of the Metropolis – otherwise known as the Head of the Met, the highest-ranking police officer in the country.

Mangan had been summoned the previous evening in a phone call from the Commissioner himself rather than some underling. She'd planned to have lunch with her teenage daughters who were both living away from home at universities in the Home Counties. Her children knew from experience that plans existed to be disrupted. A police officer's life was unpredictable at the best of times. At the moment, for Louise, the weight of work lay heavily on her shoulders. Even if it had gone ahead, the lunch would only have been a short break, albeit a welcome one. Now there would be no respite.

This was to be a discreet assignation. She'd been advised not to use her official car and had travelled on the tube, reflecting that it was just as crammed with tourists at the weekend as it was with commuters during the week.

The house in Pimlico wasn't a Met property that she was aware of. Given its location, not far from MI5 headquarters, Mangan guessed that it belonged to the spooks and that her tête-à-tête would be monitored. In all her years as a police officer she had never been called to a meeting like this; but there again, she'd never been involved in a police investigation quite like this one.

A prominent Russian film-maker had been poisoned in a London hotel. Then a Ukrainian national had been murdered by a gang of Russian thugs so sure of themselves that they'd boasted of their involvement by grotesquely leaving the name of the gang scrawled across the victim's mouth. The waitress who'd witnessed the poisoning (and probably inadvertently administered it) had vanished. When the police had gone to her flat, alerted by a remote device attached to the door, they'd found the body of a man lying in the passage. On the same Friday morning, gunshots had been fired in Crystal Palace, where some Russians had tried to abduct a young British girl, and more shots were fired outside the Ukrainian embassy in Holland Park later that day.

The front pages of all the morning newspapers carried lurid accounts of Russian gangsters 'RUNNING WILD ON LONDON'S STREETS'. The Mayor had publicly criticised the Metropolitan Police, urging them to 'get a grip', which Louise found strange given that he had overall responsibility for policing in the capital. The Home Secretary was likely to face an Urgent Question in the Commons on Monday.

Detective Superintendent Mangan went through this inventory in her head during the ten-minute walk from St James's Park station. The darkly polished double doors of the Regency house opened as she approached and a man in a brown suit led her up to the second floor. There she was left alone in a tastefully furnished, high-ceilinged drawing room to admire the expensive-looking prints adorning its walls.

After a few minutes the Commissioner came in and she was greeted with an unexpected peck on the cheek. They'd known each other for a long time and had worked together often but she wasn't expecting a display of affection. Like Mangan, the Commissioner had come up through the ranks, a process that had recently become a target for zealous politicians who claimed that the police service was the last great unreformed element of the public sector. The Commissioner had ruffled a few political feathers recently by giving a newspaper interview in which he'd mused that the reason some senior politicians and civil servants disliked what he described as the 'police meritocracy' was because they couldn't pull strings on the old-boy network as effectively as they could in practically every other sphere of public life. The Commissioner had said that he considered the absence of an 'officer class' to be a strength of British policing rather than a weakness; it was true to Robert Peel's original determination to differentiate the police from the military. The media interview had added to his reputation as a man who knew his own mind and wasn't afraid to speak it.

After the tactile greeting, Mangan was guided towards a pair of armchairs positioned in front of a decorous fireplace at the far end of the room. A tall, lean man with chiselled features and a full head of steely grey hair, the Commissioner cut a handsome figure. His dark eyes crinkled into an appealing smile as he sought to put his colleague at ease. Despite many years working in London, he'd never lost his soft Cumbrian accent.

'I'm sorry to disrupt your Saturday, Louise, but I need to have a very private conversation with you, the kind I can only have in a place like this.'

'You could have come to my office,' said Mangan, unintentionally revealing a little of the angst she felt at having had to cancel lunch with her daughters.

'No, I couldn't.' His smile vanished. 'What I have to tell you requires the highest level of security – higher than even your office can provide.'

There was a pause as the man in the brown suit came back with two cups of coffee. As he departed again, the smile returned to the Commissioner's face.

'In any case, Louise, I wanted us to talk as mates. I know what pressure you're under and I've got every faith in you to get to the bottom of this – you know I have.'

'It would help if I had the authority to bring in all the people who we know are running Krovnyye Bratya, such as Anton Sidrenko. Or we could begin further down the food chain with Stanislav Miranchuk. He was at the Strand Hotel when Smolnikov was poisoned and on the train that our witness vanished from.'

'But as you know, the main players in this outfit – congratulations on your Russian pronunciation, by the way – have links to the Russian embassy. Sidrenko and Miranchuk have diplomatic immunity.'

'And we all know that's a nonsense,' Mangan protested. 'They're no more diplomats than I am. Do the politicians want to make our streets safe or not?'

'Look, Louise.' The Commissioner rose to put his empty cup on the nearest side table. 'I'd love to authorise you to round up these characters but there would be such a political storm and at the moment nobody's keen to withstand it.'

'Bloody politicians,' Louise spat out.

'It's not just them, to be fair. The Security Services can't agree. MI5 want to take tougher action, but MI6 don't want to rock the boat. There is a perfectly reasonable argument for leaving this gang out there, convinced of their own infallibility, while we discover more about their activities. After all, it's not as if any Brits are being killed apart from that thug we found at the flat and nobody will grieve for him.'

'He was a man with a long criminal record, but he was British, and he was murdered, garrotted in fact, after being knocked out with a hammer – in Sutton, for God's sake. And that girl who they tried to kidnap in Crystal Palace was a Brit. What about all the misery these Russians invest in, the prostitution, the extortion, doesn't this damage British people? Since when have we only pursued crimes according to the victim's nationality?'

Louise Mangan's voice rose to a level inconsistent with the graceful surroundings.

The Commissioner spent a few moments studying the perfect crease in his uniform trousers before saying, 'Why don't you just fill me in on where you're up to before I tell you about the developments that I brought you here to talk about. Let's start with the Ukrainian guy.'

'We don't know much about Viktor Rubchenko. A neighbour, noticing that the door of his flat had been left open, called the police and a local PCSO went in and discovered the body. None of the neighbours could tell us anything beyond the fact that he'd lived there for a year or so and they'd rarely see him going in and out of the flat. It's one of those typical London apartment blocks where everyone minds their own business. Time of death was the early hours of Thursday; he'd had his throat cut but there were also some nasty injuries consistent with torture. The guy lived alone. There were no credit cards, bank details or mobile phone. He carried a Ukrainian identity card and there were some papers concerning his renting of the flat but nothing beyond that. We're working with the embassy to try to track down any relatives. My guess is that Viktor Rubchenko was involved in organised crime, perhaps with Krovnyye Bratya, or more probably with a rival gang that KB wants to eliminate.'

'Okay, what's the latest on our missing waitress?'

'We've had no sightings of Arina Kaplin, despite the wide circulation of the CCTV images from the train. The attempted abduction was of a girl called Melissa Thomas who actually does look a bit like Kaplin – they're of a similar height and have the same long blonde hair. She was too distraught to give much information but was pretty sure the men in the car were Russian. We don't have any images of them yet. The council's cameras weren't working – as per usual. We're still checking footage from various shops in the vicinity that have their own CCTV systems. Two passers-by rescued the girl and displayed tremendous courage. One was Melissa's housemate and the other one wandered off after the incident, so we have no idea who he is.

'There is one potentially important piece of evidence. Fingerprints taken from the wing mirror of the abductors' car match those taken from the doorknob of the flat where Viktor Rubchenko was murdered. There are two sets, so these prints could have come from one of the Russians in the car or the guy who flung himself across the windscreen.

'Then, yesterday, when our guys arrived at Kaplin's flat in Sutton they found the body of one Albert Turner, a man with a long prison record for some very violent crimes and known to be one of Krovnyye Bratya's local recruits. He'd been posing as a Parcelforce driver.'

The Commissioner interrupted. 'Was it a forced entry?'

'No. Whoever triggered the remote alarm came in with a key.'

'So, it could have been Kaplin herself?'

'Possibly. There was no trace of her in the flat and Turner didn't have a key on him, so he wasn't the one who initially opened the door. There was some damage to the door, suggesting a struggle, and as well as being garrotted Turner had also suffered a hammer blow to the head.'

'It's unlikely that the waitress could have battered him with a hammer, let alone wrapped that wire round Turner's neck and strangled him.'

'But don't forget,' Mangan interrupted, 'she's with an unidentified man. We don't know what role he's played in all this.'

She resumed her narrative. 'Nobody noticed the Parcelforce van being driven away in Sutton, but it's probably the one that was outside the Ukrainian embassy an hour or so later. We can't be totally certain because the embassy is refusing to cooperate, let alone provide us with footage from their cameras. We only know about that incident because several local residents heard gunshots and looked out onto Holland Park Road to see the van driving away. The shots were fired towards a Transit that we found abandoned in the street. A front tyre was destroyed and there was blood on the road suggesting that somebody was injured. Needless to say, that van, like the Parcelforce one, was stolen. We're trawling A & E departments in London to try to find anyone who presented with bullet wounds, but no luck so far.'

'What's your theory?' asked the Commissioner.

'The one link to all of these events is Arina Kaplin. She was the waitress at the Strand, Viktor Rubchenko was a fellow Ukrainian, the abducted girl could have been mistaken for her, Turner was killed at her flat and we always suspected that Kaplin may approach her embassy at some stage.'

'Why?'

'Because she told us she had a visa but that was a lie. She's an illegal immigrant, probably trafficked. Presuming that she wanted to avoid any involvement in the inquest into Smolnikov's death, her one chance of getting out of the country was via the embassy. As you know, relations between Ukraine and Russia, always cold following the collapse of the USSR, have gone into deep freeze since the annexation of Crimea last year.'

'I see,' said the Commissioner. 'She couldn't come to us because she thought she'd be extradited to Russia for murder.'

'Which would have been outrageous given that the murder occurred here, but I suppose stranger things have happened.'

'They certainly have, and you may as well know that the Russians are demanding the release of Smolnikov's body for burial in Moscow and it looks as if they'll get their way.'

'Doesn't that demonstrate that our young waitress is right to be sceptical? All the diplomats want to do is placate the Russians.'

'Yes,' the Commissioner said, 'but we'd have a stronger hand to play had we not released her into the custody of a couple of Russian gangsters. Who is the guy with Kaplin? Do we know?'

Mangan shifted uneasily on the damask upholstery.

'He may be an accomplice, or he may have abducted her. Between those extremes anything is possible.'

'Thank you, Louise. That's very helpful.'

There was another long pause as the Commissioner, sitting on the little armchair with his legs crossed, seemed to be watching his reflection in the highly polished toe-caps of his Dr Martens. Then he said, 'I'm under a bit of pressure from Karen. She wants me to agree to put O'Farrell in charge under her direct control.'

Louise Mangan's cheeks flushed as she absorbed this information.

'I trust you're not going to agree,' she declared.

'No, I'm not, but I wanted you to know what's going on. My Deputy Commissioner is the main advocate of letting the Russians have the waitress so that we can get on with tackling the things that are important to the public, such as knife crime.'

'Well, she seems to be an expert in the art of knifing her colleagues in the back.'

'I think she feels that O'Farrell has the Russian expertise that this case needs.'

'But he can use that under my direction,' protested Mangan, 'and work with me instead of holding things close to his chest and trying to undermine me at every opportunity.'

'Yes, he can, which is why I said no to Karen. O'Farrell probably put her up to it, but you should know that I'm on your side and so is Brian Baker.'

'Brian told me that you thought we should leave the girl to the Russians,' Mangan said.

'That is a rather crude interpretation of a conversation we had earlier in the week. Brian is more enthusiastic about Karen's position than I am, but I sounded him out about putting O'Farrell in charge and he has nothing but praise for the way you're handling all this. We're not in a good place and I do need to see some results soon, but I have no intention of following Karen Dale's advice.'

Thinking the meeting was over, Mangan picked up her handbag and prepared to leave.

'Hang on,' the Commissioner said. 'I brought you here to tell you something.'

'Sorry,' said Mangan, distracted by the news that two close colleagues were working against her. 'I thought that was it.' She put her bag down and turned to give the Commissioner her full attention.

'The Secret Intelligence Service asked to meet me yesterday. They gave me some information that, for the moment, I am only sharing with you. Karen doesn't know, neither do any of my Assistant Commissioners.

'Sergei Dzyuba, the dissident journalist who went back to the Netherlands after the meeting with Smolnikov, is dead. They believe he ate or drank something spiked with thallium, which, as you know, is slow acting. The Dutch police are keeping this under wraps until they're sure of the time trajectory, but it looks as if two people were poisoned at the Strand Hotel last Friday morning.'

'Do the spooks have any theories?' Mangan asked when she'd absorbed this news.

'Well, we know Dzyuba had attracted the enmity of the Krovnyye Bratya through the excellent piece of investigative journalism he undertook for that Sunday newspaper. You'll recall that his article actually named several of their leaders, including Anton Sidrenko. Dzyuba had investigated the organisation during his time in London.'

'He took a big risk coming back here, then.'

'Not really,' the Commissioner continued. 'He'd just started to work for the Russians in Amsterdam, providing information about a dissident there who'd built up his own drugs cartel by taking over an operation previously controlled by the Russian state. He was also a firm advocate for Crimea being part of Russia and had agreed to work on helpful propaganda to be placed in Russian and Ukrainian media. He had been assured that, because of this work, he had a guarantee of protection from the President.'

'A guarantee that has obviously been withdrawn,' observed Mangan.

'Security Service doesn't think so. The work that Dzyuba was doing wasn't yet complete and part of his usefulness lay in working with people like Smolnikov to give the CNN documentary added legitimacy. They would not have wanted him to be killed.'

'So, if he was poisoned at the Strand Hotel last week,' Louise Mangan said slowly, weighing her words carefully, 'it may have been by Krovnyye Bratya, but without the authority of the President.'

'That's the implication and it's why the Russian authorities are particularly keen to talk to the waitress, who was the only neutral witness. They are stressing that it's better for her if she falls into their hands rather than be captured by KB, who now seem to be beyond their control.'

'Surely, sir, that's why it's much better that she falls into our hands,' said Mangan firmly.

'I'm just repeating what the Russians are apparently saying,' said the Commissioner defensively. 'And there's one more thing. We're sure that the Blood Brothers have a little helper in our senior ranks.'

'Who?' asked Mangan, genuinely shocked.

'We don't know, but during the discussions between our spooks and theirs over Dzyuba's murder, the Russians imparted this nugget of information with no further elaboration. The likelihood is that they don't know the name and that they're only telling us now as part of a reappraisal of their relationship with Krovnyye Bratya. The spooks think it's someone in the command chain who is susceptible to blackmail. I'm not telling anyone else about this, only you. You'll need to be careful with any sensitive information.'

'How do you know it's not me?' Mangan asked.

'For the same reason that I'm keeping you on this case. At least sixty per cent of our work is based on intuition. I'm putting my trust in you, Louise. Don't let me down.'

22

When Gary awoke on Saturday morning, in the bedroom he'd slept in for most of his life, Arina was beside him. They'd arrived in Aylesbury on Friday afternoon having agreed to resume the roles they'd deployed in Mount Street. Gary felt bad about deceiving his mum. His silent admiration for her had never faltered, certainly not when he learned the truth about his paternity. Many girls in her situation would have understandably opted for an abortion.

While he'd wondered about his father both before and after that revelation in the car going to Swanage, Gary had no burning desire to convert the vague masculine outline in his imagination into a living, breathing human being, and felt absolutely no resentment towards his mother. On the contrary, he relished being the sole object of her affection and doubted if doubling his allocation of parents could enhance the love and security she'd provided.

Even if he was inclined to be open and honest with his mother about the danger he was in, Arina was insistent that they maintain the facade. Indeed, she'd adopted it as soon as they embarked on the journey to Aylesbury.

'They have description of me but before I change appearance,' she'd explained doggedly as they walked to Queens Park station, 'but from what you say happened with Melissa, they still know nothing about you, yes?'

Gary gave an affirmative nod.

'It is only reason that I come with you to your mother's place. Nobody knows you are involved so nobody looks for me there. Staying in hotels would be dangerous. With you I get shelter and time to think, but it will only work if we act as couple – if I am Lilia – you understand?'

When they got to Marylebone station, two police officers were patrolling the concourse. Arina pulled Gary towards her, and standing on tiptoe she planted a kiss full on his lips as the officers strolled past, smiling indulgently towards the young lovers.

'I could have you arrested for that,' Gary said breathlessly. He enjoyed the kiss but was conscious of a change in his perception of the enigmatic woman he was falling in love with. He'd originally thought of himself as her protector but now realised that any vulnerability was more perceived than actual. Gary felt let down by Arina's obvious desire to get away from him, irrational though he knew this feeling was given the danger she was in. There was so much he didn't know about her, and that he was determined to discover.

On the train to Aylesbury, continuing their subterfuge, heads close together, Gary's arm around Arina's shoulders, she'd tried to improve his mood, assuring him that everything he'd been told was true, promising to fill in the gaps when they were alone. Returning to the issue of whether to tell his mother the truth, Arina convinced Gary that deceit was essential for Rachel's own good.

'We won't be there long and the least she knows the safer she'll be.'

This settled the issue: Gary would take a woman with a gun, who the police wanted to interview, the Russian state wanted to extradite, and a bunch of bloodthirsty thugs wanted to kill, home to meet his mother.

Rachel Nelson was impressed by 'Lilia Zinchenko', the girl who worked with her son and had been forced to vacate her flat after a burst pipe caused it to flood. Gary and Arina repeated the performance they'd given the previous night – as if they were in a play that had opened in London and was now touring the provinces. But they were performing in front of a very different audience. Rachel was all eyes and ears – as perceptive as an eagle watching a fledgling's first flight.

'How long have you two worked together?' she'd asked innocently as the three of them chatted in the kitchen shortly after her guests had arrived. Just as Lilia was responding with a firm 'six months', Gary was offering a much weaker 'oh, about a year or so . . .'

Rachel had noticed the stern look of admonishment that passed from Lilia to Gary and how it cowed him into a period of silence. She didn't doubt that they worked together, it was easy to get the length of time wrong, but neither did she doubt who was the dominant partner in her son's relationship.

Having settled the two lovers in the front room with a glass of wine each while she began preparing dinner, Rachel could hear the background buzz of a quarrel conducted in whispers.

After a while, Lilia had come into the kitchen offering to help. Rachel said that if anyone was going to assist her it ought to be Gary – Lilia was their guest and should be relaxing in the front room with her wine.

'Gary wanted to come in here to help but I stopped him,' Lilia had explained. 'I know he doesn't cook so well and I wanted chat with you.'

'Well, that's very nice of you, Lilia. If you insist, there are potatoes to be peeled and boiled.'

For the next hour the two women had talked and cooked and prepared the table for the feast to come. Gary would appear intermittently, asking if there was anything he could do, only to be dismissed so that Rachel and Lilia could continue their working conversation.

Rachel had talked about what Gary was like growing up, how close he'd been to his grandfather, his passion for cricket, how he'd not put a great deal of effort into his schoolwork, and the restlessness that had taken him to London. She'd long developed an evasive answer to questions about Gary's father, which was 'I've always been a single mother'. This was duly trotted out and, as usual, had stemmed any further enquiries, although Rachel made a mental note to tell Lilia the full story once she'd got to know her better.

She had noticed how reluctant the girl was to talk about herself. Every time Rachel asked a question about Lilia's family there was a cheerful evasion – 'Oh, we are just typical Ukrainians, you know, hoping for a better life and making the best of the one we have; but I am really interested in you and the way you bring up Gary.'

And then, throughout dinner, she had sensed that the whispered argument in the front room was continuing to bubble away like the vegetable soup served as a first course.

She understood how the lovers would want to be together and had already made arrangements to leave the two of them alone for the rest of the week. Will, the divorced plumber who she'd met through an online dating app, had readily agreed to her suggestion that he and Rachel spend the week at his place in High Wycombe. They'd dated for a year in a pleasant but non-committal kind of way, enjoying each other's company without wanting exclusive access to it. Will the Plumber (as she always referred to him) was the kind of decent, dependable man her father had been, and Rachel felt reassured (if unexcited) in his company.

Her plan had been to be in his company from tomorrow evening; to spend one night sizing up the Gary/Lilia dynamic before leaving them to their own devices. However, as the evening went on, she had begun to regret this decision. It wasn't so much that she worried about inhibiting the two lovebirds if she stayed; their little displays of affection over dinner, always prompted by Lilia, had seemed forced and unnatural. The main reason she wanted to leave was to enable them to resolve whatever it was that so obviously needed to be resolved between them.

Rachel had texted Will to tell him that she'd be driving over tonight rather than on Saturday. Then, having already explained her absence from tomorrow to Gary and Lilia as something that had been planned for weeks, she'd told them that Will had suggested she drive over tonight so as to avoid some major roadworks that he'd just discovered would be starting in the morning. This fib was told just as they were finishing dessert.

'There's plenty of food and I'll hopefully get a chance to say goodbye when I get back next Saturday before you return to London.'

'As long as we're not causing you any inconvenience,' Gary had said, looking plaintively at his mother.

'Of course you're not,' said Rachel, gathering her things together. 'I hope you enjoy exploring the delights of the Thames Valley together.'

She'd embraced her son, noticing the tension in his shoulders and realising that bringing Lilia up from London must have been an ordeal for him, much more so than it was for his mother. The girl had made a favourable impression, but the sense that something wasn't quite right remained. Lilia's attractiveness was undeniable, and it was clear that Gary was mesmerised by her. But she'd done quite enough maternal observation. She left them alone that Friday evening hoping that whatever the lover's tiff was about, it could be sorted out more quickly in her absence.

After she'd gone, Gary had insisted on clearing up while Arina had a bath. Then they'd sat opposite each other drinking another coffee at the small kitchen table. The grandfather clock in the hallway struck nine. The cloud had cleared, and the low evening sun shone through the kitchen window but failed to lift the disconsolate mood.

'So, where did you get the gun?' Gary had asked, stirring his coffee distractedly.

'You should just be thankful I have it or you would be no more,' Arina replied aggressively.

'I've already thanked you – I realise you saved my life.'

'But you don't trust me, do you? How come little waitress have gun and know how to use it? She must be lying. Is that it, Gary? I save your life and you want to interrogate me?'

Arina was wearing Gary's towelling robe grabbed from a hook behind the bathroom door.

'I'm not interrogating you,' Gary had protested. 'You told me you'd fill in the gaps later and I'm just trying to have that conversation.'

'My father gave me the gun and my father taught me how to use it – okay? Just like your mother teach you to cook, my father teach me to shoot – better than you cook, I bet.'

'What about the Parcelforce van? How did you get that?'

'I saw it in the road with key in ignition when I leave my flat and I take it.' Arina's voice was growing louder.

'It was perfect way to get to embassy without arousing suspicion. You understand? I'm not car thief, I don't go around stealing vans. It was perfect opportunity and would have worked if you hadn't come running and shouting down the street.'

'I just wanted to say goodbye,' Gary had pleaded, aware how pathetic it sounded even as he said it.

'You call my fuckin' name.' Arina was shouting now. 'My name, Gary. They are watching, but they just see Parcelforce driver making deliveries, until you shout and then they see Arina Kaplin escaping.'

'I know,' Gary had said timidly. 'I didn't realise there was anyone watching. The road was so quiet . . .' His voice faltered into silence.

'I go to my room,' Arina had said. 'I'm too exhausted to talk any more. I need sleep.'

Rachel had shown Arina the spare room when her guests arrived, feeling that protocol demanded she at least go through the motions regardless of what sleeping arrangements they had planned.

'We've spent the last two nights together,' said Gary. 'Time we had a trial separation.' Arina had grunted dismissively, unable to appreciate her companion's sense of humour. Gary went to his own room a little while later, after he'd checked the cricket scores. He wanted to restore some normality to his life, to counter a dreadful sense of mortal danger.

As a boy, on clear nights like this, Gary would always leave his bedroom curtains open so that he could watch the stars. He'd track the satellites that had increasingly intruded into the firmament, observe the constellations and occasionally see a falling star, which always made him catch his breath in wonder. There were no falling stars tonight, but a spectacular full moon was bright enough to throw shadows on the wall. It had moved out of vision by the time Gary dozed off.

His dreams were vivid. He was being chased by an invisible enemy, hunted down across fields, a railway line, along a riverbank. And then he was suddenly awake, Arina's soft body pressed against him. A delicious warmth surged through him as dreams faded into reality – a reality consisting of Arina in a T-shirt and Gary, in pyjama shorts, embracing in the confinement of a single bed. They said nothing, communicating in groans and sighs as they kissed, and embraced, and explored, moving together with an instinctive sense of each other's requirements. There was lust but also tenderness – and deep affection softly expressed through a delicious intimacy.

Afterwards, lying with Arina and drifting back into sleep, Gary knew that he loved her unconditionally; that he'd do anything for her, forgive her anything. To have her close was all he wanted; to keep her close all he could ever hope to achieve.

They made love again when they woke up, less quietly and with greater passion as the morning light enhanced their desire, allowing them to see as well as touch and taste. And then they slept again.

It was 10.30 on Saturday morning by the time they were fully awake. Gary went down to the kitchen to make tea and toast, which they consumed in bed, sitting up, their backs against the headboard, Gary in his pyjama shorts and Arina wearing his dressing gown.

Arina told Gary more about herself. She told him she was born in 1991, on 24 August, the very day that Ukraine declared itself an independent country after years of being shackled to the Union of Soviet Socialist Republics. Her father was an officer in the Ukraine army, her mother a theatrical agent.

'I was only child and my father doted on me – my mother not so much.'

'What, she didn't dote on you or your father didn't dote on her?' Gary asked.

'Both. They divorced when I was ten. I love my mother, but my father I adored. He called me Kheruvym – cherub, I think you say – an angel. We always have guns in the house and papa teach me how to use them from a very young age.

'First, we'd shoot at tin cans, then at targets, and when I was about thirteen he takes me hunting for first time, to a vast forest. "Kheruvym," he say, "we are cursed to live in troubled times; you must always have gun for protection."'

Arina fell silent and Gary put a comforting arm around her. They sat like that, in silence, bolt upright against the headboard, long after the toast was eaten. Eventually, Gary asked what Arina's father was doing now.

'Nobody wanted independence more than my father, but he knew it was only illusionary after Soviet Union broke up. He was military man, he knew what power

Russia still had in Ukraine. He was supporter of Yush-chenko, who ran against Moscow stooge Yanukovych in presidential election. Yushchenko lost but election was rigged. That was what caused Orange Revolution. A new poll was held, not rigged this time and Yushchenko won.

'I was just teenager, but I knew my father must hide his allegiance because army was not supposed to take political sides. Everyone knew they were on side of Moscow, that they support Yanukovych. For them the days of USSR were good days. To my father they were days of suppression and dishonesty – days of Chernobyl. My father was always army man but wanted army to defend Ukraine not defeat it.'

'And what happened to him?'

'He died when I was fifteen. Killed. Murdered.'

Gary sensed that Arina wanted to carry on un-prompted and so stroked her arm, silently waiting for the story to emerge in its own time.

'Papa had to go to Moscow often, to so-called liaison meetings between officers of Ukraine and Russian army. He tell me they were more instruction than liaison but if ordered to go he went, with some colleagues usually.

'This time he went alone. I live with my mother but see my father most weekends. That's when we went hunt-ing. He tell me on that last weekend, the one before he die, that he was going to see a couple of guys who would help to reveal the truth about what was happening in Ukraine.'

The narrative was paused again as Arina looked down at the pillow she'd placed across her knees and was picking at as if it were a set of worry beads. After a few minutes she continued.

'His body was found in the Volga four days later. They say he had high level of alcohol in his system and must have fallen in river drunk, but my father was never a heavy drinker and was strong swimmer. They kill him.'

'The Russian Army?' asked Gary.

'Russian something – I don't know for sure. They hold inquest in Russia and don't even return body. My father is buried in military graveyard in Moscow.'

'Do you know why they killed him?' Gary realised this must be painful for Arina but wanted to know more.

'I guess whoever he met betrayed him. Lots of people die in Russia like this, dissidents, peace activists, opponents of the President. Now you know why I have gun. I already tell you why I come here as illegal, now you know why I bring the gun my father gave me.'

'So, tell me what happened when you went to retrieve it from your flat,' Gary said.

'I take a big risk there but what else can I do? It wasn't just the gun, there were other things I hide there. I get in and out as quick as I can. But as I come out, man delivering parcels comes at me. He must be with Russian gang. I defend myself – hit him with the hammer and drive away in his van. The rest you know.'

'While I was downstairs getting the toast, I checked my news app. They are saying a man was found dead at your flat.'

Arina received this information with a gasp of disbelief.

'They say he'd been driving a van that had been stolen from a Parcelforce depot that morning.'

'What are you saying, that I killed this man?' Arina's eyes flashed with anger again.

'Of course not. The guy was garrotted, for Christ's sake. That's not something a featherweight like you would be capable of. I'm just reporting what I read.'

Lying back against Gary's naked torso, Arina said reflectively, 'He must have been killed after I leave. Whoever killed him must have been close by when I was there.'

For the rest of the weekend, Gary and Arina weighed up their options. What was Arina's best route back to Ukraine? Was there any way they could go on the offensive against their pursuers? How could they best make use of Gary's anonymity? Was there anybody who could be recruited to their cause?

For the first time since being thrown together on the train they felt reasonably safe, while realising this sense of security was only temporary. They also felt a joy in each other's company that they hoped would last for ever.

23

Anton Sidrenko had arrived at the club in Old Compton Street at just after 10 p.m., fatigued from his flight on a private plane from Moscow. The atmosphere was subdued. There was no music or dancing, no background drone of animated conversation. Party nights were every other Saturday. Tonight was a business night.

Sidrenko's principal lieutenants, Vladimir Granat and Dmitry Podkolzin, were present, as was Stanislav Miranchuk and, in a separate room, nervously awaiting an audience with their leader, the three Krovnyye Bratya agents who'd made the botched attempt to abduct Melissa Thomas the previous day.

Sidrenko was seeking explanations. Speaking in his calm and measured way, he left the gathering in no doubt about his dismay at their failures while he'd been away. Miranchuk had given his account of how the waitress had disappeared on Wednesday and now Granat was telling his boss about Friday's debacle in Crystal Palace.

'I try to have somebody in each of my multi-occupied properties who I can rely on to protect my interests. They make sure my people know if any damage is being done, any antisocial behaviour, loud parties, etc. In return they get a rent reduction. It's a discreet network of snitches, if you like, to keep Grant Properties in touch with what its tenants are doing. When Stanislav told me that the girl had got off the train at Gipsy Hill, all our snitches in that part of London were contacted, given a description of Arina Kaplin and asked to contact me if an East European who looks like her appears in the area. One of these informants contacted us on Thursday. A woman answering that description was not only in the area, she was at one of my properties. I tried to contact Stanislav – where the hell were you?' he asked directly of the man sitting languorously on a low armchair opposite.

'I told you, I was busy with something,' Miranchuk answered dismissively.

'Please continue, Granat,' Sidrenko said quietly.

'In the end I decided that if Stanislav was unavailable and with you out of the country, I should make the necessary arrangements. I sent those guys the photo we have of Kaplin –' he nodded in the direction of the reception room where the three men were waiting – 'the snap that Morozov took on the train. I told them to watch the house and follow her if she appears. For some reason they decided to grab the girl they thought was her and drive off.'

Anton Sidrenko continued to exude a preternatural calm. Never known to lose his temper, the only sign of tension was a tendency to tap the middle finger of his left hand against his kneecap. That finger was tapping away like a morse-code operator as he said softly, 'Not only did they snatch the wrong girl and drive straight into a traffic jam, one of them fired a gun into the air – in case anyone hadn't noticed them.'

'You can talk to them yourself,' said Granat. 'They're not the sharpest knives in the drawer but they acted from the best of motives.'

'I'd hate to see the mess they'd cause when they act from the worst of motives,' Sidrenko responded, then turned to Miranchuk. 'I asked you to deal with this, Stanislav; to personally take charge of getting this girl back. Where were you when Vladimir was trying to contact you?'

'Concentrating on the places where I expected the girl to go – her flat, the embassy. Putting arrangements in place to capture her rather than going on a wild goose chase to Crystal Palace,' Miranchuk answered disdainfully.

And it was true that he had made arrangements for keeping watch in Sutton and Holland Park, but he had also been enjoying another night with Sidrenko's wife, Maria Paseka. Enjoying it far too much to respond to Granat's calls.

Miranchuk despised the property magnate, considering him to be part of a rich, overweight, decadent Russian elite that had gorged on the fruits of Russia's demise under Yeltsin like locusts on a wheat crop. These men never did the dirty work. They would probably faint at the sight of blood. He had checked his phone that night and seen the four missed calls. Whatever it was, he'd decided that Granat could deal with it himself for a change. Miranchuk considered a second undisturbed night with Maria that week to be too precious to sacrifice.

He went on. 'While those three dumb bastards were busy making fools of themselves and of us, my guys were in the right place at the right time.'

'And they still let her escape,' Granat retorted.

'But are we sure it was her at the Ukrainian embassy?' asked Sidrenko.

'It was either her or her buddy who killed Turner at the flat,' Miranchuk explained. 'At the embassy our guys thought it was a delivery woman until the guy turned up shouting her name. You know my theory.'

'That the guy she's with is working for the FSB?'

'Yes, the more I think about it the more sense it makes.'

Sidrenko shifted position to lean forward, elbows on knees, eyes focused on the ground in front of him as if reciting what he had to say from the polished floor-boards.

'I had discussions in Moscow,' he said eventually. 'While they're not entirely thrilled about our escapades, I was assured that whoever that guy with the waitress is, he has nothing at all to do with them.'

'So much for that stupid theory,' said Granat.

'The good news,' Sidrenko continued, holding up a hand to gesture an end to the verbal sniping, 'is that Dzyuba died yesterday. An enemy of Krovnyye Bratya has been removed. Well done, Stanislav.'

There was a burst of dutiful clapping from everyone in the room except Granat. It was applause that Miranchuk felt he fully deserved. He had devised the plan to elimi-nate Sergei Dzyuba, the troublesome journalist who had exposed the activities of Krovnyye Bratya. He'd used Denis Smolnikov and his CNN documentary as the bait to get Dzyuba to come to London and arranged for six KB men pretending to be CSKA supporters to crash the Strand Hotel. Knowing that Dzyuba only drank his own bottled water he'd ensured that the six 'supporters' each carried doses of thallium in water bottles exactly like the one Sergei Dzyuba was drinking from. The volume of water in the six bottles varied from almost full to almost empty. During the diversion, Dzyuba's bottle was replaced by whichever toxic one contained an equivalent amount. Miranchuk felt he fully deserved praise for this success but realised that without it he was likely to be in serious trouble for ignoring Granat's phone calls.

'It remains imperative to find this girl and the guy she's with,' Sidrenko said, returning to the business at hand. 'One of our men has been killed and another may need to have his leg amputated. I know I told you not to use excessive force, but this is now personal. Do we have any idea where the two of them are?'

'No, but we may have soon,' said Miranchuk. 'Morozov picked up a card that one of them dropped on the train. It's an address card for a woman called Marilyn Kelsey who lives in Fulham. We've watched the place for the past couple of days without seeing any sign of Kaplin or her boyfriend. Now we need to take it a step further by finding out what this woman knows.'

'Get our Met person to do that,' Sidrenko said. 'I don't want any more collateral damage.'

While the whole of Krovnyye Bratya knew they now benefitted from having recruited a Metropolitan Police officer to their ranks, only Miranchuk and his boss knew this person's identity. Unwilling to divulge such crucial knowledge to his two lieutenants for fear that they may one day become rivals, Sidrenko had displayed his trust in Miranchuk by making him the only other contact point.

'Perhaps we can now turn our attention to the events in Battersea on Wednesday night,' Sidrenko resumed, still in full interrogational mode.

'The murder of that Ukrainian guy was nothing to do with us,' Miranchuk protested.

'The last time we spoke,' Sidrenko said slowly, 'you told me how you'd had this guy followed home from the Strand Hotel. What are you telling me? That he cut his own throat?'

For the first time, Miranchuk displayed agitation.

'We've been focusing on getting the waitress. I planned to pay this guy a visit next week, then I saw in the papers that he'd been killed and had "Krovnyye Bratya" taped across his mouth. You know we would never draw attention to ourselves like that,' he said.

Dmitry Podkolzin, who had lowered his huge frame into a seat beside Sidrenko, spoke for the first time. 'Stanislav is right. Surely not even those idiots in the next room would be stupid enough to leave the name of our organisation on the victim. Listen, the guy was probably involved in trafficking. We have some significant rivals out there. The Albanians in particular would love to pin this on us. What does our police friend say about it?'

'They don't know anything about Viktor Rubchenko,' Miranchuk said. 'But he told me they got a clear set of prints from the doorknob of Rubchenko's flat and it matched a set they found on the car that our friends next door used to try to abduct that girl.'

Podkolzin, Miranchuk and Sidrenko all shifted their gaze towards Granat.

'Wait a minute,' he said, 'those guys would only act on my orders and I don't know anything about this Ukrainian guy.'

Miranchuk was pleased that an awkward moment for him had ended with attention being diverted towards his bête noire.

'As I was saying.' Anton Sidrenko reasserted his command over the meeting. 'Get our friendly police officer to pay this Kelsey woman a visit. She's likely to be someone who cooperates fully with the police and by sending the copper we won't risk another embarrassing incident. As for our two fugitives, the likelihood is that they're holed up in a hotel. Podkolzin and his guys have already been busy visiting every hotel in central London. Any progress to report, Dmitry?'

'Not regarding Kaplin,' Podkolzin responded, 'but I'll talk to you privately about something one of my guys saw.'

'Okay, keep looking. Remember, it's now about revenge and although it would be preferable to question them before exacting it, I'll understand if that's not possible. The important thing is to take them out.'

Sidrenko stood up, preparing to leave, before adding, 'As for those three idiots in the next room, I don't need to waste my time talking to them. Remind them that we're the Blood Brothers not the Marx Brothers and make sure they never come to my attention again.'

'Do you want me to see them on your behalf and make all the necessary arrangements?' Miranchuk asked. There had been other operatives whose time with the organisation had to be curtailed and who Miranchuk had dealt with. This usually involved removing their diplomatic status and returning them to Russia. Occasionally it involved a bullet to the head.

'Do what you like with them, Stanislav. I presume you have no objections, Vladimir?' Sidrenko asked. 'They were your men.'

Granat gave a resentful nod, just as Miranchuk expected. The property magnate wouldn't want to get involved in the messy end of the business. Miranchuk now had license to decide what to do with the three men anxiously waiting in the next room, expecting to feel the full force of Sidrenko's wrath.

Instead Miranchuk had already decided that they should have a conditional reprieve. They may not be the sharpest knives in the drawer, as Granat had remarked, but they were still knives; and Granat had made the mistake of allowing them to become Miranchuk's knives. He would ensure they were sharpened and put to good use.

24

Sunday, 19 July

Louise Mangan was finding it hard to concentrate on the sermon. In truth it was always an effort. Going to St Mary's on Sunday mornings was more an opportunity to clear her mind than to be inspired by the oration. Although Christianity was an essential part of her character, she'd long felt that its procedures and rituals were designed to be endured rather than enjoyed.

As a child she'd been compelled to attend Sunday services by her parents but, unlike most of her friends who'd abandoned organised religion in their teens, Louise found lasting comfort in the scriptures and the doctrine of the Holy Trinity.

This place of worship in Brixton, close to where she lived, was very different to the pretty village church she'd attended growing up in rural Surrey. There was nothing pretty about St Mary's. Its brickwork needed repointing, the interior smelt of damp and there were holes in the roof where the lead used to be.

The congregation consisted of the same twenty-odd souls who came every week: a retired head teacher who lived in Mangan's street and always wore the same ancient tweed suit; a Nigerian family whose impeccably turned-out children struggled to contain their obvious boredom; a few Ulster Presbyterians relocated to south London; and a group of Afro-Caribbean women whose voices carried the hymns just as their devotion sustained the church.

Detective Superintendent Mangan thought she might well be the youngest adult present, apart from the vicar who, she mused, was probably newly graduated from theological college. He was one of a procession of stand-ins who'd visited St Mary's since their regular minister had retired eighteen months ago. His sermon was satisfyingly tedious, allowing Mangan to think about her meeting with the Commissioner the day before.

Who was the traitor in their midst? It must be someone of sufficient rank to be of use to the Krovnyye Bratya, which meant all her senior colleagues were under suspicion. She'd only come across financial corruption once before; a Detective Superintendent not long off retirement who was offered a substantial sum of money to pass on some information. Once under criminal control, the demands grew more difficult to meet and the threat of exposure more terrifying, until eventually he buckled under the strain and committed suicide.

More common forms of corruption didn't involve financial inducement. They were about bending the rules to get a conviction, planting evidence, falsifying statements, bearing false witness. When she'd joined the Met almost twenty years ago, she'd been told by those who'd served in the sixties and seventies that this had been prevalent. Some had even spoken of 'the good old days', complaining that having to play by the rules assisted the villains who had no such constraints. Louise had never been in doubt that such a culture had existed or that breaking it had been essential to the extensive reforms she'd witnessed during her time as a police officer.

Exposing the traitor was a second-order issue for Mangan. Her main focus was on the case itself and the news that Dzyuba had been poisoned. He'd told the police in Amsterdam that because he lived with the constant fear of assassination, he rarely consumed food or drink that he hadn't prepared himself. At the Strand Hotel he was careful to bring his own bottled water rather than drink from the jugs on the table.

But if Dzyuba was the target and not Golovin, the theory that Smolnikov had drunk from the wrong cup required a rethink. Before he died, Smolnikov had said he suspected Dzyuba of poisoning him. Could it be that they had poisoned each other? Her thoughts turned to the young waitress who'd become embroiled in all this. Karen Dale wanted to sacrifice her to the Russians and the Commissioner seemed sympathetic to what Mangan described as the Pontius Pilate Option. She wondered again why Kaplin had walked away from police protection. Had O'Farrell encouraged her to leave the Strand Hotel?

Since her meeting with the Commissioner, trust had become a more precious commodity and it had already been in short supply with regard to O'Farrell. In the six months since becoming her ADS, she'd been aware of his simmering ambition. Mangan was used to the kind of silent scepticism that women in her position had to endure from some of their male subordinates – the arched eyebrow, the suppressed smirk, the feeling that every decision she made was being subjected to a more rigorous analysis than any of her male equivalents had to go through.

But O'Farrell's approach was more sinister. He simply acted as if he was the DS. It had been noticed. Brian Baker, the Assistant Commissioner who had been a kind of father figure for Mangan ever since he'd been her sergeant in the early days of her career, had mentioned it. His advice was to have a quiet word with the Commissioner about having O'Farrell moved. The man was unpopular with colleagues, Baker had told her, so she needn't worry about her authority being usurped. However, Baker said he had rarely seen such an obvious mismatch. Mangan was reluctant to follow that advice, which felt too much like giving in.

Now it was too late. If she tried to move him after what she'd been told, the Commissioner would think she was turning this case into some kind of vendetta.

She knew O'Farrell had spent the previous day checking CCTV footage from the shops in Crystal Palace close to where the attempted abduction had been thwarted. She'd received a report from him stating that nothing of interest had been discovered. As the sermon neared its end, Mangan decided to pay a visit to the incident room at Crystal Palace. It was only a couple of miles away and going there would pass the time until her daughters arrived for the dinner in a local restaurant that she'd offered in compensation for the lunch she'd had to cancel yesterday.

'. . . and that is why God's love is unconditional and why our response must be to accept the burdens that life places upon us and face up to them with a Christian equanimity born from our deep faith in His everlasting glory.'

The sermon finished on what Mangan felt was an appropriate note. After a couple more hymns, she'd be able to leave this cool sanctuary to pursue her newly planned afternoon activity.

In another church, of a different Christian persuasion, not far away in Knightsbridge, Stanislav Miranchuk stood next to Ivan Ilkun.

'I'm pleased you came here to see me,' Ilkun whispered, 'but please, let's not discuss business until the service ends.'

Miranchuk admired the glorious interior of the Russian Orthodox Cathedral of the Dormition of the Mother of God and All Saints. Looking around at the congregation he saw several prominent Russian ex-pats, amongst them a respected banker, a senior overseas representative of Gazprom, the state-owned energy company that wielded huge influence across Europe, and a famous ballerina who was currently appearing with the Bolshoi at the Royal Opera House.

Impressed by the fine vestments of the bearded priests, the brocade cuffs and elaborately decorated cassocks, Miranchuk was nevertheless aware of the incongruity of his presence. He had never been baptised, having been born at a time when the Russian Orthodox Church had already been subjected to decades of destruction and oppression under Soviet rule. In the past, men from the security services such as Ilkun would have been at religious ceremonies covertly, to take names, rather than overtly, to pray.

Miranchuk watched as many in the congregation took communion, queuing to have breadcrumbs soaked in wine spooned into their mouths by the priest.

Ten minutes later the two men were walking through Hyde Park in the sunshine.

'Forgive me for asking, but why didn't you take communion?' Miranchuk asked.

'There's nothing to forgive. I'm delighted that you're taking an interest in what must seem to you to be strange and unnatural rituals. The Church is kind enough to provide a private, closed communion during the week for me alone. The President has made the Orthodox Church another arm of the Russian state. He apparently takes communion privately in the Kremlin and even has his own personal confessor. Loyal servants such as I are also privileged to receive a few . . .' he paused, searching for a phrase, 'celestial perks, shall we say. The Russian Orthodox Church is important to the presidential reforms. It serves as a counterpoint to Western liberal values.'

Miranchuk noticed that two men a hundred metres behind were shadowing their movements. Following his companion's eyeline, Ilkun said, 'Unfortunately, it is felt that I need to have protection. Strange things have been happening in this city. Moscow believes that it's time for the reckoning. The question is, whose side will you be on when it comes?'

'There need not be any trouble between us,' Miranchuk said. 'Why destroy what has been a fruitful relationship for FSB and Krovnyye Bratya?'

'I'm afraid the murder of Dzyuba has changed everything. But you must know that, Stanislav; why else would you have come here to see me?'

'Because we are old comrades and you wanted us to stay in touch.'

'At Stamford Bridge I thought we had time before the rupture came, that you could make up your mind over the summer. That's all changed. You've got until the end of the week to decide. You have my number, call me. If I hear nothing, I'll pray for your soul at next Sunday's service.'

By four o'clock on that sultry Sunday afternoon, Louise Mangan had already spent a couple of hours watching several versions of the same scene. CCTV footage had been downloaded from three private cameras housed in a bank, a newsagent's and a pizza takeaway on Westow Hill.

A car attempted to pull out of a side street into the line of traffic being held by a red light at the junction with Crystal Palace Parade – a spot where, as she'd been told by an attendant PC, four London boroughs meet – Croydon, Lambeth, Bromley and Southwark.

Mangan found this piece of information as soporific as the footage.

The PC also told her that he'd been with Assistant Detective Superintendent O'Farrell the previous day while he'd studied the same grainy images, checking the faces of the men who emerged from the car against a sheet of photographs of twenty-two known Krovnyye Bratya operatives. Some of the photos were passport sized, issued by the Russian embassy and purporting to be of diplomats. Others were surveillance shots taken surreptitiously by the security services.

O'Farrell's report, emailed to Mangan on Saturday evening, said that none of the occupants of the car had been identified against this rogues' gallery. This wasn't a surprise as many of the gang's foot soldiers were as yet unidentified. Besides, as O'Farrell's report pointed out, 'Krovnyye Bratya is not the only gang operating in London. Some Romanian and Albanian outfits have a greater involvement in trafficking young girls for prostitution. This incident may well be totally unconnected to Arina Kaplin and the poisoning at the Strand Hotel.'

His conclusion was that there was 'nothing remarkable here beyond the undoubted heroism of the two guys who'd foiled the abduction'. Louise Mangan disagreed and couldn't suppress a flush of indignation at the thought of O'Farrell being lined up to take over this investigation. His ambition ran well ahead of his ability. Why would a gang of people traffickers try to snatch a woman off the streets in broad daylight when they had a ready supply available in drug dens and brothels across the country?

Those poor girls had been groomed not kidnapped. The intended victim here, Melissa Thomas, had no connection to drug dealing or prostitution. She did however resemble Arina Kaplin; she was of a similar height and build with the same distinctive long blonde hair.

The camera in the pizza parlour faced Mount Street, the road out of which the car had emerged. The actual abduction had been too far down the road to register, but what was visible was the car speeding towards the junction and the two men running after it. Mangan trawled through the copious notes. Only one of those men had been interviewed, a Mr Murray, aka 'Knuckles'. Nothing was known about the lad who'd thrown himself across the windscreen apart from his name, which according to one of the Turkish barbers was Gary.

A thought suddenly struck her. The houses in Crystal Palace were large, reminiscent of the area's former glory when a single family, including servants, occupied an entire building. Now those buildings were multi-let. It was perfectly possible for two girls with long blonde hair to reside in the same house. From what they knew, Kaplin had escaped the close attention of Krovnyye Bratya at Gipsy Hill station less than a mile up the road. The Russians were desperate to find her and the mysterious stranger she'd left the train with. What if Melissa Thomas hadn't been plucked off the street because she looked like Arina Kaplin but because she looked like Kaplin AND had emerged from the house where it was thought she'd been hiding?

Mangan noticed the time. She would need to rush in order to get home before her daughters arrived. She would come back to Crystal Palace tomorrow in order to take a closer look at – she searched the notes until she found the address she was looking for – 27 Mount Street.

25

Monday, 20 July

Stanislav Miranchuk received the text message at 11 a.m.

Can I book a hair appointment for 3 p.m.?

He replied in the affirmative and the arrangement was made. He would meet Maria Paseka in the cafeteria of Marks & Spencer on Regent Street. This was the code they used to arrange meetings when Anton Sidrenko, Maria's husband, was at home. The subterfuge even went so far as involving an actual hairdresser's, off Regent Street, which had two entrances, one leading off the main street and another accessed from a mews at the back of Savile Row.

Maria would walk in the front door for her hastily arranged appointment and leave through the back door for her assignation.

She and her lover knew the extent of Sidrenko's surveillance capability – indeed Miranchuk was often part of it. He had always been confident that if any suspicion emerged about Maria having an affair, he'd be the first to know. He was about to be proved wrong.

When Maria arrived at the table that he'd commandeered in the furthest corner of the large cafeteria she was wearing dark glasses to cover her bruised eyes. As usual, they conversed in Russian.

'He knows I spent the night with someone, but he doesn't know it was you,' Maria told Miranchuk when he arrived back at the table with a couple of skinny lattes.

'How can you be sure of that?' he asked.

'Because he spent so much effort trying to find out.'

She told him of her suspicion that somebody had seen her checking out of the hotel they'd stayed in on Tuesday night. The booking was under a false name and she and Miranchuk had arrived and left separately.

'I tried to pretend that I'd been out with some girl-friends and had drunk too much to travel home but he knew that was rubbish – particularly as our flat is only a short taxi ride from the hotel. In any case, I'd claimed to have been home every night when the crafty bastard asked me what I'd been up to while he was away. He'd been all smiles and affection when he first came in.'

Miranchuk suddenly remembered what Podkolzin had said on Saturday night about having some informa-tion that he'd talk to Sidrenko about privately. Podkolzin had been put in charge of checking hotels in the search for the two fugitives. That must be it. Maria had been seen checking out – if she'd been seen checking in, they would surely have had unwelcome visitors to their room during the night.

Maria was telling him how shocked she'd been by her partner's behaviour.

'He came home late on Saturday after meeting you

and the others at the club, and as I said, was all sweetness and light until we were eating dinner on Sunday. The maid had left after cooking and serving our meal, so we were alone. We'd not long begun to eat when Anton suddenly said very softly, "Who is he?" so quietly I could hardly hear. I tried to laugh it off and gave that lame excuse about being out with the girls, but he carried on relentlessly – "Who is he? Who is he?" his voice getting louder and louder.'

'I know he has women all over the place and thought he wouldn't mind so much about what I did.'

'It must be good to know he cares,' Miranchuk said sarcastically while rolling a sugar sachet mindlessly through his fingers.

'He has given me a good life and although Anton has always had a cold heart, he'd never raised a hand against me in all the years we've been together – until last night. But the physical pain is nothing compared to the humiliation.'

'What did he do to you?' Miranchuk asked calmly.

'As you can see, he punched me in the face,' Maria said quietly, staring down into her coffee cup. 'He just put his knife and fork down, got up, walked round the table and punched me. Then he grabbed my hair and dragged me into the bedroom. And then he beat and raped me, all the time asking for a name.'

There was a long silence before she spoke again.

'My body is bruised all over, but he was careful not to break any bones. And this morning he acted as if nothing had happened. He was distant as he always is, but there was no talk about us breaking up or any reference to yesterday.'

'Where is he now?' Miranchuk asked.

'He's gone to Manchester on business. He left at about half ten. I had to get out of that house as soon as I could. I had to see you.'

'I'm glad you took the risk,' Miranchuk said. 'You can't go back. He'll be planning a more serious effort to get a name out of you.'

'Oh, but I gave him a name. I said I'd spent the night with Vladimir Granat.'

'What? Vladimir? Did he believe you?'

'Granat, or Grant as he likes to call himself these days, has made several attempts to seduce me. The fat pig slobbers over me every time we meet. I know Anton has noticed. And he knows that Vladimir collects women even more enthusiastically than he collects properties. Very young women, usually, but he does have the odd stately home.'

A rare smile broke across Miranchuk's face.

'Brilliant,' he said. 'What's Granat going to say if he's confronted? He'll deny it, but he was bound to do that anyway. Anton was already suspicious about his behaviour towards you and I doubt he'll be in the mood for checking alibis.'

'So, you can relax,' Maria Paseka said, touching her lover's knee beneath the table in a gesture of affection. She was wearing a lemon-yellow dress beneath her light summer raincoat which she let slip from her shoulders like a discarded bath towel. 'And we can continue to see each other.' The slight intonation in her voice left the comment suspended between question and statement.

Miranchuk's feelings for this woman went beyond desire. He had never experienced such deep emotions and this incident had made him feel more protective towards her and more contemptuous of Sidrenko.

'Will you leave him?' he asked.

'I have no life without him in England and I don't want to go back to Russia, so no, I will not leave him. I will stay.'

'But he might do this again.'

'I have known Anton since we were eighteen-year-old students inspired by the prospect of glasnost. We've been through a lot together. He has never hurt me before and I doubt he will again, but I hate him now: I hate him because he raped me. The first physical contact we've had in two years and it was rape – as if the only thing that excited him about me was that I'd been with another man. But I will suppress my loathing and stay, because I have no other option.'

'You can come away with me,' Miranchuk said, placing his hand gently on her arm.

'You know that's not possible, Stanislav.'

Indeed, he did know that nobody could leave Krovnyye Bratya; that death was the only escape. He wondered at his own importunity. This was a time for careful consideration, not impulsive gestures.

Maria was talking now of the need for them to cease any contact for a while, until things had settled down. She mentioned the prospect of Sidrenko kicking her out, but thought that he'd have done this on Sunday if he intended to do it at all.

Miranchuk was only half listening now. He was going over his conversations with Ivan Ilkun at the church yesterday. So much of Ivan's assessment made more sense now. Miranchuk's mind was focused on revenge for what had been done to Maria, but this could be harnessed to self-preservation in the fallout that was to come. Given that Sidrenko now suspected Granat of being his wife's lover, there may be an opportunity to dispose of them both while securing his escape route through Ilkun. His old FSB friend had given him a week to decide, but as things turned out, he'd only needed a day.

26

Gary was trying to explain cricket to Arina.

'But how can you waste so many days on a game?' she asked, having endured a long explanation of the rules.

'Not so much a game, more a way of life,' Gary pleaded. 'And death.'

He recounted the story of a batsman named Andy Ducat who'd died during an innings at Lords. The score-card eventually read 'Not Out – Dead'. Gary relayed this gleefully as a fine example of the idiosyncratic nature of his favourite sport, but Arina remained stubbornly unimpressed.

They were sitting at the small kitchen table eating breakfast, continuing to bask in the warmth of each other's company. The last two days, tucked away like hibernating animals, may have taken Gary's mind off the danger they were in, but Arina had never ceased to be vigilant. Periodically peering through the net curtains, she'd asked Gary to explain any activity considered suspicious, such as neighbours walking to their cars or people passing by a little too slowly.

On Sunday afternoon the doorbell had rung, inter-rupting a game of cards they were playing in the front room. Arina's gun had been placed under a cushion on the settee. Retrieving it even before the chime faded, she'd crept into the passage to observe two silhouettes caught in the frosted glass of the front door, while Gary went upstairs to look through the landing window. He saw a pair of Jehovah's Witnesses who soon moved on to the next house. Gary explained that their dark suits and the *Watchtower* magazines they carried pointed to their identity, and how council estates like his were regularly visited to seek potential refugees from Armageddon, but Arina, who had never heard of the Witnesses, insisted on keeping watch until they'd cleared the street; then they went back to playing cards. Arina had taught him the games they played in Kiev, all of which turned out to be Ukrainian versions of Newmarket or Kings or some other card game he'd grown up playing with his grandparents.

When they'd gone to bed the night before last, Gary had placed the Queen of Hearts on Arina's pillow as a gesture of his love. She responded by telling him about Ukraine's national poet, Taras Shevchenko, reciting one of his romantic verses.

'And then remember me,
with gentle whispers and kind words,
in the great family,
of the newly free.'

Gary had never liked poetry. He thought Arina's recital was charming but what he really wanted was for the King of Hearts to be on his pillow the following night. It never appeared and Gary was surprised to feel a deep sense of disappointment. It seemed to suggest that his love for her wasn't reciprocated, although eventually he convinced himself that it was more to do with Arina's practicality. They only had one pack of cards and Arina had already returned her Queen of Hearts to it. Taking out the King would have spoilt the next game, he told himself. Nevertheless, her failure to properly acknowledge his gesture worried him. They could easily have used the Jokers as replacements.

This was the way their weekend had passed, alternating between the deeply serious and the utterly frivolous. They'd explored various scenarios as to what to do next. Should Gary, who was able to travel without fear of recognition, go to the Ukrainian embassy to explain Arina's dilemma and enlist diplomatic support? He was keen to do something to compensate for scuppering her escape but Arina pointed out that the embassy may still be under surveillance and that, in any case, without Arina actually being there to explain her plight, the embassy was more likely to call the police.

Gary had asked if there was anyone back home that Arina could contact for help. They'd even considered whether he should fly to Kiev. Arina thought that her mother would be powerless to help, and in any case, Gary would struggle to overcome the language barrier; as for the Ukrainian 'authorities', they were divided between the corrupt and the incompetent. Arina's only feasible means of escape, they'd decided, was on one of the cargo vessels docked in ports such as Tilbury and Liverpool which regularly sailed to Ukrainian ports. After breakfast they'd spend the day developing a skeletal plan.

Gary watched Arina as she moved around the kitchen fetching spoons for the cereal and cups for the tea. She fascinated him: the way she cursed in Ukrainian when the toast began to burn, or rocked on the balls of her feet as she waited for the kettle to boil; her habit of lifting a hand to smooth down the long hair she used to have. He liked her new look, the cropped black hair that accentuated those amazing eyes and offset the tilt of her chin and the paleness of her alabaster skin, every inch of which he had explored and caressed.

Last night, when debate gave way to desire, they had made love on the living-room floor, the stairs and the upstairs landing. Now Gary found himself fantasising about unbuttoning the fuchsia blouse she wore, lifting her simple black skirt and laying her gently across the kitchen table.

A ping indicating the arrival of an email on his phone ended Gary's reverie. He didn't receive many. All were read immediately, whereas his friends were always boasting about the number of 'unreads' they had no time to peruse.

His mother had sent a message the previous afternoon to check that everything was okay. Apart from some advertising stuff that went straight to his junk file, that had been the full extent of his weekend inbox.

This one was from Knuckles, telling Gary that as he was 'resting at the minute' (as if he were an actor rather than a gofer), he now had time to check the electrics at Ms Kelsey's if Gary could pass on the address.

Indicating that he had a call to make, Gary moved

to the living room to escape the music playing loudly on the kitchen radio.

'Knuckles, how's it going?' he said when his house-mate answered.

'It's deadly quiet here,' Knuckles said. 'Like a grave-yard in a monastery. Jason's still abroad, Mel's in Swansea and you're Christ knows where.'

'I'm having a few days away with Lilia,' Gary said, more in deference to Arina's strict instructions than any distrust of his friend.

'Look, mate,' he continued, 'it would be great if you could sort that electrical fault out tonight, but I'm not interested in following it up any more.'

'Ah, the attraction has faded, has it? Decided to deal with one woman at a time?'

'Something like that. I'll be calling the office later to tell them I'm not fit to come back to work yet and I'll pass a message to Ms Kelsey to say you're about to pay her a visit.'

'Great. If there really is something up with the wiring it's best to make sure she's not fried alive,' Knuckles said cheerily. 'What's her address again?'

Gary felt a stab of annoyance at the recollection that he'd dropped The Ice Queen's card on the train, but he'd scrutinised it long enough to remember the address.

'Number 16 Ellerby Street, Fulham,' he relayed con-fidently.

'Look, Gary.' Knuckles sounded nervous. 'There's something I have to tell you. I've messed up. I know you didn't want me to say anything about your involvement in stopping those bastards the other day, but I went and blurted it out to Melissa.'

Gary gave a sigh of disappointment. 'Now she'll mention it to the police, and I'll have all that hassle to contend with,' he said.

'No – she promised not to – although I don't know why you shouldn't share my hero status. It's just that I was talking to her yesterday, trying to help with the trauma the poor girl is still experiencing, and I inadvertently said, "me and Gary" and she latched on straight away. "What did Gary do? What did Gary do?" She went on and on until I had to tell her. But I said you'd go feckin' potty if the police knew, because you had this strange aversion to coppers. She said it was because of your secret life as a mass murderer.' Knuckles chuckled. 'It was the first time Mel sounded as if she might be getting back to normal.'

'Look, you're forgiven,' Gary said. 'But make sure you fix those electrics this evening and don't forget to drop the bit about me doing a follow-up check.'

'Okay. The poor woman will be inconsolable at getting me instead of you, but I'll let you know how it goes.'

Early-evening sunlight slanted between the gaps in the high buildings like floodlights onto a stage as Louise Mangan walked down Mount Street. It was Monday evening and she had only now managed to escape from Victoria to travel to the outer extremities of south east London and return to the line of thought she'd been pursuing the previous afternoon. She'd come alone, having told her office that she was heading home after a gruelling day.

A vigilant journalist on one of the broadsheets had made the link between Dzyuba's death in Amsterdam and his presence at the Strand Hotel. The coincidence of his poisoning and Smolnikov's had been made public and aired in Parliament where the Urgent Question had been debated as expected.

A Foreign Office minister had responded rather than the Home Secretary as part of the government's effort to portray this outbreak of violence as a symptom of Russian rather than British lawlessness. The Parcelforce van used by the man murdered in Sutton and from which gunshots had been fired outside the Ukrainian embassy had been found abandoned in a north west London back street. It was currently being examined by forensics but Mangan wasn't holding her breath for any clues to emerge from that quarter.

At the daily case call, O'Farrell had repeated his view that the attempted abduction in Crystal Palace was unrelated to their search for Arina Kaplin. She'd not mentioned her suspicion about 27 Mount Street, not even to Brian Baker, who was about the only senior officer she felt she could trust following the Commissioner's Saturday-morning revelation. Instead she'd come here alone. She wore a light cardigan over her simple blouse and skirt combination and carried a satchel-type handbag draped across her shoulder. A thick summer breeze had begun to cool the air.

An old man occupied a cushioned chair directly opposite number 27. Mangan stopped beside him posing as a passer-by who had a simple interest in observing the scene of a recent news story. Terry introduced himself and soon made it clear that he was an authority on all things to do with No.27.

'So it's where all the commotion was on Friday,' Mangan said.

'Yes,' said Terry, 'I was sitting right here when it happened. Saw Melissa come out and those men grab her.'

'Do you know your neighbours very well?' Mangan asked.

'Oh yes, lovely kids, all of them. Only Knuckles there now, with the others away; and I saw him go out not long ago.'

As Terry didn't seem at all curious about Mangan's interest she thought she may as well go for broke. 'The real hero on Friday was Gary, wasn't it?' she asked tentatively.

Within ten minutes she'd not only learned that 'Gary' was Gary Nelson, and that he did indeed live at that address, but also that he was a paragon of virtue and an expert in domestic electrical appliances.

'I'm not surprised the girls go for him,' Terry concluded. 'He came home with a lovely blonde last Thursday.' Mangan feigned nonchalance.

'Oh really? Sneaked a girl in, did he?' she said.

Terry laughed. 'I thought it was Melissa at first. Same long hair. I thought it was funny, her being home so early, but sure enough she came home a few hours later so I'd got that wrong.'

'You know what?' Mangan told Terry. 'If he was at home, I'd put a little note through the door to thank him for his bravery. There's too little appreciation shown to youngsters like Gary.'

'He's not been home all weekend,' said Terry, 'but when he helped me I wrote to his employer so that they knew what he'd done. You should do the same. It might help him get promoted. I've got the address somewhere. Hang on there a minute and I'll get it for you.'

By the time Knuckles arrived at 16 Ellerby Street the day's heat had dissipated as if some celestial hand had turned down the temperature gauge. He'd driven to Fulham in a gleaming black Volvo, a company car from Pinewood that he'd somehow managed to retain during his current break between film projects.

There was a parking space almost opposite Marilyn Kelsey's house into which Knuckles backed, ignoring the 'Residents Only' sign. As he was about to get out of the car, having stretched over to the back seat for his tools, the varnished red door of number 16 opened, and a policeman emerged.

The uniform was 'full dress' – all epaulettes and fancy buttons and the copper was adjusting a peaked cap that Knuckles knew was worn by officers rather than infantry. A glamorous woman came out onto the front doorstep behind the departing visitor, said her farewells and went back inside. This was obviously Ms Kelsey and

Knuckles decided to wait a few moments before becoming the next interruption to her evening.

He watched as the policeman walked to a car parked further down the street.

A few minutes later it came past, the officer's eyes focused on the road ahead. It seemed odd to Knuckles that such an obviously high-ranking police officer should be driving himself.

A couple of hours later, Knuckles was drinking the hot chocolate that Marilyn Kelsey had prepared for him in thanks for a job well done. He'd refused the fifty pounds offered, settling for the hot drink as his only reward. After a rigorous examination, the electrical fault had been located and fixed. Ms Kelsey purred her approval and Knuckles used the opportunity to ask about her earlier visitor.

'Sure, he looked a fine specimen of a policeman,' Knuckles said, explaining how he'd pulled up just as the officer was leaving.

'Yes, he was rather grand. He said he was in counter-terrorism and called because one of my address cards had been found on a train and the man who dropped it was of interest to them.'

'Hey, I don't mean to pry, Marilyn,' said Knuckles, using her first name as she'd insisted. 'It's none of my business.'

'Don't be silly. I can assure you that I'm not a master criminal. Anyway, as I told him, I give my card to somebody at least ten times a week, how can I possibly know who dropped it?'

Knuckles nodded his head in affirmation.

'But actually, I'm pretty sure I do know. I think it was your friend and mine.'

'Gary?' Knuckles exclaimed.

'Yes. I told the policeman that it would help me if I knew where it was found. He said it was on a train from Victoria to Sutton and I know that's the train that Gary takes to get home to Crystal Palace.'

'It is indeed. Did you tell him?'

'No, I did not,' said Marilyn Kelsey indignantly. 'I'm not in the habit of shopping my staff to the Old Bill.'

She sat back in her chair, crossing her legs and gazing up towards the ceiling.

'If Gary's been a bad boy, he'll need to answer to me,' she said with a smile that was close to a smirk.

Knuckles told her about Gary's act of heroism, suggesting that it may be why the police were trying to find him.

Ms Kelsey laughed.

'Like you, I'm not English, but I doubt if one of their little peculiarities is to use senior police officers to pursue commendations. Anyway, poor Gary is ill. I'm on holiday this week but I heard from the office that he's signed off for another week with something called Russian flu which sounds horrendous.'

Later, as she showed Knuckles to the door, Marilyn Kelsey said, 'Do pass on my best wishes to Gary for a speedy recovery and tell him that if anybody in authority is going to interrogate him about dropping that card, it will be me. Thumbscrews may well need to be deployed.'

27

Detective Superintendent Louise Mangan loved the view from her office window at New Scotland Yard. She was sufficiently high in the twenty-one-storey tower block to see St James's Park and Buckingham Palace. Like most of the three thousand staff working in this cheese-shaped plot in Victoria, she would be sad to move out.

After almost fifty years, the headquarters of the Metropolitan Police was to move to the Embankment in 2016. New Scotland Yard would move back into the vicinity of Old Scotland Yard, albeit to much smaller premises.

The Tuesday-morning weather, dark and miserable, matched Mangan's mood. She'd spent another night dwelling on the fact that one of her superiors had tried to replace her with one of her subordinates. She'd not seen Deputy Commissioner Karen Dale since the Commissioner's revelation of the attempted coup, but she knew that when they did meet later it would be an awkward encounter as it would be with ADS O'Farrell. He must know about the plot to put him in charge – indeed, he was likely to have been its instigator. Mangan was pleased that the Commissioner had confided in her, but it had added internal distrust and suspicion to the already burdensome nature of this case. She now felt unappreciated from above and below.

It seemed like a breakthrough had been achieved the previous evening, but after tossing it around with most of her bedding during a restless night, she wasn't so sure. All that had been revealed was the name of the man who had intervened to rescue Melissa Thomas and that this man had arrived home the previous day with a blonde on his arm.

Nothing suggested that he was involved with a Russian crime syndicate either as friend or foe. His housemates would need to be questioned again to find out more about the mystery blonde, although it was possible they wouldn't have seen her, that she'd never strayed from Gary's room. It was even more possible that the woman wasn't the one Mangan was looking for.

She couldn't even be sure that the attempted abduction had anything to do with what now appeared to be a double murder at the Strand Hotel. However, what was beyond doubt was that Arina Kaplin had left a late train at Gipsy Hill with an unknown man. This lad Gary may well be him and this possibility needed to be investigated, albeit unconventionally in the sense that Mangan had decided that she needed to pursue this offline for now, without Dale or O'Farrell knowing.

Assistant Commissioner Brian Baker had already popped his head round her door to say good morning and ask if there had been any developments he should know about. Louise liked and trusted Brian but had revealed nothing, either about her liaison with the Commissioner (which could not be mentioned) or her discovery in Crystal Palace (which could).

The turncoat in their ranks was apparently a senior officer, which meant that she could at least trust her detective constables. The two working on this case were known to everyone at New Scotland Yard as Torvill and Dean. Their actual names were Tonkin and Din. They were around the same age, had come through police college together, arrived in New Scotland Yard at the same time and had become inseparable friends despite being very different people. Geoff Tonkin was a bald, overweight south Londoner who'd joined the Met after two years in the forces. Rushil Din's family left India for Walsall when he was two years old. Slim and handsome, he'd been recruited straight from university. Neither of them minded the nomenclature that had attached to them from Hendon onwards. Indeed, they answered to their nicknames as readily as to their real names.

Mangan called them into her office.

'I want you to find out everything you can about a Gary Nelson of 27 Mount Street, Crystal Palace. Geoff, you check if we have anything on him by way of a criminal record, DNA sample, witness reports, etc. Rushil, you need to go to his workplace, though I'd be surprised if he's there. He wasn't at home yesterday and his elderly neighbour said he hasn't seen him since the attempted abduction on Friday.'

Mangan told them that Gary Nelson was 'wind-screen man', as they'd dubbed him, and that DC Din should tell Nelson's employer that he was being sought in connection with his possible entitlement to a police commendation.

'Don't set any hares running, but this may be the guy who walked off the train with our disappearing waitress. If he's there, call me and keep a hold of him till I arrive.'

'Shall I staple him to his desk?' Din asked, a broad smile on his face.

'No, just file him under "pending".'

Later that morning, when Mangan entered the conference room for the daily case review, Deputy Commissioner Karen Dale and Mangan's ADS, Connor O'Farrell, were already there, seated together, chatting amicably over tea and biscuits. Brian Baker having already given his apologies, the only other attendees were a detective sergeant and a clerk to take notes.

Mangan didn't engage in the usual small-talk preliminaries. She'd pledged herself to remain professional in front of her two adversaries, but this positivity didn't stretch to friendly banter.

The 'Morning, Supe' that O'Farrell chirruped as she walked in hadn't helped lift her mood. She hated the abbreviation, which made her sound like a tin of Campbell's condensed.

Karen Dale opened the meeting and invited O'Farrell to report on his examination of the CCTV footage over the weekend.

'It didn't throw up anything of real interest in respect of the Strand Hotel poisoning. I had one of the spooks who has a deep knowledge of Russian organised crime with me and neither of us saw any faces we recognised. The car they were in was of course stolen, and Forensics are still working to find any useful DNA. The only significant fingerprints were on the chrome wing mirror. One set matches the prints found on the doorknob of Victor Rubchenko's flat. I think this is all about that murder and nothing to do with Smolnikov's poisoning at the Strand.'

'Go on,' said Dale, 'explain yourself.'

O'Farrell stirred his tea methodically, as if winding a clockwork toy. 'Rubchenko was a Ukrainian. We know very little about him, but what we do know is that he was probably associated with people smuggling. In the same way as the two countries are at loggerheads over the annexation of Crimea, so Russian and Ukrainian gangsters are at war as well. They used to rub along, but now Krovnyye Bratya are determined to wipe out the Ukrainians.

'Other competitors include the Albanians, who are already established here, and the Chechen Mafia who are keen to get a foothold, but there isn't the same level of vicious animosity as there is with the Ukrainians.

'Perhaps more importantly, the biggest Russian criminal organisation, the Solntsevskaya, operate all over the world but until now they've been content to leave this country to KB. The spooks say that's all changing and that they're now keen to muscle in here.'

O'Farrell looked directly at Mangan.

'So, Supe, we've got ourselves bogged down looking for this waitress who, in the grand scheme of things, is unimportant. What happened at the Strand was Russian on Russian. What happened at Crystal Palace involved the attempted abduction of a British girl, and from the fingerprints on the wing mirror of the car they used, it seems that one of the guys was also involved in the murder of Viktor Rubchenko.'

'So, they were from Krovnyye Bratya, the outfit that killed Rubchenko?' Karen Dale asked.

'I think it's safe to say that if KB had killed him, they'd be unlikely to advertise the fact by putting their name on the body,' O'Farrell replied.

Louise Mangan noted the brazen way that her Deputy had adopted her argument as his own. She said, 'But those prints could have come from the guy who threw himself across the windscreen.'

'There are two sets of prints on that wing mirror,' O'Farrell explained, speaking slowly, as if to a class of remedial students. 'The driver will have needed to handle the mirror because they weren't electrically adjusted. So, two sets of prints – one set from a gangster trying to kidnap a young girl off the street, and the other from a young guy who happened to be passing by. Which of the two was most likely to have been found on Viktor Rubchenko's front door after he'd been murdered?'

The question was left hanging as Dale turned her admiring gaze away from O'Farrell to say, 'On the face of it, there does seem to be a clear connection to the murder in Battersea rather than the poisoning at the Strand;

and this does seem far more important than finding the waitress, wouldn't you say, Louise?'

Mangan leaned forward, placing both elbows on the table, and looked directly at O'Farrell. 'I disagree,' she said. 'I think the guy performing the heroics in Crystal Palace is the same one who walked off the train with Arina Kaplin, which would link both incidents. In any case, I will not abandon that girl because Connor considers her to be unimportant. She's in danger and we have to find her – particularly as we lost her in the first place.'

The meeting dragged on unproductively as various bits of bureaucracy were dealt with. Dale had sparked an unnecessary discussion about the importance of the issues raised in the wider political and geopolitical context.

By the time it finished, lunch was being served in the huge ground-floor canteen and Torvill and Dean had returned from their assignments.

Louise Mangan, returning to her office with a hastily grabbed cheese roll, found them waiting like a couple of eager retrievers after a shoot.

DC Tonkin had found references to several Gary Nelsons but none matched the profile of the Crystal Palace version.

'Our Gary seems to have led a blameless life devoid of any interaction with the forces of law and order,' Tonkin said.

His friend admonished him good-naturedly.

'You sound like an Old Bailey brief, never using one word where four will do. Why don't you just say you drew a blank?'

Tonkin laughed. 'Because I wanted to keep you quiet for as long as possible. The only reason you don't use long sentences is because you don't know enough words.'

'Okay, kiddies, let's get on with it,' Mangan said, chewing a chunk of her roll. 'This in itself suggests that our Gary is not obvious criminal material. So, nothing from Torvill, how about Dean?'

DC Din consulted his notebook. 'Gary Nelson works there all right, but he's currently off sick. His boss is on holiday, but I spoke to HR who let me have a look at his file. He's worked there for about four years and does indeed live at 27 Mount Street. Well thought of by the company and judging by a letter on file this isn't the first time he's acted as a good Samaritan. He apparently fixed a serious electrical fault for an elderly neighbour.'

'Yes, I know all about that. Is there anything that might indicate his actual whereabouts?' Mangan asked.

'There is. They have his letter of application on file, sent before he moved to London. It's from what I presume to be his family address in Aylesbury.'

'Excellent,' said Mangan, leaning across to see the address in Din's notebook.

She'd been thinking hard about whether she could carry on pursuing her own line of enquiry without sharing the details with senior colleagues. Much of the morning meeting had been spent wondering if she should counter O'Farrell's argument by revealing what he had failed to uncover. But the Commissioner had warned her that somebody in the upper echelons was working with Krovnyye Bratya and she was reluctant to take the risk of handing Gary on a plate to those vicious thugs. In any case, she couldn't yet be absolutely sure that Gary Nelson was the guy with Arina Kaplin.

'Do you want me to pass the address to the Thames Valley guys?' Din was asking as Mangan gazed across the rooftops of SW1 lost in thought.

'No,' she said abruptly. 'The three of us are going on a little trip – to Aylesbury.'

28

Tuesday, 21 July

Tobias Parnaby had a collection of three vintage cars, which he kept in what used to be the stables of his nineteenth-century manor house in Stoke Mandeville. It was hardly an extensive collection, partly because Parnaby was a capricious collector. His enthusiasm for classic cars had begun in the late 1980s and ended in about 1993. It had evaporated in the same way as his subsequent passions, first for rare stamps and then fine paintings. Tobias Parnaby had always lived a little beyond his means, but he wasn't short of a bob or two. The dental practice was lucrative and the contacts he'd made outside dentistry had been cultivated to provide an impressive crop of Board positions with a variety of companies.

The car he had wanted to use for his trip to London with Rachel Nelson was a 1950 Riley coupé – until Mrs Parnaby intervened. Why, she asked, was he even contemplating driving off in an old convertible on such an important journey in grey and gloomy weather with rain forecast? Her husband had imagined himself at the wheel of the Riley with the roof down, tossing witticisms into the conversation, captivating Rachel with his air of debonair sophistication. He imagined she would be wearing a chiffon scarf that fluttered gently in the warm breeze. As it turned out he was driving his distinctly non-vintage Audi A4 beneath a slate-grey sky when he picked Rachel up at 10 a.m. She'd told him how she'd exiled herself to Will the Plumber's house and it was from there that they set off for London.

Her mood was one of trepidation. Tobias Parnaby had tracked down Gary's father through his network of important contacts. Having forged a close friendship with the Chief Constable of Thames Valley Police, through their association with a police charity of which Parnaby was a trustee and the Chief Constable a patron, he had called in a favour. Parnaby had invented another story about his dental nurse, this time about her needing to trace a relative, which had the virtue of being close to the truth. Could the Chief Constable find out if a Daniel Henry Collins was a serving officer with the Metropolitan Police and, if he was, to be reasonably sure it was the man they were looking for, when had that officer been recruited?

The Chief Constable had produced the required information the previous day. Daniel Henry Collins, who joined the Met as a twenty-one-year-old in 1991, was now an inspector in the Insurance Fraud Enforcement Department of the City of London Police, having transferred there from the Met a decade ago.

As they drove along the M40, the gregarious dentist gave Rachel a little lecture on the origins and purpose of the City of London force. It was, he told her, 'a piece of institutionalised nostalgia that existed only because it had always existed'. Going back to its foundation with the modern police service in the nineteenth century, Parnaby explained how this tiny constabulary served only nine thousand residents in the Square Mile of the City of London, but that this population swelled to half a million through the influx of those who worked there on weekdays.

Rachel was mildly interested up to the point when he started to talk about the tunic buttons of the City of London police being brass as opposed to the white metal of the Met. She had completely zoned out by the time her boss was wittering on about the absence of the Brunswick Star on the cap badge, only tuning back in as Parnaby was explaining where they would meet the father of her child.

'Given that it polices London's historic financial district,' he was saying, 'its speciality of investigating fraud is hardly surprising. Daniel Collins is based in the Guildhall, which is a magnificent and ancient town hall which also happens to be the headquarters of the City of London Police.'

Rachel asked about the meeting arrangements and was assured that Daniel was expecting them at 11.30.

'He knows you want to ask him about the dance he attended at Aylesbury College, but I'm afraid there was no easy way to pre-warn him about the specifics. That's all down to you.'

Rachel had spent a sleepless night worrying about this encounter. How could she even broach the subject of Gary to this stranger who she hadn't seen for almost a quarter of a century. She hoped there would be some kind of instant recognition; that a flicker of the flame that burned between them that night had survived. It would at least help to create the right atmosphere for what she had to tell him. She was pleased that Parnaby was with her. There was a tweedy dependability about him that comforted and reassured. This quest to find Gary's father had largely occurred at his gentle insistence, and although she knew his reasoning was correct, she also knew she should have done this many years ago. Daniel Collins would be entitled to berate her, either because she hadn't told him about Gary sooner or because she was telling him now. Her stomach ached with nerves as they pulled into a car park near Moorgate station and took the short walk to the Guildhall.

Having signed in at the reception desk and donned their lanyards, a young woman led them through a maze of corridors to the office of Inspector Daniel Collins. At first, when the door opened, she thought there'd been a mistake; that they'd come to the wrong office – because the bald, round-faced man holding out his hand in greeting was definitely not the one who'd seduced her in the college grounds all those years ago.

Had Rachel Nelson been more prone to tears she would have shed them then and there, in that office, in front of the stranger called Daniel Henry Collins. The release of pent-up sentiment, combined with relief that she didn't have to say to this Daniel what she had prepared herself to say to her Daniel, caused her to totter but not to fall.

Tobias Parnaby held her arm and guided her to a chair. Inspector Collins looked on kindly as the young woman who'd shown them in went to fetch a glass of water. After a couple of sips Rachel recovered her composure. She felt this poor man was owed nothing short of full disclosure so she told him her story with the occasional intervention from Tobias. By the end she even managed a smile. There was an element of comedy about the way that door had been opened by a man so very different from the one she'd been expecting. The passage of time would of course have changed the way Gary's father looked. But the baldness wasn't the issue, she'd have recognised her Daniel even without those dark locks. It was the shape of him, the bone structure, his posture. Mr Parnaby made a weak joke about the fraud inspector turning out to be a fraud, which eased the tension after Rachel had finished her explanation.

'You may be the wrong man, but you were the only Daniel amongst that coachload of Metropolitan Police trainees listed as coming to the dance from Hendon that night,' Parnaby said.

Daniel Collins remembered the dance very well. He'd danced with one of the three women who'd come on the coach from Hendon that night. The forty-seater had contained two classes of sixteen. The girl he'd danced with was from the other Hendon class and they'd formed a lasting friendship.

'No real romance,' he explained. 'We both went our own way after the course, but we still catch up at the odd reunion and send each other Christmas cards. I'll give her a call now, if you like, just to see if she can help.'

He took his mobile into the next-door office to make the call in private, while Rachel and Parnaby sat in silence, contemplating defeat. All of this was very interesting, thought Rachel, but if there wasn't another Daniel amongst the Hendon visitors there was nothing more to pursue. Gary's father may have used a false name or pretended to be a copper. They hadn't worn their uniforms so how would she have known? But she couldn't bring herself to believe that her Daniel was that deceitful. In any case, as she reiterated to Parnaby, she'd seen her lover board the coach and blown kisses to him as it drove away that night.

Inspector Collins returned after ten minutes and asked Rachel if she had the list of names with her. She had. The sheet that she'd smuggled out of the college was in her handbag. She handed it to Collins.

'Mystery solved,' he announced after perusing it for a few minutes. 'My friend reminded me that there was another Danny who was in her class. The guy's name was Daniel Martin, but Hendon had got it back to front, listing him as Martin Daniels. There was much merriment about police bureaucracy not even managing to get the students' names right. For the duration of the course he was known as Marty rather than Danny, just to rub it in. I didn't know him well because he was in the other class, but my friend says he was tall and "dishy", to use her term, with black curly hair.'

He passed the sheet back to Rachel, pointing out the name.

'Does anybody know where he is now?' asked Parnaby.

'Afraid not. He's never been to a reunion and my friend says nobody has heard from him in the twenty-odd years since the course ended.'

On the drive back to Aylesbury there was silence in the car. Rachel felt wrung out, like a damp cloth. After the emotional commitment she'd made to pursuing this cause, they were at another dead end. At least she now knew the real name of Gary's father and had the perfect excuse to stick with the status quo; to refuse to participate any further in a quest that had in any case been thrust upon her by Mr Parnaby. The problem was that the status quo was what she now felt so guilty about. She had selfishly kept Gary to herself and could no longer bear the prospect of him never knowing who his father was and blaming her, rightly, for his ignorance.

'Do you want to take this any further?' Mr Parnaby was asking, using the voice he reserved for his most needy patients.

'Where would we even begin? If Daniel Martin was still with the police one of his classmates would have known,' Rachel responded.

'While you were in the Ladies', before we left, Inspector Collins gave me a useful lead. Their main tutor at Hendon is apparently still there.'

'But what could he tell us about a class he took almost twenty-five years ago?'

'I'm not sure, but your man obviously stood out by virtue of the mix-up with his name, and this time we do have his real one.'

Rachel said nothing as she gazed out of the car window.

'If you want to give up now, I wouldn't blame you. If you want to take it a little further, I'm perfectly willing to take a trip to Hendon on your behalf. As you well know, I'm used to having to drill a little deeper.'

As they left the M40 on the final leg of the home journey, at about 4.30 in the afternoon, Rachel's mobile rang. It was one of her neighbours from the Mandeville Estate letting her know that the police were outside her house.

29

At about the time Rachel Nelson was getting ready to go to London with Tobias Parnaby, her son was easing himself into a fourth day of secluded refuge at her house. Gary still wore his night attire of mis-matched T-shirt and shorts as he stood in the kitchen spooning marmalade onto a slice of toast and checking his phone.

Arina was engaged in the sacred ritual of applying her make-up in the bathroom. Gary failed to see the point as she wouldn't see anybody but him all day. Besides, he thought that if anything her face looked even more beautiful in its unadorned state.

He'd reached this conclusion in the course of another tranquil night sleeping beside her. Arina had fallen asleep first and Gary had spent a good twenty minutes gazing at her profile, admiring the long mascara-free lashes, the perfect shape of her luscious lips and the tight, smooth texture of her neck and chin. Although it was out of sight, Gary knew she'd have the gun somewhere close on her side of the bed and that, however deeply she appeared to be sleeping, she remained attuned to every noise in the street outside. At around three in the morning when a car door slammed, Gary had opened his eyes just wide enough to see Arina move swiftly to the landing window, where she had a better view of the street below. Gary feigned sleep, regretting that he hadn't told Arina about the guy four doors down who worked unusual hours and had never learned to close a car door quietly.

When she returned to bed as softly as she'd left it, Gary knew Arina would lie awake picking over the events that had transformed her from waitress to fugitive. She'd be planning her escape while Gary relished this self-imposed imprisonment. Perhaps it was the sense of security that he'd always felt growing up in this house or, as Arina kept saying, his untroubled innocence, but he sensed the danger they were in less vividly and, as a consequence, appreciated this blissful interlude more profoundly.

Now, standing at the breakfast bar, his drifting thoughts were interrupted by the ping of an email entering his inbox.

It was from Melissa:

Hi Gary,

Not sure where you are or what you're doing. Knuckles says you're not at the house and unless you've gone on a secret mission with your mate Jason (ha! ha!) who also seems to be away, I assume you're with the lovely Lilia somewhere having a good time.

I just want to say thanks for what you did. You and that mad Irishman saved my life. When he told me that it was you who stopped the car with that incredible act of bravery, I felt really bad about all the harsh words we've had over the years in Mount Street.

Do forgive me for not noticing that it was you when it happened. I was busy discussing a Russian holiday with a couple of chaps in the back at the time.

Anyway, thanks, mate. If you two are ever down this way do come and see me in Swansea. I think I'll be here for a while. Although the police say it was a case of mistaken identity, they can't be certain and are taking no chances.

I'm at my parents' and Dad says this must be what it's like to be in the Royal family. There are two coppers in a car out front and two more in our back garden, in a little hut they came and built specially. I told Dad I'm saving myself for Prince Harry, so he'd better get used to it.

I'm still reading loads but have gone off crime novels! Me and my mum do get out and about most days, shopping and suchlike, trailing my police entourage behind us. The doctors say I have to rebuild my confidence. Don't think I could do it in London just yet, at the scene of the crime, so to speak. But I do miss you guys and wish we could be having our Tuesday-evening meet-up tonight. If we did, I would actually buy you a drink and sit next to you and be nice to you.

That would make a change wouldn't it?

Stay in touch,

Lots of love,

Mel X

Gary reflected on the fact that he'd had to help rescue Melissa from being kidnapped to get a civilised word out of her. Then his mobile rang. It was Knuckles.

'Hey, Knuckles, how did it go last night?' Gary said by way of greeting.

'Oh, it went all right. In fact, it went sweet as a feckin' sherbet dip, I'd say. A loose wire that I fixed, a dodgy plug that I replaced, and your woman's house could be in the Ideal Home Exhibition as the model of an electrically safe dwelling.'

'You're a star,' Gary said, 'and I owe you – big time.'

'You certainly do, my friend. Particularly as I almost had a brush with the law.'

Knuckles told Gary about pulling up outside Ms Kelsey's house to find a police officer on the doorstep, and his subsequent conversation with Marilyn about her uniformed visitor. Gary made him repeat the story again with particular emphasis on the address card and where the officer said it had been found.

'What was the copper's name?' Gary asked, barely able to contain his excitement.

'How the feck should I know? I didn't ask and your woman didn't tell me.'

When Arina came downstairs shortly after the conversation with Knuckles ended, Gary was pacing the kitchen floor.

'Who were you talking with?' she asked.

Gary gave her a verbatim report of his exchange with Knuckles.

'But your boss told the policeman nothing – that is good, no?'

'Good, yes, but don't you see? How come a senior police officer had that address card? It's hardly likely that a member of the public would bother to hand it in as lost property and even if they did, why would the police collect it? The only people on that journey who would be keen to know who dropped the address card would be those Russian guys. I must have dropped it as we got up to leave the train, which was when one of them picked it up.'

'Those guys were gangsters, probably Krovnyye Bratya. The police might have caught them and found the card.'

'But that's not what Ms Kelsey's visitor told her. He said it was found on the train.'

'So, policeman is working with gangsters,' Arina said.

'Yes, and that's why he was driving himself last night – because he was freelancing. This is probably the same officer who let you wander into the arms of those thugs in the first place.'

Within an hour, Gary and Arina had finalised their plan. They must separate. Arina would go to Liverpool to try to get onto a Ukrainian cargo ship and Gary would go back to London. First, he'd visit The Ice Queen to find out more about her police visitor.

'Fulham is a posh area,' he reasoned aloud to Arina, 'with residents who have enough money to install the most sophisticated anti-burglary devices and enough possessions to warrant the expense.'

After explaining the meaning of the word 'posh', Gary went on to say that his boss may not just be able to give him the name of the officer, she may also have a camera image. He then needed to take that information to the police officer in charge of the investigation.

Arina was initially sceptical about this element, thinking it possible that the entire senior layer of the Metropolitan Police was in cahoots with organised crime. Gary said that the dodgy officer was a rare exception and that the British police were probably the least corrupt in the world. Arina wasn't entirely convinced and, as she emphasised, Gary had no way of knowing that for certain.

'Since when were you expert on police?' she'd asked more out of mischief than spite. But she wanted to believe Gary's observation and had already decided to trust his judgement on the issue.

They had originally been planning to stay together, but the phone call from Knuckles had changed everything. The need to separate became obvious. They could now go on the offensive against those who wished them harm; turn the tables on their attackers.

Arina pointed out that, when she was out of the way, Gary would be at liberty to tell the police everything. He'd no longer need to hide.

Eventually they would be reunited, somewhere, at some time. Who knows? they mused, if Gary's intervention led to the exposure of police corruption and a focus on the criminals who were really responsible for the death of Denis Smolnikov, it could lead to Arina being able to return to Britain legally.

In any case, by proposing separation, Arina had put a stop to Gary's propensity to drift into a mush of romantic sentimentality. She emphasised that they had no other realistic alternative. In a sense, they had to separate to stay together.

She could have also pointed out that her life depended on it. For Arina to get on board a vessel home would be difficult enough; for the two of them to do it would be practically impossible. Her only alternative to escape was being captured and probably killed. She'd planned to tell Gary this to justify separating when they got to Liverpool. Now it could remain unsaid.

They talked about the best time to activate the plan and decided to spend one more night in Aylesbury and leave the next day. By midday they were even at the stage of planning a special dinner that evening, of raiding the fridge and freezer that Rachel had left so well stocked to produce a three-course feast in celebration of the end of their sojourn in Aylesbury.

'I cook you my speciality,' Arina said. 'Ukrainian fish balls.'

'I didn't know fish had testicles.'

Gary was still trying to explain this joke when a text came through from Jamil at the office.

Police have been here. Ice Queen is on holiday, but they saw that prick Darren from HR. I just heard him say that your home address in Aylesbury is on the file and he thinks they're going to check if you're there. Thought you ought to know. Sounds exciting.

Arina, who'd been reading the text message over Gary's shoulder, went immediately to the landing window to check that the coast was clear.

'Okay, we leave now – this minute,' she announced while gathering items into her knapsack.

The plan they'd developed for tomorrow had them travelling to London together, Gary having explained that the only way Arina could get to Liverpool was via Euston. They'd planned to walk to Aylesbury station, but Arina said that would now be too dangerous.

'We need car. They may be watching for us at station.'

'I could order a taxi,' Gary suggested as he threw his clothes and toiletries into his bag.

'Do you know anyone close by who could lend you a car?' Arina asked. 'Your mum maybe?'

Gary balked at the idea of involving his mother, but instead rang his friend Duncan McDonald and arranged for him to pick them up from the shopping arcade on the Mandeville Estate, Arina having stressed they should get out of the house straight away.

Gary had told Duncan that he and his girlfriend needed him to drive them to London right now. It was an emergency and he'd explain everything on the journey. Fortunately, Duncan, who had a great deal of control over the hours he worked, was about to go for lunch, and reckoned on being with them in about twenty minutes.

The two fugitives left the house, moving through the streets that were so familiar to Gary as if they were entering a war zone. Arina made Gary slow down and walk at a reasonable pace without looking as if he'd just robbed a bank. Gary knew she had the gun in her knapsack and implored Arina not to use it, making this plea as they headed for the shopping arcade.

'It's the police who are on their way,' he hissed, 'not the Russians. If we're apprehended, you must not on any account use that thing.'

Arina nodded assent but Gary remained nervous. The woman beside him seemed unable to differentiate one group of pursuers from another.

Fortunately, they encountered no one on the short walk to the shops. At 1.15 p.m., Duncan's grey Mercedes pulled up. Gary got in the front passenger seat, Arina in the back on the driver's side.

What the hell is going on?' Duncan asked as they pulled away.

'Head for London and I'll tell you on the way,' said Gary, unsure how much he should confide in his oldest friend. 'Oh, and please do try to drive in a way that doesn't attract the interest of the local constabulary.'

Detective Superintendent Louise Mangan's car pulled up outside Rachel Nelson's house on the Mandeville Estate at 2 p.m. DC Geoff Tonkin had driven her unmarked car, its flashing blue hazard lights the only indication that it was a police vehicle.

Having ruled out subcontracting this task to their Thames Valley colleagues, protocol demanded that the local force at least be informed of a Met presence in their territory.

DC Din, who'd remained at New Scotland Yard, had been told to carry out this piece of diplomacy but not until an hour after Mangan had left so that her arrival wouldn't be pre-announced by a marked Thames Valley police car arriving on the scene.

Such a car duly turned up with two PCs on board ten minutes after Mangan and Tonkin arrived.

Having received no answer when they'd knocked, the two Met officers were contemplating whether to seek a warrant to enable a forced entry. An audience had gathered in the street, consisting mainly of children, the school holidays having just begun. A few parents had also materialised, keen to know what had brought the police to their street.

A quick vox pop revealed that this was Rachel Nelson's house but that she'd been away since the weekend. One of the more observant residents thought that Gary, her son, who the officers had been asking about, may be staying there with his girlfriend. They were seen arriving on Friday, but nothing had been seen of them since. Then a woman strode over from the house immediately opposite, bristling with barely disguised hostility. What were the police doing chasing after Gary? He was a good boy who'd never been in trouble. There were other kids on this estate that the police should be concentrating on.

'We want to talk to Gary about an incident near where he lives in London,' Mangan explained. 'Gary may be able to help us.'

'Gary wouldn't be involved in any so-called incident,' the neighbour said. 'He never did any harm to nobody.'

She told the officers that she'd contacted Rachel Nelson, who would be arriving soon. The police should be ashamed of themselves, bringing all this disturbance into decent people's lives.

Within half an hour, Tobias Parnaby's car pulled up and Rachel invited Mangan inside, having had her initial fear about her son being involved in an accident dispelled.

Introduced as 'my employer, Mr Parnaby', the dentist also entered the house along with DC Tonkin and his notebook.

The offer of tea having been declined, the two women sat in what Rachel's parents had always referred to as 'the parlour', Rachel in the armchair and Louise Mangan on the sofa opposite. Tonkin sat awkwardly next to his boss. Tobias Parnaby stood by the door, quietly observing how the two women were sizing each other up. He guessed they were of a similar age and noticed that the Detective Superintendent had the same casual elegance as her host. Mangan wore a blue worsted suit with a tight knee-length skirt. She carried a natural air of authority and Parnaby reflected that any stranger arriving in the room would immediately know which person was the senior police officer.

Mangan asked if Rachel knew where her son might be.

'Why? Has he done something wrong?'

'No, quite the opposite. He carried out an act of heroism that any mother would be proud of.'

Rachel noted the comment, keen to know more, but it didn't diminish her prickly suspicion.

'Then why are you here?' she asked, looking her visitor straight in the eye.

Mangan knew she could go no further with the pretence that she was trying to find this woman's son in order to baste him with praise.

'Look, Mrs Nelson—'

'Miss,' Rachel fired back a little more aggressively than she'd meant to.

'Sorry, *Miss* Nelson.' Mangan restarted the sentence, filing away the small detail of Rachel's unmarried status. 'We think your son might have got himself involved in something dangerous. I suspect,' she went on, careful to say 'I' and not 'we', 'that he's with the woman we've been looking for in connection with the poisoning of that Russian chap in London recently.'

Rachel was shocked, but retained her composure as she absorbed this information at the same time as trying to calculate where Gary and Lilia might be. She guessed they'd be out 'exploring the delights of the Thames Valley' as she remembered saying to Gary.

'Have you got a warrant for Gary's arrest?' Tobias Parnaby asked from his vantage point by the door.

'No,' snapped Mangan, irritated by his intervention. 'This is about protecting, not arresting.'

She decided to tell Rachel Nelson everything: all they knew about the poisoning at the Strand Hotel, how the waitress had innocently served the poisoned coffee to the unintended victim, and the danger this had placed her in. About the involvement of Russian gangsters and the train journey to Gipsy Hill. She told Rachel Nelson about the murders in Battersea and Sutton and the attempted abduction in Crystal Palace and what Gary had done to thwart it. She said she knew that Rachel's son was with Arina Kaplin, the waitress who may well have changed her appearance and be using a different name.

'Arina will be frightened of us because she's here illegally and must be worried that we'll send her back to Ukraine, where she's from, or to Russia, who'll be keen to extradite her. But we won't do that, not if she cooperates and testifies as to what happened at the Strand Hotel. She probably doesn't realise the danger she's in. The Russian authorities want to talk to her even more than we do.'

Mangan shifted forward in her seat, bringing her face closer to Rachel's.

'From everything I know about your son, he's obviously a decent law-abiding lad who's got himself mixed up in something that's spiralled out of control and he doesn't know how to extricate himself. I don't think he's committed any crime – neither has the woman he's with, but if we don't find them, some pretty unsavoury characters will. You need to help us to help him.'

Mangan knew she'd said more than she should but there was something about Rachel Nelson's quiet, watchful presence that obliged her to be completely frank; it made her feel that honesty was the only route she could take if she wanted this woman's help. She also knew that she'd promised more than she could deliver in respect of deportation or extradition. These were issues that would be decided by politicians and the judiciary, but she intended to argue fiercely that removing such possibilities should be the quid pro quo for Arina's full co-operation.

As for Rachel, she found it difficult to suppress the mounting horror that came with each fresh revelation about the danger Gary was in. A tissue that she'd been clutching in her lap was twisted tighter and tighter as she tried to control her emotions. Only a huge effort of self-discipline prevented her from bursting into tears and throwing herself upon the mercy of this woman, pleading with her to make everything right again. While she sensed instinctively that she could trust Mangan, and there seemed little doubt that Lilia was this Arina woman who the police were looking for, Rachel felt there must be some good reason for Gary not to have been truthful with her. She wanted to ask these visitors to stay, call in reinforcements, do whatever was necessary to protect her son, but she concluded that she should do nothing until she'd spoken to Gary. She feared that with police cars outside she was unlikely to get the opportunity.

'I'd like you to leave now,' Rachel said. 'I don't want Gary coming home to this kind of reception. I'm sure that with the assurances you've given me I'll be able to convince my son to cooperate.'

'He has been here then?' Mangan asked.

'Yes, and he'll probably be coming back soon.'

But Gary wouldn't be coming back soon. By then Gary was miles away, in Duncan's car, approaching London.

'Remember how, in our first year at Mandeville Comp, we upset Nutter Nolan by refusing to give him and his gang the 10p a week they were demanding for "protection" in the playground?'

Duncan smiled at the memory as he navigated a roundabout.

'You mean when six of his fifth-year goons tried to trap us in the gym after school?'

'Yeah,' said Gary, 'and you found a side door that led out onto the main corridor.'

'The Great Escape, we called it. Even Nutter Nolan couldn't help but be impressed.'

'Well, today, my friend, you are that side door and the M1 is the corridor.'

Gary went on to explain the predicament Duncan was rescuing them from, skirting over much of the detail to claim that Arina was about to embark on a voyage home to Ukraine and that he would be contacting the police as soon as he'd waved her off. The explanation was more aspirational than factual but would hopefully avoid Duncan thinking he needed to drive them straight to a police station for their own safety.

'And for the purposes of this analogy, would Nutter Nolan's gang be Russian by any chance?' Duncan asked.

'Kind of,' said Gary, 'but some of the teachers are involved as well.'

Arina poked her head into the space between the front seat headrests.

'I don't know what you two talk about, but fact is, Duncan, you may be saving my life. I have to get home and without Gary and now you, I would be captured by bad Russians or handed over to them by police.' She placed an affectionate hand on Duncan's shoulder.

'I can't believe I'm in a car with the famous missing waitress and this dipstick here next to me has got himself involved in all this,' Duncan said.

'Dipstick? What is dipstick?'

Duncan assured Arina that it was a term of endearment.

An hour later the car arrived at Euston station and the two fugitives were saying farewell to Duncan, who swore complete confidentiality, offering to drive them again if they needed him.

'One thing's for sure,' he shouted to Gary through the open window as he pulled away, 'a Sunday pint with you will never be as boring again.'

With half an hour to wait until Arina's Liverpool train, she and Gary went for a coffee. As they sat at a table stained by the spilt refreshments of previous travellers, Arina took Gary's phone.

'I prefer you don't have this, but we need to stay in touch. So, in case they get your number, I turn your location setting off. Remember it is only to be used in emergencies and for me to text you to say I am on boat. Then you can go to police, yes?' Gary nodded his assent. 'Also, I give you this.'

Arina took a roll of banknotes out of her knapsack

and passed it beneath the table to Gary. 'This is eight thousand pounds from money I had at flat. You will need for hotels and perhaps for bribes.'

Gary tried to reject the offer, saying it must represent her entire savings and that he hoped not to have to bribe anybody, but Arina insisted he take it.

'My father ensured I was looked after in his will and I bring lots of cash when I come to England. Don't worry, there is plenty more. Anyway, what you don't spend you can give me back when we meet in Kiev.'

The station tannoy directed passengers for Liverpool towards their platform. Arina and Gary embraced awkwardly, half crouching as they rose from their chairs. Arina insisted that she walk unaccompanied to her train so as not to attract attention. Gary wanted them to hug and kiss, as if that would leave an indent of her body after she'd gone; as if the soft intimacy of his lips on hers would seal the love he'd discovered over the past week; but Arina was already striding across the station concourse. She didn't look back.

Gary's phone indicated a missed call and he dialled into his voicemail, holding a hand over one ear to block out the station noise.

'The police were here,' he heard his mother say breathlessly. 'They've just left, but I'm sure they'll be keeping watch because they are very keen to talk to you and Lilia, or whatever her real name is. I'm worried about you, Gary, and I don't know why you haven't said anything to me about all this. We need to talk – don't be afraid to come home. I've talked to the policewoman in charge of the mess you've got yourself into and she says your girlfriend will be all right. If you're not coming home, at least ring me.'

Gary decided that the first thing he should do was find a hotel. He needed food and sleep before planning the visit to Marilyn Kelsey.

He checked into the Premier Inn at King's Cross, had a steak dinner in the restaurant and, before settling down to sleep, texted his mother.

Don't worry. I'm safe. Talk tomorrow.

By then he hoped to have some information that the policewoman who his mother had mentioned, the one in charge of this case, may find interesting.

After boarding the train with no seat reservation, Arina settled into the first empty seat she saw, next to the window in the standard class section. There were plenty going spare on this, 'THE 17.07 TRAIN TO LIVERPOOL LIME STREET', as the train guard announced at deafening volume.

Sitting, knapsack on knees as the whistle blew and the train began to move, Arina was surprised by the arrival of another passenger in the empty seat beside her. She was irritated by what she saw as an intrusion. There was space elsewhere in the carriage.

A sideways glance revealed that she'd been joined by a bearded cleric. She noticed his highly polished shoes beneath the cassock as he crossed his legs, pulling the little lever to lower his seatback to a more comfortable angle before opening a book. Arina tried to read the text out of the corner of her eye while pretending to gaze straight ahead. She saw that the book was printed in Cyrillic script. A few minutes later, when the train had gathered pace, the man closed his book and turned towards Arina. Speaking in the language of the book, he introduced himself.

30

Wednesday, 22 July

Jason flew into Gatwick from Zurich at just after 11 a.m. He couldn't face the thought of the train ride to Crystal Palace and was considering whether to splash out on a taxi. He'd spent more time partying than working on the trip and the rare English humidity that morning intensified his hangover and made the prospect of commuting even more unappealing than usual. There was thunder in the air.

To his surprise, as he emerged into the arrivals hall, Jason saw a placard with his name being carried by a large besuited man at the front of a jostling crowd of drivers.

'That's me. I'm Jason Cowan-French,' he told the man, 'but I didn't order a car.'

'Mr Grant wanted to make sure your journey home was comfortable,' the besuited man said with a heavy foreign accent.

Mr Grant owned the house Jason lived in. They'd never met but, through the managing agents, Jason had agreed to be his eyes and ears at 27 Mount Street shortly after moving in. They had told him about the property magnate's many multi-occupied premises having a 'lead renter', someone to keep an eye on things and let them know about any antisocial behaviour that might disturb the neighbours, or any incidents that Mr Grant needed to be aware of.

In exchange for fulfilling this role, Jason received a ten per cent reduction in his rent. It seemed a reasonable arrangement although, in accordance with the request for this to be discreet, Jason had never told his house-mates about it.

The role hadn't required him to do anything until the previous week when he'd been asked to attend a dinner in a private suite of the Queen's Hotel in Crystal Palace to which the 'lead renters' from all ten of Mr Grant's properties in the area had been invited. One of Grant's associates hosted the dinner. She asked them to look out for someone who'd been all over the news; the waitress at that London hotel who'd served drinks laced with poison and killed a friend of the Russian president. This woman was apparently in the vicinity and Mr Grant had been approached by the police to help find her.

As a responsible citizen grateful to Britain for the opportunities it had provided, Mr Grant was of course keen to help the forces of law and order in any way he could. The cooperation of those in attendance at this dinner, who were his most trusted local tenants, would be appreciated. A grainy photograph of the woman in question, of sufficient quality only to convey her strik-ing blonde hair, was distributed together with a phone number to ring if they picked up any information on her whereabouts. It was a pleasant dinner paid for by their host and the task they'd been given seemed reasonable enough.

Jason hadn't expected to actually have to do anything about it, but last week Gary had arrived at 27 Mount Street with an Eastern European woman who fitted the description they'd been given. Gary's girlfriend – what was her name? Lulu, Lilian? No – Lilia, that was it; Lilia had the accent, the grey eyes and, most distinctively, the long ash-blond hair of the waitress that the police were looking for.

On his way to the airport, Jason had obediently called the special number they'd been issued with and reported what he'd seen. He hadn't given the matter another thought. This Lilia woman apparently worked with Gary at his dull and dismal job in Accounts Payable. She was unlikely to be the waitress/poisoner and it was even more unlikely that boring old Gary would get himself involved in anything even mildly exciting, let alone all this Russian intrigue.

The car he was about to travel in was probably a gesture of thanks from Mr Grant for at least taking the trouble to participate. Jason had mentioned to who-ever was at the other end of the phone that he was off to Zurich for a week and they must have thoughtfully arranged to get him home in comfort – luxury even, thought Jason, as his bulky companion led him to a black Jaguar waiting at the drop-off point. He saw the uniformed chauffeur in the driving seat but not the third man sitting behind the blacked-out rear window. As Jason got into the front passenger seat something was placed over his face and held tighter and tighter until, as the car pulled away, he drifted into unconsciousness.

As he came to an hour later, Jason found himself in what appeared to be a warehouse. From the roar of aircraft engines close by he guessed he must still be somewhere on the Gatwick site. His hands were cuffed behind his back and a piece of thick rope bound his ankles to the metal chair he was sitting on.

He could see three men, one of whom he recognised as the driver with the placard from the arrivals hall. This trio were standing round him like hospital consultants at a patient's bedside. When they noticed his eyes open, they called to another man who was sitting some distance away checking messages on his phone.

Stanislav Miranchuk put the phone in the inside pocket of his grey linen suit jacket and walked unhurriedly towards the bedside-like gathering. Jason could hear rain rattling on the tin roof. Flashes of lightning illuminated the only sky visible through the narrow windows set high above the plain brick walls.

'Ah, Jason, you are with us again,' said Miranchuk. 'Thank you for your help last week. My three friends here acted on the information that you kindly passed on to us, but they're rather upset with you because it got them into lots of trouble.'

'Are you Mr Grant?' Jason asked, his voice only managing to croak the words as he struggled to suppress the terror he felt and the pain pounding against the inside of his skull.

'No, I'm not Vladimir Granat, or Mr Grant as he's known to you. I only wish I was. Then I could be enjoying an expensive lunch somewhere instead of doing his dirty work. No, I am merely one of Mr Grant's minions but we'd both like to know why you pretended that a woman who apparently lives with you at 27 Mount Street and is very obviously British was the Ukrainian girl we've been looking for. Was it some kind of practical joke? If it was, my friends here are struggling to see the funny side.'

Miranchuk pulled a chair across, placing it so close that Jason could smell his aftershave. The Russian was amused that Jason thought him to be acting on 'Mr Grant's' orders, whereas in reality, Granat was completely unaware of this extra-curricular activity and would soon be facing the wrath of Anton Sidrenko.

'Look, all I did was report the woman that Gary, my housemate, turned up with that afternoon. She was Eastern European, Russian I thought, and had long blonde hair. Mr Grant asked us to report any woman of that description and I just did as I was asked.'

Miranchuk received this information with a quiet sense of satisfaction. He was now sure that he'd come to the right conclusion in thinking that 27 Mount Street may still be key to their efforts in tracking down Arina Kaplin. As he'd suspected all along, there were two blondes at that address and Granat's thugs (who now worked for him) had picked up the wrong one.

'That's very interesting. You must tell me more about this Gary chap. My friends here picked up the woman you described as she left your house the next morning, but it wasn't who we were looking for – it was a British girl,' he responded.

'Oh my God, that must have been Melissa. She's one of my housemates and she does fit the description we were given – she has long blond hair as well. What's happened to her?'

'Don't worry. She was unhurt and we have no further interest in her. But I'm very interested in your friend Gary.'

Jason told him as much as he knew. Where Gary worked, the train journeys that he made in and out of Victoria every day, what he looked like, the kind of clothes he wore.

'And you have a phone number for him?' Miranchuk asked.

'Yes,' said Jason, 'but you'll need to let me get my phone from my case.'

The handcuffs were removed, and Jason's case passed to him. As he pulled out his smartphone Miranchuk took it from him, 'just in case you press any distress codes'. He tapped into Contacts himself and found the one mobile number listed for Gary Nelson.

There followed a lengthy conversation in Russian between Miranchuk and his three associates. It was ten minutes before Jason once again became the centre of attention.

'I'm sorry we had to be a little forceful but now we will get you home. My friends here were keen to exact revenge, but I knew that you were an ally rather than an enemy,' Miranchuk said sweetly. 'I do hope you're not thinking of going to the police. If you do, we will know, and my friends here will find you and do what they wanted to do originally. Also, I took the liberty of copying your contacts file. If you make an enemy of us, you make your family and loved ones our enemies, you understand?'

Jason nodded as the rope around his ankles was untied and he was allowed to stand up.

'You will go home and report anything you discover about Gary to me personally. My name is Stanislav and I have put my number into your phone. If you try to help us, we will reward you. If you try to harm us, we will kill you. The choice is yours.'

31

Wednesday, 22 July

The morning rush-hour traffic had peaked by the time Gary made his way to Marilyn Kelsey's house in Fulham. Rested and breakfasted, he felt, if not rejuvenated, at least restored and ready for whatever lay ahead. In an early-morning call to his mother she'd told him that she'd stayed at home in case he and Lilia returned, and Gary had urged her to go back to Will the Plumber's house in High Wycombe until all this had blown over. If the police had managed to find their way to the Mandeville Estate, the chances were the Russians would as well, and Gary didn't want his mother to be there when they did.

Rachel urged her son to contact Detective Superintendent Mangan, who'd left her personal mobile number for this purpose. Gary punched the number into his phone and promised to call her. Once he'd visited Ms Kelsey's house he hoped to have something important to say to this woman who his mother placed so much trust in, but thought it best not to tell his mother yet, so as not to raise expectations. When Rachel had asked where he and Lilia were, Gary said that the least she knew the better.

He now regretted involving his mother by taking Arina to Aylesbury and didn't want to drag her in any deeper. The conversation ended with his reassurance that they were both safe and a promise to call or text every day. The deep, unspoken bond with his mother had always been the most stable aspect of Gary's life. That she was now at least aware of his situation was curiously comforting, although in reality it did nothing to lessen the danger that he and Arina were in.

Turning into Ellerby Street, Gary looked out from under his hooded top, paying particular attention to the cars parked in the Residents Only bays to see if anyone was watching Marilyn Kelsey's house. He'd pondered whether it would be best to make this visit in the morning or the evening, deciding eventually on going as early as he decently could. If he still had that address card with all the contact details he'd have been able to ring ahead to announce his visit, but The Ice Queen had told Knuckles that she planned to spend her week's leave at home and the stormy weather should have put paid to any plans for an away-day. There was a rumble of distant thunder as Gary rang the bell of number 16. He glanced around looking for the security camera that he hoped to find pointing towards the red varnished front door, and was dissappointed not to see one.

Louise Mangan was in her office going over the events of the previous day with DCs Tonkin and Din. They had arranged for the house in Aylesbury to be watched after they'd all left late the previous afternoon. Mangan was sure she'd been right to trust Rachel Nelson, that eventually the rapport they'd established would pay dividends, but in reality, there was no alternative. As that annoying dentist chap kept pointing out, the police had no authority to remain in the house once they'd been asked to leave.

They could have waited outside but that would have broken the spirit, if not the letter of the understanding reached with Rachel Nelson. The Thames Valley guys were keeping an eye on the place, but at 10 p.m. Rachel had texted to tell Mangan her son still hadn't returned. There was no necessity to pass on this information, only the commitment Rachel had made to keep the policewoman informed. Neither was there any obligation for Rachel to have gone further by informing Mangan that Gary and Lilia had taken all their stuff and so obviously wouldn't be returning to the Mandeville Estate.

'Our birds may have flown but at least we now know who the birds are,' DC Din was saying. 'We've got that photograph of Gary Nelson from his work file, so we can get that distributed along with a mock-up of how Arina may look with short black hair, thanks to the description that Miss Nelson gave us.'

'I don't want any photographs distributed – nothing that could help the Russians get to them first,' Mangan ordered.

'Are you sure?' Tonkin asked. 'Presuming that it was her driving that Parcelforce van, she's got a gun that she's already used once.'

'Yeah, and don't forget that guy was killed at her flat,' added Din.

'I'm perfectly aware of that, but it only demonstrates the danger they're in. I know I'm banking an awful lot on that meeting yesterday, but I think Rachel Nelson will be of more help to us than photographs and identikit mock-ups. Listen, guys, I'm out on a limb here and I need you to trust my judgement.'

'Always,' Torvill and Dean said, almost in unison.

At that moment, Assistant Commissioner Baker appeared round the door asking for a quick chat. Mangan cleared the two DCs out of her office immediately. She'd been hoping to get the opportunity for a quiet word with Brian Baker. Acutely aware of how far she'd flown solo, Mangan badly needed to tell somebody of a higher rank about these latest developments. She'd considered asking for a meeting with the Commissioner, but conscious of how busy he was and distrustful of Karen Dale, his deputy, she'd already been thinking about unburdening herself to Baker and seeking his authority as a kind of safety net.

The Assistant Commissioner's large round face was sweating from the exertion of climbing several flights of stairs. 'You could wait all day for the lifts in this place and I've been in the basement with the spooks,' he said, mopping his face with a handkerchief that could easily be mistaken for a bedsheet.

'Anyone I know?' asked Mangan.

'We were actually honoured by the presence of K himself.'

'I didn't think we applied an acronym to the head of MI5 any more.'

'It's my little gesture against progress, Louise. Our lot stopped that nonsense after the war, but MI6 do still have their C, which many of their guys think is the first letter of the expletive they use to describe him.'

Baker lowered his heavy frame into a chair. 'The Director General of the Security Service, Sir William Mason himself, came to talk to us.'

'Doesn't he normally come to your Wednesday-morning gatherings below stairs?' Mangan asked.

'He's usually only wheeled out for meetings that the Home Secretary attends,' Baker explained. 'But the Commissioner was there so it was a meeting of equals, I suppose. It was the Commissioner who asked me to come and see you.'

'I'm glad you did, Brian – do you have half an hour to spare?'

'Anything for you, Louise. Why don't you tell me what you've got for me first?'

Mangan told him that Arina Kaplin's accomplice and the man who'd intervened so effectively in the kidnapping attempt were one and the same. She explained how she'd identified him as Gary Nelson and discovered where he and Arina had been hiding.

The Assistant Commissioner mopped his face and sipped the tea that had been placed in front of him, listening carefully to Mangan's narrative without interrupting the flow.

'Do Karen or Connor know about this?' he asked when she'd finished.

Unable to break the confidentiality of what she'd been told by the Commissioner, Mangan kept as close to the truth as she could.

'You know how sceptical those two have been; how they would gladly leave that girl at the mercy of Russian gangsters. They believe that the attempted abduction of the girl in Crystal Palace is entirely unconnected to the poisoning at the Strand Hotel.'

'But you can now prove that they're wrong,' Baker said.

'Yes, but only because I was allowed to get on with the job away from the constant sniping and back-stabbing. Karen and Connor both have other cases they can be getting on with.'

'Louise, you can't withhold important information from colleagues on your team.'

'You are part of the team and I'm telling you. I need a few days, Brian. I promise that if I haven't found Kaplin and Nelson by this time next week I'll tell the team everything.'

Brian Baker reflected for a moment before saying, 'They buried Denis Smolnikov in Moscow yesterday. In a lead-lined coffin, apparently, to stop the polonium contaminating the soil. That's why Sir William graced us with his presence. We were shown footage of the event. The President attended, all the top military brass – it was like a bloody state funeral.

'Sir William told us he's under pressure from the more cautious side of our security services to sort this out. MI6 believe that Krovnyye Bratya murdered Sergei Dzyuba at the Strand Hotel, hoping that the thallium would take long enough to work for it not to be linked to London, but nobody has a clue who killed Smolnikov, or how or why.'

'What about the theory that Smolnikov poisoned the coffee meant for Igor Golovin and the waitress mixed up the cups – that Smolnikov swallowed his own poison?'

'That has such a lovely symmetry I think we all hoped it would be true, but the Russian FSB have told our people that the CNN documentary that Smolnikov was working on had the President's approval. Golovin was to be the star participant. Dzyuba, who brokered the meeting, had come to London from Amsterdam with a guarantee of safety. He wouldn't want Golovin killed and it's unlikely that Smolnikov would either.'

'So, if the Russians think our theory is wrong, what's theirs?' Mangan asked.

'They think we had Smolnikov killed.'

Seeing the sceptical look on Mangan's face, Baker quickly added, 'You have to bear in mind that they operate in a world of extra-judicial killings and suspect that every other country does as well. They say if it wasn't Krovnyye Bratya and it wasn't them, who else could it be? Having been on the receiving end of these kind of accusations for so long it makes sense for them to peddle this line and the ceremonial funeral yesterday was part of the political capital that the Russians intend to make out of this.

'Sir William says that they seem very relaxed about the evil deed itself. They're keen to pin it on a country rather than a person and don't even seem that upset about Smolnikov's demise, despite his supposed close relationship with the President. The Russians are enjoying themselves.'

'I expect all this vindicates the suggestion that we should let the Russians have the waitress, as a gesture of goodwill. Sacrifice her on the altar of international relations,' Mangan said, barely able to suppress her contempt for such a proposal.

'All that is now academic, Louise,' Baker responded. 'The Commissioner wanted you to know that, according to Sir William, based on high-level intelligence picked up at the funeral yesterday, the Russians are no longer demanding that we hand over Arina Kaplin because they already have her.'

The film was just beginning as Gary took his seat. After leaving Marilyn Kelsey's house he'd wandered around for half an hour before deciding to enter the comforting darkness of this cinema on Fulham Broadway.

He had no interest in what was showing – a Marvel film starring Scarlett Johansson – but needed to reflect on the morning's developments. But he needed somewhere conducive to meditation albeit through the clamour of superheroes preventing the destruction of some planet or other.

Ms Kelsey had come to the door that morning wrapped in a purple kimono and dishevelled by sleep.

'Bloody hell! The things you find on your doorstep,' she'd exclaimed before inviting Gary in and offering tea along with an instruction to speak quietly because Jack, her boyfriend, was sleeping off a hangover upstairs. She explained that they'd celebrated his birthday the previous evening and hadn't got to bed until 3 a.m.

Gary had then embarked on a convoluted and entirely fictitious explanation of why he was there before The Ice Queen intervened.

'Save that bullshit for the office,' she'd said. 'I know you're mixed up in something that you probably shouldn't be, so just tell me what it is that you want: are you here to check out your friend's electrical work? Do you need money? A reference? Or have you come to tell me all about the symptoms of your Russian flu?'

Gary asked if she had CCTV.

'Funny you should say that, it's exactly what that copper asked when he came on Monday.'

'And what was the answer?'

'I told him that we didn't, but that was a lie.'

She went on to say that she'd distrusted the police ever since her father had been arrested on a trumped-up charge when she was a small girl growing up in Melbourne.

'My dad was a pilot who flew freight all over Australia. One of the companies he worked for was involved in a smuggling racket. Dad knew nothing about it. He just flew the bloody planes. But they tried to pin the whole business on him. He taught me never to blindly follow the authority of a uniform. Plus, this copper the other evening didn't give me a name or show any identity, as if the uniform was enough. That added to my suspicion.

'He was interested in the address card, and as I told your mate Knuckles, it was obvious that you'd dropped it on the train going home but it was also obvious that he knew nothing about you, so I certainly wasn't going to enlighten him.'

As for the CCTV, she hadn't been lying. There were no clunky cameras spoiling the outside of her house.

'I know they're supposed to be on display as a deterrent, but I don't buy that. Christ! Every house around here has one, so if it's such a great deterrent how come Fulham is such a burglar's nirvana?' she'd asked, pulling the kimono tighter as she pottered round the kitchen addressing Gary, who sat at the breakfast bar like a presiding magistrate.

'Jack upstairs may not have been able to fix my electrics but he's a dab hand at digital gadgets. We don't live together, by the way – in case you get the wrong impression. We're just good friends who wouldn't be if we saw too much of each other.

'Anyway, he got someone to fix up a whizzy system that allows me to monitor every part of this house 24/7 through my mobile. As soon as you rang the bell, I got a clear picture of you registered on this little beauty,' Ms Kelsey had held up a wafer-thin device. 'Here you are in all your glory,' she continued, leaning across Gary's shoulder to show him a still photograph of him pressing the doorbell a few minutes before. She stood up to slide her finger across the screen.

'And here is Officer Whatsit. He only asked if I had CCTV and as this is in a different league, I don't think I was fibbing. I can give you video footage or a photo and, incidentally, it works whether you ring the bell or not – you just have to stand anywhere near this house, and I've got you – watch the birdie! The cameras are tiny and set into the brickwork. The discerning burglars around here always go for the houses with those awful CCTV cameras. They're about as useful as one of those alarms that drone on for hours without anyone taking a blind bit of notice.'

Thinking back now, sitting in the cinema, Gary reflected on this encounter and remembered how much he'd always longed to be alone with Ms Kelsey, away from the workplace; how he'd lusted after his bright, funny, attractive boss and how she'd flirted with him outrageously at the office.

That all seemed as distant from reality as this film that he'd paid to watch. It was pre-Arina, back when his life was staid and predictable, the way he hoped it could be again.

He decided he'd probably been deceiving himself about The Ice Queen. Her mildly flirtatious behaviour towards him was simply part of her irreverent approach to life in general.

Having got what he'd come for, Gary had left Ms Kelsey with sleeping Jack. At the door her sassiness had resurfaced.

'Do come back to us when you're fit and well, Mr Nelson. The business can't survive much longer without you,' she'd said, standing on tiptoe to kiss his cheek. 'And remember, the safest wildebeest in the herd is the one in the middle.'

And now, during the cacophonous climax of the film, Gary contemplated what to do with the photograph that

Marilyn Kelsey had transferred from her phone to his: the image of a uniformed police officer in profile that was so clear you could almost see the worry in his eyes.

Gary wished he could share this good news with Arina but they'd agreed that the only contact would be when she confirmed that she was Ukraine bound. That was when Gary would go to the police to give himself up and reveal the image of the bent copper.

Thanks to his mother, Gary had the personal contact details of Detective Superintendent Louise Mangan. All he had to do for now was keep his head down and hold his nerve.

32

A soft evening breeze ruffled the row of elm trees that Stanislav Miranchuk walked past on his way to Santini's restaurant. The traffic heading towards Hyde Park Corner was relentless, a dense mass of engine noise, like a turbulent river flowing towards a waterfall.

The turbulence matched Miranchuk's mood. Since Maria had told him about being assaulted by her husband, this loyal agent of Krovnyye Bratya had been considering how best to bring about its decapitation. While his encounter with Jason at Gatwick that morning gave the impression of continued loyalty, he was about to engage in an act of betrayal.

Ivan Ilkun had responded to Miranchuk's request for an urgent meeting by suggesting an early dinner at a restaurant he knew away from the usual Russian haunts of Knightsbridge – a place where the combination of the location and the hour would ensure some necessary privacy.

Entering beneath Santini's dark blue canopy, Miranchuk could see that Ilkun was the only diner, sitting at a table in the furthest corner with a glass of rosé and the evening paper. His bodyguards were presumably outside keeping watch as they were nowhere in sight.

'My apologies for bringing you to a place devoid of borscht and cabbage rolls, but hopefully you'll enjoy the pasta,' the FSB man said as his guest settled himself at the table, wiping his horn-rimmed glasses on a trailing edge of the pristine white tablecloth.

They conversed in Russian except when ordering the food. Ilkun explained that the Bolshoi was in town and he needed to accompany the Ambassador to the Royal Opera House for a performance that evening. They would therefore order a single course to ensure that their ninety minutes together was focused more on talking than eating.

Miranchuk said that having been sceptical of Ilkun's dire predictions he could now see that Krovnyye Bratya was exceeding any presidential authority it once may have had and that the principal problem was its leadership. He was prepared to actively engage in its replacement if that was what the FSB wanted.

Ilkun replied that it was, but they also wanted Miranchuk to take charge.

'Krovnyye Bratya can be good for Russia – we don't want to scupper the ship, just appoint a new captain who will ensure it stays within the fleet.'

'You do know that I was the one who organised the poisoning of Sergei Dzyuba,' Miranchuk said.

'Of course, we are aware of that, but you didn't know that the President had guaranteed Dzyuba's safety. Anton Sidrenko did. He was told that we had turned a hostile journalist into an important ally. He was told in words of one syllable that Dzyuba must come to no harm in London. Nevertheless, he decided to go ahead with the elimination because Krovnyye Bratya regarded Dzyuba as an enemy and so there arose a direct clash between the interests of your organisation and those of the Russian state. In such circumstances there can only be one winner.'

Ilkun sat back while the food was served. He wore a dinner jacket, the double-cuffed sleeves of his white shirt protruding far enough to reveal an expensive-looking pair of silver cufflinks.

When the waiters had departed Miranchuk said, 'Denis Smolnikov knew we were acting without the President's authority. Is that why you had him killed?'

'We didn't kill Smolnikov, although given the outrageous way he traded on his friendship with the President we may well have got around to it eventually. As things turned out, Smolnikov's demise in London has been advantageous. Did you see the turnout for his funeral yesterday? Russia has united in grief and anger over the death of the heroic film-maker. After years of allegations against us, the West now finds the tables turned. Russia is the accuser rather than the accused. A diplomatic triumph.'

'But if you didn't kill Denis, who did?'

'Well, at first we were inclined to believe the theory that he poisoned himself with coffee meant for his intended victim, but who was his intended victim? That is the sixty-four-thousand-dollar question. Dzyuba was

Krovnyye Bratya's primary target and he was poisoned with thallium not polonium. Why would your mob set out to murder two people using different poisons at the same gathering? It makes no sense.

'Now we know what happened. The final pieces of the jigsaw are falling into place. It was an audacious plot, carefully planned over a long period. You were an FSB man, you know how good we are at foiling plots against Russians abroad.'

'You mean when FSB isn't carrying them out,' Miranchuk interjected.

Ilkun smiled. 'Accepting that proviso, of course,' he said. 'The plot to kill Smolnikov was so meticulous that had you not been suspicious about the guy in the Strand Hotel blazer we may never have discovered the truth, and by then it was too late.'

'So you murdered Viktor Rubchenko,' said Miranchuk.

'We sent a man to kill him having been given the address by your friend Morozov.'

'Andrey?'

'Indeed, Andrey Morozov,' Ilkun responded calmly. 'He works for us.'

'And Albert Turner?'

'Your thug with the Parcelforce van? I'd like to say that we cleared up your mess, but actually it wasn't us. We assume it was the lovely Arina's accomplice finishing off her work. That girl certainly knows how to wield a hammer.' Ilkun glanced at his watch before continuing, 'Look, Stanislav, we could spend all our time discussing these fascinating details, but let's concentrate on the job in hand. I can tell you all about Smolnikov's murder another time. Can we get back to Krovnyye Bratya? We're ready to remove Sidrenko, which is why this dinner is so timely.'

'How? You can't just gun him down in the street.'

'Nothing so crude, Stanislav. And don't worry, his wife won't be hurt.'

For the first time in their conversation Miranchuk looked uncomfortable. 'You know?' he asked.

'Of course, and we very much admire your taste – and your stamina.'

Miranchuk, who considered himself beyond embarrassment, could feel his cheeks flush.

'Ah, a man capable of being discomfited by his indiscretions, how rare and how charming. But your affair with Maria Paseka is of no importance to us. You need to understand that it's not just her husband we need to remove. As you well know, Krovnyye Bratya is a three-headed beast. Granat and Podkolzin have to go as well.'

There was a pause as the waiter brought some freshly grated Parmesan.

'You ask how we plan to deal with Sidrenko,' Ilkun resumed when the waiter had gone. 'With him and the other two this very much depends on whether you intend to work with us or not. If you decide not to, that's fine. You may even decide to prove your misguided allegiance by telling your comrades about this conversation. It would be a foolish thing to do but it won't change the eventual outcome.

'I have been your advocate within FSB, convincing colleagues that with you in charge we can work in harmony once again. If I am wrong, you need to say so now, Stanislav – are you in or out?'

'I'm in,' said Miranchuk without hesitation.

The two men shook hands and Ilkun said there was time for a vodka to celebrate. When two frosted glasses arrived, the two former associates discussed the removal of Sidrenko, Granat and Podkolzin.

'Everything is in hand for Anton,' Ilkun said. 'He's due to come to Moscow again in a few days. He won't be returning to London. We've managed to construct an impressive charge sheet around his extensive business activities.'

'Has he not been paying his taxes?'

'No, although to be fair to him, many of the taxes he owes have been applied retrospectively. At the end of his fair and unbiased trial he'll receive a substantial prison sentence, and in the meantime his bail application will be refused and his passport confiscated.'

'What about the other two?' Miranchuk asked.

'Now that you're on board I thought you might enjoy dealing with Granat yourself, given the obvious contempt you have for him.'

'I wasn't aware it was so obvious.'

'Morozov told us all about it. By the way, Andrey will continue to work with you, which means that, along with those three Granat men you've commandeered, you'll have your own little platoon.'

Miranchuk said he'd be very happy to continue work-ing with Morozov and that he already had a plan for the disposal of Vladimir Granat and knew exactly how to deal with Podkolzin if he must.

In twenty minutes of whispered conversation Miran-chuk explained his plan for a double murder. Ilkun added some suggestions before announcing that he had to leave to get to the ballet.

'Should I not pursue Kaplin and her companion any-more?' Miranchuk asked.

'The elusive Miss Kaplin has been captured,' Ilkun announced. His dinner guest was shocked by this new piece of information.

'But when? And how?'

'Once again, let's leave that for another time. We still know nothing about her companion.'

'His name is Gary Nelson and he lives at 27 Mount Street, Crystal Palace,' Miranchuk said, keen to demon-strate that at least he knew something his FSB friend didn't.

'That's very interesting but no longer our priority. You must tell me all about it – after you've dealt with the more immediate issue of clearing your path to the leadership of Krovnyye Bratya.'

After calling for the bill, Ilkun pushed back his chair and, looking past his dining companion into the middle distance, said reflectively, 'It's such a shame that Russia has never managed to form a bond with this country. They used to condemn us for being communists, now we are condemned for being capitalists. Did you know that Lenin declared England our greatest enemy?'

Miranchuk shook his head.

'Always remember, my friend, that the skulduggery we engage in here is a pale reflection of Britain's interference in Russia over the past century. But I do wish things were different. I admire this country in so many ways. But now I really must be off.'

'Ah yes, to the Bolshoi,' said Miranchuk.

'This job does have its compensations. Isn't it amazing that the country of Tolstoy, Tchaikovsky and Kandinsky has somehow acquired an international reputation for thuggery.'

'And ballet,' Miranchuk reminded him.

'Yes, I suppose so – bad guys and ballerinas, our gifts to the world.'

33

Gary walked through the gates of the Oval at 10.30 a.m. on a perfect day for cricket. A smudge of flimsy cloud was the only stain on an immaculate blue sky from which blazed an uncompromising sun. Having slept in a different hotel for each of the three nights since he came back to London, it had taken a few seconds to get his bearings when he woke up that morning. He'd decided that it would be dangerous to stay in one place too long but was quickly tiring of this nomadic existence.

Gary missed Arina desperately and was longing to speak to her. Yesterday he'd gone so far as to tap out a text telling her that he'd got the photograph of Ms Kelsey's visiting policeman and ending with terms of sweet endearment and a couple of kisses. As his thumb hovered over the send button, he had imagined his lover's stern reproof and censured himself.

This was no time to be departing from the careful plans they'd made. He would hear from Arina when she'd managed to get aboard a ship bound for Ukraine and not before. That was what they'd agreed and today was probably the earliest she could be expected to succeed. It could take much longer, and in the meantime he

273

must try to replicate Arina's strength and determination. Making contact now could endanger her as well as him. Loneliness was something he'd have to live with.

A few days of cricket would help. Flush with the cash Arina had given him, he had no problem with the entrance charge and travelling across London didn't constitute much of a risk. He'd felt a twinge of trepidation passing a couple of coppers as he came into the Oval, but this was London in summer and he guessed that although the police may be looking for him using the photo from his work file, the chances of being recognised in the crowds were negligible. The sunglasses, baseball cap and three-day beard growth made it even less likely.

On Thursday he'd spoken to his mother. It was a long conversation in which Gary had told her everything. The way he'd rescued Arina on the train, their visit to Viktor's flat, the attempted abduction of Melissa, the shooting outside the Ukrainian embassy, how they'd sought sanctuary in Aylesbury and how he'd be free to talk to Detective Superintendent Mangan as soon as he knew Arina was safely out of the country.

There'd been a long silence at the other end of the line as Gary finished.

'Mum – are you still there?' Gary had eventually asked.

'Yes, I'm here, son, and I'm proud of what you've done, but I'm so frightened for you. Why not go to the police now, straight away? That girl of yours seems perfectly capable of looking after herself. Anyway, you don't have to tell the police where she is. You need protecting from those Russians and only the police can do that.'

'But if Arina doesn't manage to get herself on a ship I need to be free to help her.'

'The police will make sure she's not taken to Russia. The detective superintendent gave me her word.'

'Arina doesn't trust them to do that, Mum, and neither do I.' Gary had reminded his mother how this woman could have been home in Kiev now if she hadn't spurned safety at the embassy to rescue him.

The call had ended with Gary promising to ring every day to confirm that he was safe. And he'd kept his promise like the dutiful son he considered himself to be. He was glad that his mother had followed his advice by continuing to live at Will the Plumber's house in case any Russian pursuers made their way to Aylesbury. Gary's call to his mother at about 5 p.m. every day was as much to assure himself of her safety as to assure her of his.

The Oval was a wonderful sanctuary. He felt entirely safe here, watching cricket in the sunshine. Surrey were having a great season and this game looked like being another step towards promotion back to the top division.

The only interruption to his state of serenity was a missed call from Knuckles. Gary's phone was switched to silent mode in accordance with cricketing protocol and he waited until the game had stopped for lunch before calling back. Knuckles was at Pinewood working on another game show.

'This is one of the weirdest things I've ever been involved in,' he told Gary. 'Four celebs playing virtual snooker for charity. If they pot the black, they win seventy thousand pounds. I'd tell you who the celebrities are, but I doubt they've heard of themselves.'

'How are things at Mount Street?' Gary asked.

'Well, Jason's back. God knows what happened in Zurich but he's a changed man. All the old Jason cockiness seems to have seeped out of him.'

'You mean he's not a pain in the arse anymore?'

'No, he's just as feckin' annoying but much quieter – and more nervous. I dropped a pan in the kitchen last night and he almost collapsed in a heap. Anyway, why I called was to tell you that Mel has invited us down to Swansea, the three of us, you, me and jittery Jason. She emailed to say that it feels like she's under house arrest and that seeing us would really cheer her up. Permission has been granted by the boys in blue as well as her parents and she said you can bring Lilia if the two of you can't bear to be parted.'

As usual, Knuckles rattled the words out like bullets from a Gatling-gun. Gary, waiting for a pause in the intensity in order to interject, had a fleeting image of an ideal world where he and 'Lilia' were together and free to go on such a jaunt like any other couple.

'And here's the thing,' said his friend in conclusion. 'Jason has offered to pay – for the train fares, the hotel we'd have to stay in because there's not enough space at Mel's – everything. How about it?'

'When are you planning to go?' Gary asked.

'Next weekend. Jason's free and this snooker thing will be finished by then. We can't leave it too long or Mel will go round the twist.'

Gary said that he'd love to join them but doubted he'd be able to.

'You owe me a favour, Gary,' Knuckles said with an edge to his voice that Gary hadn't experienced before, 'and Melissa wants to see us. You can bring your bird and it won't cost you a penny. There's obviously something going on here. If you can't come to Swansea at least tell me why.'

Gary promised he'd tell Knuckles everything soon and that, as far as the visit to Melissa was concerned, he wasn't ruling it out. It didn't completely pacify his friend, but at least the call ended amicably.

Gary spent the rest of the break for lunch booking himself into his next hotel, returning to his seat just in time to see the first ball of the afternoon.

Nothing else disturbed the serenity of a perfect afternoon's cricket until teatime, when Gary's vibrating phone announced a new message. It was a text from Arina. All it said was:

On board ship heading for Odessa

Anton Sidrenko's gaunt features displayed no emotion, although Miranchuk thought he saw a flash of exasperation in those dark eyes.

'I fly to Moscow early tomorrow morning,' Sidrenko was saying. 'By the time I return next week I want this over and done with.'

The two men were alone in Sidrenko's inner sanctum, a small, sparsely furnished garret above the main suite of rooms in Old Compton Street. It was the place reserved for the most intimate of conversations. Two of Sidrenko's henchmen stood guard outside the door.

The sound of a Bruce Springsteen track intruded from the party below. Krovnyye Bratya was hosting another Saturday-evening gathering.

For Miranchuk this meeting was the culmination of all his efforts to ensure that when Sidrenko decided to eliminate the man who he thought had cuckolded him, it would be Miranchuk who was asked to do the eliminating.

Given his role within the organisation, this was always likely, but he'd taken nothing for granted. There was a chance that Sidrenko would become suspicious about his wife's confession, acquired, as it had been, under duress. So, to back up Maria's story, Miranchuk had used the past few days to drip-feed a supply of corroborating information.

In respect of that fateful Thursday night, he'd told Sidrenko that he had tried to return Granat's calls but couldn't get through. He'd kept quiet about this at the time because of Granat's position of authority but on reflection thought his boss should know. Such was his concern that night, he'd even sent Andrey Morozov to Granat's Knightsbridge home to check if he was okay but

Morozov reported that when he called at one o'clock in the morning Granat wasn't at home.

Since the dinner with Ilkun on Wednesday evening, Miranchuk knew he had an ally in Morozov, the FSB infiltrator, who'd now joined the three bone-headed former Granat men to form Miranchuk's own private bodyguard.

Morozov had been primed to give the right answers should Sidrenko question him about this, but Miranchuk's word had been enough. As for Granat, he was unlikely to have the chance to put forward a case for the defence. He was downstairs now enjoying himself with a couple of buxom girls young enough to be his granddaughters. With every leering gesture he was providing evidence for Maria's allegations. She hadn't come to the club this evening. Her wounds remained too visible for Sidrenko to even suggest that she should.

Maria knew her husband well enough to know that he wouldn't tolerate the humiliation of having his wife seduced, particularly by a close associate. If Sidrenko was going to exact his revenge it was better to sacrifice Granat, who she hated, to protect her real lover. She therefore had no qualms about cementing the lie, telling her husband that she'd been lonely and that Granat's persistence had worn down her defences; that he'd got her drunk and taken advantage of her emotional turmoil.

In truth, the cold contempt she professed for Granat was now directed at her husband. That Sidrenko could believe she'd share a bed with a lecherous slob like Granat only added to her detestation. While she felt she had no alternative but to stay with her husband, she wanted revenge and would have rejoiced had she known what was about to happen to him.

As for her lover, Miranchuk could hardly believe his good fortune. By ordering him to murder Granat, Sidrenko was unwittingly helping to ensure Miranchuk's succession. His boss was playing a central role in his own demise.

But Miranchuk had another 'removal' to make and this was one that Sidrenko knew nothing about. It was bound to be less straightforward. Dmitry Podkolzin could look after himself. He'd come to Krovnyye Bratya from the military, where he'd acquired a fearsome reputation for violence. He was a fitness fanatic and his functions within KB included overseeing what was euphemistically known as 'safety measures'. Podkolzin had overall responsibility for the organisation's security.

Podkolzin and Miranchuk had often worked closely together on eradicating those who needed to be eradicated: rivals from other gangs who'd overstepped the mark, traitors within their ranks, those who had seriously upset the President. While Podkolzin had long ceased to get involved personally, such activities, the poisoning of Dzyuba for instance, required his authorisation.

Miranchuk respected Podkolzin every bit as much as he despised Granat.

Nevertheless, as Ilkun had pointed out, if there was a vacuum at the top of the organisation, Podkolzin would be sucked into it. His muscular figure was all that stood between Miranchuk and the crown. He must be got rid of, and both removals had to take place, if not simultaneously, within hours of each other.

Miranchuk was confident that Sidrenko would not have told his other lieutenant about Granat. Had he been prepared to bear the humiliation such an admission would entail, Podkolzin would probably have been asked to do the job. But if Podkolzin heard about Granat's demise and suspected that it presaged an assault on the organisation's leadership his defences would be up. Careful timing was therefore crucial.

All of this was running through Miranchuk's mind as he listened to Sidrenko waffle on about one or two issues that he planned to address upon his return from Moscow, issues that were inconsequential because there would be no return. His attention became focused once again only when Sidrenko changed the subject.

'Our man at the Met tells me that the FSB have captured that waitress, Arina Kaplin,' he said.

'That's interesting, and the kind of important information that he was bound to tell you rather than me,' Miranchuk replied, faking an air of surprise.

'Indeed, but I've told him that he's to contact you in my absence as usual.'

Miranchuk responded by reporting on his success in at least identifying the man that Kaplin was with.

'You thought he was with the FSB.'

'I was obviously wrong.'

'Why obviously?' asked Sidrenko.

'Oh, because they have her but not him,' Miranchuk said, realising that to reveal his contact with Ilkun would be foolish, 'and because they separated. Have the FSB said anything to you about her capture?'

'No, but I think they will. I was at the ballet on Wednesday evening and Ivan Ilkun was there with the Ambassador. He couldn't have been more friendly. I think the short period of tension between us has ended. I always said they'd get over their anger at Dzyuba's murder, but I have to confess I didn't think it would be so soon. Ilkun, who virtually runs the show over here now, couldn't have been more charming. He told me we should discuss working more closely when I get back.'

'That's good news,' said Miranchuk, admiring Ilkun's mastery of the Machiavellian. He'd obviously gone out of his way to put Sidrenko at ease, just before putting him into captivity.

'Do you still want me to deal with this Nelson guy?' Miranchuk asked.

'I want to find out who killed Denis Smolnikov. He was one of us, a "blood brother" as they would say in this country. This guy Nelson must have had some involvement, as he must have had in Sutton where our man was killed. I want him "dealt with" as you so charmingly put it. Do you know where he is?'

'No, but I have his mobile number. Our technical guys are trying to pinpoint his location through that.'

'Okay, well done, Stanislav. Deal with Granat and I'll promote you into his newly vacated position, alongside Dmitry.'

Were Miranchuk a more demonstrable man he would have found it difficult to suppress a smile. He wouldn't be serving alongside anybody. Now was his chance to be emperor rather than envoy. His plans for a double disposal were in place. They would be activated the very next day.

34

Sunday, 26 July

It was audacious, foolhardy even, but as Gary contemplated where to go for what he expected to be his final night as a fugitive, the idea became ever more tantalising. In a flurry of feverish phone activity in the slanting sunlight of the Oval the previous evening he'd ascertained that there was a room available and, thanks to the opulence bestowed on him by Arina, the two-hundred-pound-a-night room rate was affordable. And so, Gary had stayed at the Strand Hotel.

It took an almost superhuman effort to control himself when he'd read Arina's text. The urge to leap from his seat, punch the air and bellow like a ten-year-old was barely contained. A Surrey batsman hit a four a minute later and Gary allowed some of his exuberance to escape by clapping and cheering a little louder than anyone else in the ground.

He'd tried to ring Arina without success and assumed she was too far out at sea, but sent a text message anyway to say how much he loved her. Not caring if his words were lost in the atmosphere, he needed to put his adoration in writing; it was the first time he'd used such language to anybody, and he did it as much to record the fact as to share it.

Later, when his plans were more fully formulated, he'd sent another text.

Booked into the Strand Hotel for my final night on the run. It's the last place any of them would expect to find me. We'll stay here together when you come to London as a free woman. Xxx

Checking in with his single piece of luggage at 9.30 p.m., he'd replaced the casual top worn at the cricket with his only collared shirt in a gesture of respect for this fine old hotel. As usual he signed in as Duncan McDonald, using his friend's address in Aylesbury and paying by cash in advance. Then he went to a nearby Italian restaurant for a slap-up meal with half a bottle of wine. It was all very decadent, but Gary felt entitled to celebrate. Besides, he needed the right environment to plan his next move. Ninety minutes in that restaurant fulfilled both objectives.

Now, awake in the quiet opulence of the Strand Hotel on Sunday morning, he thought through the day ahead. He would ask his mother to be his intermediary with the policewoman. She had established a good relationship and it would be better than him calling out of the blue. Gary was determined not to rush into this. If he was right about that police officer being linked with Krovnyye Bratya, the photograph on his phone would provide damning evidence.

How deep did the corruption go? For all he knew, the policewoman might be involved. He was banking an awful lot on his mother's judgement. But there was no viable alternative. He'd considered walking into New Scotland Yard and simply giving himself up. The problem with that idea was its randomness. It must surely create a greater chance of him ending up in front of one of the traitorous officer's accomplices or even the officer himself. Another alternative would be to simply email the photograph to the Detective Superintendent but he didn't want to entrust this crucial nugget of evidence to the vagaries of the internet. Besides, he'd still be left with the dilemma of how to give himself up. Dealing with Mangan direct and asking his mother to set up a meeting with her had to be the safest route.

As far as the timing was concerned, he had an entirely illogical desire for Arina to be out of British territorial waters before handing himself in – illogical firstly because nobody but him knew that she was on her way to Ukraine and he had no intention of telling anyone else; and illogical secondly because he hadn't a clue if there was such a thing as British territorial waters or how far they extended. It was just a phrase he'd heard. Nevertheless, giving Arina another thirty-six hours at sea before going to the police seemed sensible.

Gradually the outline plan that he'd made in the restaurant the previous evening acquired substance. The Strand seemed unaffected by its recent notoriety. The reception room that had been the crime scene was closed to the public but the police officer who'd guarded it for a while had gone and all the black and yellow tape had been removed. The friendly receptionist who Gary chatted to stressed the fact that nobody had died in the hotel and told him that, after a few cancellations in that first week, business was booming. The incident seemed to have enhanced the hotel's reputation rather than damaged it.

Gary had gone to reception to book another night's stay, having decided to set things in motion for Monday lunchtime. While chatting to the young receptionist, who was obviously Eastern European, it struck him that she'd have been one of Arina's colleagues and perhaps a close friend. He was thinking of raising the subject of the missing waitress just so that he could talk about the woman he loved and gain a sense of how others saw her. As the question formulated in his mind, a cat jumped onto the counter and sat staring at Gary with the intensity of a hypnotist.

'Ah, that's our Oskar,' said the receptionist. 'He just wants to stare into your soul.'

Gary rang his mother at his usual reporting-in time of 5 p.m.

'I need you to be my go-between with that policewoman,' he said, having got past the preliminary inquisition on his health and safety.

'You mean Detective Superintendent Mangan? She's not just any old policewoman, Gary.'

Suitably admonished, the younger Nelson explained why it was best for his mother to speak to the Detective Superintendent on his behalf. Rachel said she would, and asked what she was to say.

'First and foremost, tell her that I'm willing to give myself up, but also – and this is important, Mum – that I have a photograph of a senior colleague of hers who I think is working for the Russian gangsters. I need to hand over the evidence and then give myself up to her in person. She needs to meet me on her own and on neutral territory. Make sure she understands – with no other officers present.'

'Okay, I'll do that straight away. Where are you?'

'No, Mum, not straight away. It's important that she doesn't have long to think about it. That should make it easier for her to come on her own. I don't want the bent copper to get wind of this and she doesn't yet know who he is. Neither do I, for that matter, I've just got a photograph. It's important that you don't ring her until noon tomorrow, and then tell her to meet me at 3 p.m.'

'But she might be busy at that time,' Rachel said.

'Mum, will you stop being thoughtful. She won't be too busy to meet me. Oh, and tell her to carry a scarf so that I recognise her.'

'But where is she to meet you?'

This was a question that Gary had laboured over, but as he sat in his room and pictured the quiet bar and restaurant area downstairs his mind was made up.

'Tell her to meet me in the Strand Hotel.'

Vladimir Granat always spent Sunday evenings at his office in the City. Grant Properties occupied the entire tenth floor of a 1960s concrete monstrosity off Gresham

Street and the company's founder liked to work on the accounts when nobody else was around, thus avoiding unnecessary interruptions.

There were those in the company who believed that he was cooking the books more than checking the finances, but all those who worked for him knew that this was when their boss liked to be in the office, alone except for the security man way down on reception and the two bodyguards who always came with him to stand sentry at his office door.

This evening the security guy had been told to expect visitors. Anton Sidrenko had asked that Granat speak with Stanislav Miranchuk privately about some financial difficulties that Miranchuk had got himself into. There was no better time for such a delicate conversation than Sunday evening and no better place than this office perched high above the London pavements that still held the day's heat even as the sky began to darken into night. Indeed, Sidrenko had suggested this venue when he'd rung his lieutenant from the airport that day before boarding his flight for Moscow.

Granat knew that Miranchuk disliked him. There was nothing subtle about the way this hostility was transmitted, but it had never been reciprocated. The opposite was true. The property millionaire admired the sultry solemnity of his younger colleague. Terrified by any form of violence himself, he'd nevertheless found Miranchuk's aura of suppressed savagery appealing. This homoerotic attraction could well have been fuelled by

Granat's prodigious sexual appetite that was usually, but not exclusively, focused on women. Leaving aside any sexual undercurrent, he felt good about the prospect of doing Miranchuk a favour, helping him resolve whatever this delicate problem was, and thus for Miranchuk to be forever obliged.

At a quarter to eight, fifteen minutes before the meeting was due to take place, Granat freshened up in his en suite bathroom, splashing cold water onto his fleshy face and tidying his white hair, so sparse it needed to be rearranged rather than combed.

Emerging into the office, he closed and locked the door leading onto the small balcony that had a sumptuous view of St Paul's Cathedral.

Miranchuk arrived downstairs with a trio of henchmen. The security guard on reception waved them through, hardly bothering to look up from the magazine he was reading. Coming out of the lift on the tenth floor, Miranchuk told Granat's bodyguards that they were being relieved on the orders of Anton Sidrenko. It had been cleared with Granat; there was no need to interrupt him.

The men were happy to comply; it was a warm night and they could do with a cold beer. Two of Miranchuk's men replaced them on either side of the office door. Miranchuk knocked and went in accompanied by the third.

Granat, coming from behind his desk to shake hands, recognised Miranchuk's companion who, until recently, had worked for him.

'I thought you wanted a private conversation, Stanislav. Why have you brought him with you?'

'I thought you'd like a reunion,' Miranchuk said, watching carefully in case Granat reached for a gun.

'Guards!' Granat shouted.

Miranchuk went back to the door.

'Do come in, chaps, your former boss wants to say sorry for abandoning you so neglectfully last week.'

When Granat saw all three of his ex-employees eyeing him with barely concealed contempt the colour drained from his face. When Miranchuk gripped the back of his neck he began to whimper. As the other three began pushing him towards the balcony door, he screamed.

'Nobody will hear you, Vladimir,' Miranchuk said softly, as if coaxing a lover. 'Where's the key to the door?'

'Why? Why?' Granat cried.

'Because I want to open it,' Miranchuk explained calmly.

'No – why this? Why me?'

One of his assailants had already found the key in Granat's pocket as he was held almost upside down.

Miranchuk stepped onto the balcony to check that there were no prying eyes. The dome of St Paul's glittered in the fading sunlight but none of the adjoining buildings were this high. There would be no witnesses.

He looked over the waist-high railings. Granat's office was at the rear of the building. Far below was a dismal yard, empty but for five enormous rubbish skips. Taking a leg or an arm each, the four men rocked Granat

backwards and forwards a few times in the office to calculate the swing they'd need to clear the railings. Then
they fastened the doors back, stepped through with their
spread-eagled captive, and with one final heave hurled
Vladimir Granat over the balcony and into the warm
summer night.

35

Monday, 27 July

It was early, too early for Granat's body to have been discovered, let alone identified. It would be another hour before a janitor, taking some rubbish out to the bins, discovered the pulped remains of the founder and executive chairman of Grant Properties.

Broadcast media would eventually be buzzing with the news, but for now, apart from the four men who had murdered him, nobody else knew that Granat was dead.

Miranchuk sat patiently at the wheel of the stolen Range Rover in the sweet morning air of rural Hertfordshire, waiting to bring his plan to completion, like a raptor ready to swoop.

Dmitry Podkolzin never varied his morning regime. Each day would begin with a five-mile run. Leaving his mock-Tudor mansion at precisely 7 a.m., he'd turn into a long, narrow country lane that stretched across farmland at the rear of his house.

As a man who'd inevitably acquired enemies, he should have alternated this routine, but of all the leading figures in Krovnyye Bratya, Podkolzin was the most impervious to danger. He was a man with a false sense of his own indestructability. A martial arts expert during his army days, he'd spent a few years as a professional wrestler after discharge and soon found himself in demand by those of his nouveau riche countrymen who considered a personal bodyguard to be a fashion accessory.

But Podkolzin was a bodyguard with brains. Having protected a senior executive of one of the many Russian banks that had sprung up in the 1990s, he became a major investor and was soon running a bank of his own as Russia's resource wealth was transferred into the hands of bankers at knock-down prices.

A native of St Petersburg (or Leningrad, as the city had been called when Podkolzin was born in 1965), he'd then become embroiled with the notorious Tambov organised crime outfit that was so powerful in the city. Some businessmen fell reluctantly under Tambov control; others, like Podkolzin, grasped the opportunity with relish. Using his powerful physique ruthlessly, he came to be admired and feared in equal measure within Russia's second city. He'd only left to avoid imminent arrest during the early days of the President's tenure when some of Podkolzin's activities attracted the disapproval of the new, more disciplined state regime. While he didn't consider himself a dissident and wasn't on any hitlist so far as he knew, Podkolzin left Russia never to return. His experience with Tambov had been the perfect introduction to Krovnyye Bratya and the wealth he'd accumulated gave him the kind of financial independence conducive to success in Londongrad.

He'd married a British girl and settled into country life. Even in his fifties there was no relaxation in the fitness regime he'd always followed as rigorously as his moneymaking activities. After the five-mile run, he'd lift some weights and do half an hour of exercises before breakfast.

As he jogged along the country lane listening to music on his headphones, the Range Rover cruised a quarter of a mile behind. Miranchuk was waiting for the long, straight stretch of road that he'd noticed during his Saturday-morning reconnoitre. There was little traffic anywhere on this road and on this section Miranchuk had calculated that he'd have time to drive past Podkolzin, turn around in the entrance to a field further on and come back towards his victim, who was running against the traffic. This stretch benefitted the potential assassin by running alongside the wall of a farm building with no grass verge to provide refuge.

Podkolzin must have seen the approach of the car that would kill him. He may even have recognised his comrade behind the wheel, although by the time the Range Rover hit him it had accelerated to 60 mph and there was very little time for the indestructible Podkolzin to register anything at all.

Louise Mangan had spent the weekend waiting to hear from either Rachel or Gary Nelson and trying to get more information about Arina Kaplin. Since Brian Baker had told her about the Russian claim to have captured the waitress, Mangan had felt her authority seeping away.

Baker had ended their meeting on Wednesday by agreeing not to tell Dale or O'Farrell about what she'd discovered, but had put a time limit on his discretion. She only had a few more days to produce the fugitive. In the meantime, the alleged capture of Kaplin was common knowledge amongst her team. For Connor O'Farrell it was a vindication; grist to his over-productive mill.

At their team meeting on Friday he'd suggested they should downgrade the Strand Hotel investigation and concentrate instead on the murder of Viktor Rubchenko and the attempted abduction of the girl in Crystal Palace 'by the same people'. The Assistant Detective Superintendent had been almost mutinously emphatic.

'As I've been saying all along, the guy who took Kaplin off that train at Gipsy Hill is obviously a Russian – either from a rival gang or, perhaps, the FSB. By now she'll be back in that country where she belongs.'

'Except that she's Ukrainian,' Mangan had observed tartly.

'That minor detail doesn't change the basic facts – she was in this country illegally, witnessed a murder involving Russians and is now in Russian custody. There's nothing more to be done by way of detection and much more we can do by way of deflection.'

'What do you mean?' asked his admirer, the Deputy Commissioner.

'What I mean is that we've spent too long on the back foot. The Ruskies have had a field day, blaming Britain in general and the Met in particular for Smolnikov's murder. We need to stop being defensive and go on the attack, emphasising that there was no British involvement in the poisoning at the Strand and that we have clear evidence linking the same Russian thugs who murdered Viktor Rubchenko in Battersea with the attempt to abduct Melissa Thomas in Crystal Palace.'

Mangan wouldn't have been surprised to see Karen Dale burst into applause at the end of this peroration. The only response Mangan could make was to mouth some platitudes about the obvious need to focus on Russian organised crime that sounded like a weak endorsement of her deputy's argument.

Brian Baker had tried to bolster her authority by reminding the meeting that they had no proof that Kaplin had been captured and that, like the theory that it was a Russian who'd been accompanying her, it was currently pure conjecture, but his intervention failed to alter the mood of the meeting. O'Farrell acted as if he were the superintendent and Mangan felt like his assistant.

Ever since that difficult meeting, Mangan had been trying to get an appointment to see the Commissioner. Hopefully Brian Baker would have passed on the gist of their conversation the previous week and he would therefore know all about her work to identify Gary Nelson. Only the Commissioner would understand why she was withholding this information from senior colleagues. She needed to hear if any progress had been made in identifying the traitor in their ranks. There may at least be some process of elimination that would allow her to reveal the progress she'd been making to Dale and O'Farrell. In addition, she wanted to know more about the supposed capture of Arina Kaplin.

Breaking into the Commissioner's diary had proved difficult. On Saturday she'd received a call from his office to say that he was at a conference in Belfast – would a telephone call suffice? Mangan refused to deal with such sensitive stuff in a phone call. Yesterday she had at last managed to make a firm arrangement. The Commissioner would be flying back to London late on Sunday night and there was a slot available for a meeting at 12.30 on Monday lunchtime.

As usual, Mangan had got to the office early to ease her way into the week ahead. By the time she'd read all the reports and updates she only had a few hours to wait, then the reports began to come in – of an apparent suicide in the City and a hit-and-run in Hertfordshire. The identity of the two victims was yet to be confirmed, but word was spreading around New Scotland Yard that they were Russian.

Mangan was still absorbing this information when Rachel Nelson rang. Gary's message was safely relayed. He would meet the Detective Superintendent at three o'clock in the bar of the Strand Hotel. Mangan was to come alone and carry a scarf for identification. These precautions were necessary, Rachel explained, because Gary would have a photograph of a senior policeman who he was convinced was working with Russian gangsters. She emphasised her son's concern. For all he knew, Mangan might be mixed up in this corruption.

'Gary only trusts you because I told him that I trust you. He's always relied on my judgement. Don't let me down,' Rachel said in conclusion.

Mangan promised she wouldn't and the call ended.

She paced the room, excited about what she'd just heard and impatient at having to wait another twenty minutes until her meeting with the Commissioner. Everything was falling into place. She'd found Gary Nelson despite the doubts and disruptive behaviour of Dale and O'Farrell. From this afternoon he would be under police protection, able to reveal everything he knew about the events of the past few weeks. And, incredibly, he'd somehow managed to identify the KB informant in the senior ranks of the Metropolitan Police.

Now she really did have something to tell her boss.

There was no cheery greeting for Mangan as she was shown into the Commissioner's office.

'What a bloody mess, Louise. Russians falling off balconies, being ploughed down in peaceful country lanes – what the hell is going on?'

By now the two murdered men had been positively identified and various security correspondents in the broadcast media were making guarded comments about their links with organised crime.

Mangan grasped her moment, the words falling from her lips in a tirade: about finding Gary Nelson, forging a close bond with his mother, the phone call she'd just received, and that she'd be going to the Strand Hotel in a couple of hours to bring Nelson under police protection and discover the identity of the corrupt copper.

To her consternation the Commissioner seemed unmoved.

'So, you're being asked to go alone to the scene of the original crime, the hotel where two Russians were poisoned, to meet a man we know nothing about, and who your senior colleagues, including my deputy, think is linked with the Russians, and you want my endorsement?' he said, his Cumbrian accent suddenly sounding anything but soft.

'Yes,' said Mangan. 'I don't know why he's chosen the Strand Hotel but the reason he's not simply coming here to give himself up is that he has a photograph of the senior officer who works with us and moonlights with Krovnyye Bratya.'

'*Claims* to have a photograph,' the Commissioner corrected her. 'Did he give you a name?'

'No, but it's not just the photo; it was taken somewhere our copper shouldn't have been – actual proof of this man's treachery. You took the trouble to tell me that we had an informant. I've not whispered a word about it to anybody. The only other person to have referred to it besides you is Gary Nelson in a phone call to his mother. How would he know that if he'd made the whole thing up?

'This lad isn't working for the Russians or the security services. He's a young clerical assistant from Aylesbury who's somehow got himself mixed up in all this. Dale and O'Farrell may suspect him of being "The Spy Who Came in from Accounts Payable", but they know nothing about him.'

Mangan's face was flushed with the effort of trying to convince this man of her case.

The Commissioner's features softened as he said, 'Okay, calm down, Louise. I'm just nervous, it doesn't feel right. If you solve this thing and at the same time unmask the bastard who's working against us, you'll have earned a medal. I've been setting traps, but he or she hasn't fallen into any of them. I was even beginning to think that the spooks were wrong, but even though they haven't got any more information, they are adamant that this person exists. Apparently only two people within Krovnyye Bratya know who it is.'

'With a bit of luck, you will too – very soon. If you let me go to the Strand Hotel, I'll be back by four o'clock with Mr Nelson in tow and the photograph.'

'I'll clear my diary so you can bring Nelson straight in here,' the Commissioner said, 'but I'm still worried about you going alone, particularly with all the mayhem that's happened this morning. There seems to be a killing spree going on and I don't want you to become embroiled in it.'

'I'll not break my word to Mrs Nelson. Anyway, if Gary sees a bunch of coppers he'll vanish again, and we'll have missed our opportunity. He may only be an office worker, but he's made a good job of evading us up until now.'

'Okay, okay – you go to your rendezvous, but be bloody careful.'

After ten minutes of deep contemplation following Mangan's departure, the Commissioner concluded that he couldn't allow her to go to the Strand Hotel alone.

With so much riding on the outcome, it would be a dereliction of duty for him to allow one of his best officers to undertake this liaison without some kind of backup. It needn't be in full view. If it wasn't required, Mangan need know nothing about it. If it was, it could save her life.

Deputy Commissioner Dale had arrived for a routine meeting they already had scheduled. The Commissioner had made his decision. He asked Dale to arrange for a couple of armed plain-clothes officers to follow Mangan discreetly. Given that the Krovnyye Bratya informer was almost certainly a man and therefore not Karen Dale, he also decided it was time to take his deputy into his confidence.

'The guy Detective Superintendent Mangan is meeting has some crucial evidence about someone here passing information to KB. That's why it's important for her meeting to go ahead and for our guys to stay in the background unless they're needed. It's important to send the right officers.'

'The two DCs working with Louise, colloquially referred to around here as Torvill and Dean, are very good,' said Dale, 'and I'm sure they're Authorised Firearms Officers. I could send them.'

'Do that. But make sure they stay in the background unless something happens requiring their intervention.'

DCs Tonkin and Din were in a meeting about the two fatalities discovered that morning along with Assistant Commissioner Baker and ADS O'Farrell when the indiscreet Deputy Commissioner made a grand entrance,

telling the room at large what the Commissioner wanted
Torvill and Dean to do and why he wanted them to do it.

Stanislav Miranchuk had arranged to meet Morozov
and the rest of his personal bodyguard in Old Compton
Street at half past one and was on his way there now.
After disposing of Podkolzin he'd abandoned the car in
a country lane, walked to the station and was back in
London by mid-morning. As usual, he'd travelled across
the city by public transport. London's streets always
seemed even more congested than Moscow's and, in any
case, Miranchuk felt less safe in a car.

The elation he felt wasn't discernible on his face or
in his demeanour. His steps were measured, his features
stern. Today he would take control of one of the most
powerful criminal gangs in the world – although Miranchuk himself wouldn't have described the organisation in
that way. To him it was a pillar of the Russian nation,
about to be returned to state control, rescued from the
decadence it had been allowed to descend into.

Miranchuk wore a beige suit, the top button of his
shirt already unbuttoned, tie tugged loose, revealing the
blue tattoo on his neck. Walking along Oxford Street
having emerged from the tube, he stopped suddenly as if
a window display in one of the shops had caught his eye.

Ever since leaving the station he had had the sense
that he was being followed. He used the reflection in the
shop window to scrutinise the scene behind him. The
shadowed summer street was teeming with commuters,

shoppers and tourists. He knew that if he was being followed it wouldn't be by a man in a fedora with a belted
gabadine mac and dark glasses. He was looking for the
inconspicuous but, seeing nothing suspicious, walked on.

His mobile rang. It was Ivan Ilkun. The FSB man
had promised to let him know when Sidrenko was taken
into custody in Moscow. He'd also promised some carefully coordinated assistance. The FSB, working from the
Russian embassy, would inform the managerial tier of
Krovnyye Bratya – the accountants and technicians –
that Sidrenko wouldn't be returning and Miranchuk was
their new leader. Anybody who objected would lose their
diplomatic immunity and perhaps their lives. The King
was dead, long live the King.

'Good morning, my friend, and congratulations on
a job well done.' Ilkun's deep voice sounded even more
reassuring than normal.

'For my country,' said Miranchuk.

'Of course, always for Mother Russia. Anton
Sidrenko was arrested at 06.00 hours Moscow time.
He's in custody. The bail he's applied for will not be
granted. His mobile phone has been confiscated and
although he may know that the little plan you cooked up
together to get rid of Granat succeeded, he won't know
about Podkolzin. He won't yet have realised that he's
been ousted in a palace coup.'

'Fine.' Miranchuk was characteristically monosyllabic.

'I'm so glad you're not getting over-excited,' Ilkun
observed tartly.

'Sorry, it's great news and thanks for letting me know. But I'm on my way to Old Compton Street and running a bit late. Have you started your ring around yet?'

'Don't worry, Stanislav, it's all set for this afternoon.'

Ilkun was about to end the call when Miranchuk asked, 'Are you having me followed?'

'No, of course not. Why would we have you followed when we know precisely where you're going? What makes you ask?'

'Oh, nothing. Just an intuition I have.'

'Sometimes I think the FSB, and the KGB before it, were guilty of over-training us. We see darkness where there is only sunlight. And today, my friend, for you, the sun is blazing. Anyway, you've got your own defence force with those three stooges you hired and Morozov. Make sure they stay with you.'

'I understand,' said Miranchuk. 'They should all be there by the time I get to Old Compton Street.'

'Perfect,' said Ilkun. 'Remember – only sunlight from now on, for you and Maria.'

Miranchuk returned the phone to his jacket pocket. He'd thought about ringing Maria Paseka to tell her about her husband's arrest; to reveal how her lover had avenged the degradation she'd been forced to suffer. He hadn't told her anything about what was planned. It would have been reckless to do so in advance and reck-lessness was not in Miranchuk's nature.

He would go to see her this evening – openly, honestly, with no further need for subterfuge. To hold her in his arms, make love to her, stay the night; tell her that he was now in charge but that she remained First Lady of Krovnyye Bratya.

Turning into Old Compton Street, he stopped on the corner and looked back surveying the scene – some workmen in the road fixing a telephone cable, a vagrant in a shop doorway, an endless stream of pedestrians, nothing to justify his suspicion. Then his phone rang again. It was almost 1.30, time for his meeting. But this was a call he had to take. The police officer so carefully compromised and then ensnared to work for Krovnyye Bratya was on the line. After taking the call, Miranchuk only paused at Old Compton Street long enough to tell the Three Stooges and Morozov where they were going next.

They had to be at the Strand Hotel by 3 p.m. at the latest.

36

Monday, 27 July

The reception area of the Strand Hotel remained an oasis of calm irrespective of how busy it was. The hotel's tranquillity seemed to impress itself on guests arriving after long, difficult journeys or departing in haste to catch trains and boats and planes. The Strand slowed everything down to a pace consistent with its quiet, understated elegance.

Gary Nelson (known in this vicinity as Duncan Mc-Donald) was checking out. Having paid for his room in advance there were only a few sundries to settle: room service, a bar bill, some laundry. He stroked the pure white chest of Oskar perched elegantly at one end of the reception counter.

A group of ten Japanese tourists arrived, all wearing surgical face masks, their tour guide barking instructions as they congregated looking like delegates to a bank robber's convention.

It was 2.55 and Gary had remained in his room way past check-out time. After settling the bill, he asked if he could leave his bag behind reception. Taking a ticket stub in exchange, he decided to visit the Gents' for a quick tidy-up before meeting Detective Superintendent

Mangan, who had yet to arrive for their 3 p.m. appointment. Situated down the passage to the left of reception, the toilet was empty and very clean, carrying an antiseptic aroma of powerful disinfectant and fragrant air freshener. The soft muzak which permeated the reception area and the bar intruded into this sanctuary as well.

One other man came in while Gary was combing his hair. They took no notice of each other until the man, turning from the urinal and fixing his flies, looked up. Gary had his back to him, but their eyes met in the mirror – exactly as they had through a car windscreen in Crystal Palace ten days before.

After a three-second delay, Gary got to the door first. His exit was impeded by the sheer bulk of the Russian, until Gary drove his elbow hard into the guy's fat, sweating face. The man yelled but Gary was free and running towards reception, where the masked Japanese tourists were queuing to check in. As Gary ran past, one of them stepped forward calling, 'Gary, this way.'

The beautiful eyes above the mask were Arina's.

A Japanese woman was complaining loudly about her face mask being stolen while she was in the Ladies'. Three thoughts flashed through Gary's mind in an instant. First, Arina wasn't on a boat to Ukraine, she was here; second, the staff knew her, hence the need for the mask; and third, Arina must know every nook and cranny of the hotel she'd once worked in.

He followed her down the passage to the right of reception. Miranchuk, who'd just come into the reception area, saw the commotion and slipped quietly back out of the hotel, leaving Morozov to lead the chase followed by the squat Russian who Gary had encountered in the toilet. Their two colleagues were about to follow when the cry went up – 'STOP, ARMED POLICE, STAY WHERE YOU ARE.'

DCs Tonkin and Din were on the scene and in fine voice.

Gary followed Arina down three passageways, the two Russians panting heavily in pursuit and falling further behind. At every corridor junction the pursuers had to stop to check which way their prey had gone, whereas Arina knew all the twists and turns on the way to her destination, which was a fire-escape door that led into a back alley. As the lovers stepped through it Gary saw a heavy-wheeled skip that Arina intimated should be pulled across the door they'd just emerged from. The door opened outwards and with the skip in place it would be impossible for those in pursuit to follow them. As they finished manoeuvring the skip into position the muffled sound of Russian curses could be heard from behind the door, confirming that the ploy had worked.

Arina told Gary to stay behind her as they ran into the quiet streets of Pimlico.

'We need to get to the main road,' she shouted breathlessly over her shoulder. Gary was confident they could outpace the men they were fleeing, even without the blocked fire door. He and Arina were so much younger and fitter.

He gestured to Arina to slow down.

'Isn't it better not to draw attention to ourselves by running?' he asked as Arina allowed him to catch up.

The maze of turnings and little squares all around seemed to be as tranquil as the mews they were in.

'Okay, we can catch our breath, but there is a car waiting near the railway bridge a little further on,' Arina said, sucking air into her lungs. The face mask had been discarded and Gary longed to kiss the lips he had missed so much, but he knew that this was neither the place nor the time. Arina was wearing a thin denim jacket over a white T-shirt and Gary guessed that a gun would be tucked into the waistband of her sky-blue jeans.

'How come you're here and not on that boat?' he asked.

'Gary, this is not time for chat. Do you have photo of police officer?'

'Yes, it's on my phone.'

'Krovnyye Bratya will kill you to get that. Do you understand? We need to get to a safe place, then we can talk.'

She was already leading him towards the main road. They walked unhurriedly but purposefully, monitoring the few cars that passed. It was a hot afternoon and the tree-lined street offered shade as well as cover. Gary convinced himself that they were safe. The armed police that they heard as they ran from the hotel foyer should by now have captured all their pursuers. But then he remembered that Mangan had broken her promise to come alone, and he worried that they were now in more danger from the police than from the Russians.

They could see buses and taxis running across the top of the road as they came closer to the junction. The contrast with the serenity of the street they were in was as if they were navigating a gently flowing stream that was about to empty into a tidal river. As they turned into the main road, three police cars sped past, sirens wailing, heading for the Strand Hotel. Arina suggested that Gary cross over so that they were walking in the same direction but on opposite sides of the road. It would make them less conspicuous. When they reached the other side of the railway bridge, they could then reunite to drive away in the car that was waiting for them there.

Gary saw two men at a bus stop who looked suspiciously like the kind of Russian heavies they were fleeing from, but the men took no notice of his approach and, just as Gary was about to gesture his concern to Arina, who he knew would have her eye on him from across the road, the overweight duo boarded their bus.

Gary and Arina walked on, separated by the B324 but soon reaching the bridge. As Gary prepared to cross the road and join Arina, a figure appeared from behind a news vendor's stall on her side of the road. Gary just had time to register where he'd seen this man before: on a train heading towards Gipsy Hill station. He recognised the closely cropped hair, thick horn-rimmed glasses and the small blue tattoo on his neck that seemed somehow to have turned to neon – a signal passed at danger.

Gary could see what was about to happen before it happened, but a passing bus blocked his view and prevented him getting to the other side of the road in time.

He shouted a warning just as a shot was fired and, once the bus had passed, Gary saw Arina fall to the pavement. Miranchuk hadn't seen Gary, who was out of his eyeline and running at him from behind as the Russian took aim once more in an effort to finish Arina off. A surge of raw energy sent Gary leaping onto Miranchuk. The impact sent the gangster sprawling, his gun rattling across the pavement into the gutter. Miranchuk, left breathless by the blow, scuttled like a crab towards the pavement edge in a bid to retrieve his weapon, but Gary retained enough of the power surge to leap on Miranchuk's back and, with an arm around his throat, pull him away from where the gun lay.

The two men wrestled ferociously but Gary was no match for the Russian, who didn't carry the disadvantage of having been rushing through the streets for the previous fifteen minutes. Gary could feel a brutal, unremitting strength being turned against him. Within seconds he'd lost the advantage of surprise and was being dragged towards a low parapet forty feet above the busy railway line. As Gary was pulled along, he caught sight of Arina, her leg covered in blood, aiming her gun. But he and Miranchuk were close together as they pushed and punched at one another; too close for Arina to fire at the Russian without the risk of hitting Gary. She collapsed, and as she did so she fired into the air as if attempting to attract somebody's attention.

The report of the gunshot made both men stumble. Gary fell back onto the wide parapet, his head over the edge. Miranchuk's spectacles had already dropped from his face, a face now grotesque in its expression of concentrated violence. As he held his captive's throat in a choking grip he was moving the rest of Gary inexorably towards the precipice. Gary kicked and struggled, realising that soon his attacker would only have to release his grip for Gary to fall onto the tracks below. Breathless and in pain, he could feel his strength fading like air from a punctured balloon. He tried kicking out once more, but his tired legs could only manage a feeble tap against an assailant who'd seemed to have preserved all his energy for this one, final struggle. Gary could hear a train approaching on the tracks below and knew he could soon be under it.

Suddenly, there was another man on the parapet; a bearded man in a hooded top. Miranchuk, looking down at his victim as an eagle looks down upon the prey in its talons, hadn't seen him, but Gary had. He saw the bearded man hook a piece of wire around Miranchuk's throat while whispering something to him in Russian. Gary watched his assailant's face contort as he was dragged along the parapet away from his intended victim, allowing Gary to roll away from the edge. Miranchuk was desperately trying to get some purchase on his attacker, to find some point of vulnerability; but the bearded man remained expertly positioned behind and above him, out of range of the wild and frantically flailing fists and elbows aimed towards him: and all the time the wire was tightening, forcing Miranchuk to abandon his attempted blows and reach instinctively up to his neck in a futile attempt to loosen the grip. In all probability the life had already been choked out of Miranchuk by the time he was sent hurtling over the side. And if the fall didn't kill him, the approaching 4 p.m. train from Victoria to Gatwick certainly would.

There was an eerie silence. Gary eventually forced himself upright, manoeuvring his body carefully off the parapet and back onto solid ground. The bearded man had disappeared, taking Arina with him. All that was left of her were bloodstains on the pavement.

A crowd of spectators had gathered, and a taxi driver was asking Gary if he was all right. He was; and he could feel his iPhone secure under the buttoned flap of his back pocket. Then he heard the jarring tone of approaching police sirens and within minutes a woman with a scarf draped across her shoulder was taking Gary's arm to lead him away.

Later, in the police car on the way to New Scotland Yard, he'd show Detective Superintendent Mangan a photograph on his phone and she'd spend the rest of the journey in shocked contemplation of the image it revealed.

37

Three months later

The drab October weather was more winter than autumn as Gary Nelson made his way to New Scotland Yard. In the aftermath of the confrontation at the Strand Hotel three months ago, he'd spent many hours under gentle interrogation within its walls telling the police everything they wanted to know; but they weren't telling him the only thing *he* wanted to know – how was Arina?

Gary had been keen to get back to some semblance of normality following his second near-death experience. On the Saturday after his ordeal he'd even gone to see Melissa in Swansea with Knuckles and Jason. Newly released from three days of questioning, he couldn't think of anything better to do, other than mope around feeling gloomy. The 'Met Triumphs Over Russian Gangsters' story was already all over the papers.

Under the headline 'GANG LEADER DEAD AND HENCHMEN IN CUSTODY AFTER SHOOT-OUT ON LONDON RAILWAY BRIDGE', *The Sun* had reported that:

> In one dramatic showdown, heroic Detective Superintendent Louise Mangan nabbed the Russkies responsible for four murders, an attempted abduction and multiple other crimes.

On that weekend in Wales, Jason, who'd been a shadow of his old bombastic self, had made an emotional confession. The four housemates were dining in a Swansea restaurant and Gary had been telling his friends about 'Lilia', how they'd met and most of what happened (leaving out the more intimate details). Knuckles intervened to explain Gary's involvement in rescuing Melissa when Jason suddenly burst into tears. Through much sobbing and the tactile encouragement of his fellow diners he admitted his role as Granat's snout and told them about his terrifying experience at the airport. He said that he'd arranged and paid for this weekend because of his sense of guilt.

Gary freely offered the forgiveness that Jason tearfully begged for and Knuckles said he'd have done the same to get a rent reduction and a free dinner at the Queens Hotel, but Melissa was furious. Given that it was Jason's phone call that had led to her being snatched off the street, this was hardly surprising. Jason agreed to repeat his confession to the police as soon as they returned to London.

Now, twelve weeks later, Melissa was back at 27 Mount Street and life was returning to normal, except for a noticeable change in the dynamic. Jason's position as unofficial head of household had passed to Gary. Nowhere was this more apparent than in the attitude of Melissa, whose previous prickly resistance to Gary's charms had morphed into an affectionate concern for his welfare.

But Gary only had one woman on his mind. He was

now on his way to find out what happened to her, for Louise Mangan to fulfil the promise she'd made to reveal everything the police and security service knew once they'd had time to piece it all together.

Mangan had remained in contact with Rachel Nelson. According to Gary's mother, the Detective Superintendent was tipped for promotion and her two detective constables, Tonkin and Din, had been nominated for a police medal. Rachel and Louise had become firm friends, talking on the telephone at least twice a week. It was Rachel who told her son that Mangan was now ready to brief him.

When he reached New Scotland Yard on that drizzly day in October, Gary was immediately shown to a room where Mangan was waiting alone. Gary thought she looked drained and anxious. Her long brown hair was piled into a bun and she was wearing a sombre, dark dress, belted at the waist, with plain, flat slip-on shoes. While she greeted him with genuine affection, Gary could tell she wasn't relishing this encounter.

'Thanks for doing this,' he said as they settled on either side of a long teak table.

'It's the least we can do, given all you've done for us. Can I just warn you though – some of this might be difficult for you.'

Without further ceremony, Mangan pressed a button on a small handheld gizmo and a photograph of Arina appeared on a screen at one end of the oblong room.

'This is Natalia Tarasova, previously known to us as Arina Kaplin and, I believe, Lilia Zinchenko at one stage of your adventures together.' Mangan smiled in an attempt to lighten the mood, but Gary stared impassively at the photograph. Arina looked exactly as she had when he'd first seen her on the train into work, her long blonde hair once again flowing down to those slim, elegant shoulders.

'She is, as you know, Ukrainian, the daughter of Captain Roman Tarasova, an officer in the Ukrainian army, sympathetic to the Orange Revolution and active in trying to secure its success.

'In 2006 he travelled to Moscow to meet two men who he thought were sympathisers prepared to help ensure that the Russian people understood what was happening in Ukraine, and perhaps pass him military secrets about Russia's intentions towards his country.

'Captain Tarasova was never seen alive again. His body was pulled from the Volga a few days after his arrival. The Ukrainians tell us that one of the men he went to meet was Denis Smolnikov.'

A photograph of Smolnikov flashed onto the screen.

'She told me about her father being murdered, but not about Smolnikov being involved,' Gary said quietly.

'That's because she had to maintain the pretence of being a waitress caught up in the events at the Strand,' said Mangan. 'Whereas, in reality she caused them. Arina Kaplin, the illegal immigrant who'd found work at the Strand, was the persona she'd adopted as an agent of the SBU, the Ukrainian secret service. She came to London with one purpose only – to assassinate Denis Smolnikov.'

Gary shifted in his chair but said nothing.

'As I said, this may be difficult for you, but whereas some of what I tell you is informed conjecture, this bit is beyond refute. Our security services have a good working relationship with their Ukrainian counterparts thanks to Britain's strong condemnation of Russia over the annexation of Crimea. The Ukrainians have no reason to lie about all this. Indeed, they're immensely proud of their achievement and of Natalia, as we must learn to call her.

'She wanted to avenge the murder of her father,' Mangan continued, 'and so motive matched opportunity because the Ukrainians wanted to strike at a prominent Russian target, someone close to the President, who had actively worked against their country. The fact that Smolnikov was a celebrity in Russia was an added bonus. However, it had to happen abroad so that the Russian authorities couldn't cover it up, and to maximise its international impact.

'They knew that Smolnikov visited London often, that he used the Strand Hotel for his regular business meetings and that he considered this city to be safe territory for his activities and so was less likely to be on his guard.

'Natalia Tarasova was smuggled into England over a year ago. One other SBU agent came separately, a man known as Viktor Rubchenko, an experienced officer in an elite SBU specialist group called Alpha. He masterminded the entire operation. Natalia didn't know him, all she had was a telephone number, an address and an entry code, only to be used after the assassination when both agents needed to leave the country. Smolnikov was a hugely significant target and they couldn't run the risk of any messages being intercepted, so they communicated in code. This is where our experts have had to use a bit of conjecture.

'The SBU obviously don't want us to know all their secrets, but if we piece together what you told us, what the Ukrainians have revealed and what we knew already, we're convinced that the code related to the way she applied her morning make-up.

'It wasn't difficult for Natalia to get a job at the Strand Hotel. Once in post nothing was to happen for a year. During that time, she would fully adopt her waitress role as Arina, learning more about the hotel, Smolnikov's visits and the arrangements that were made for them, for instance the beverages that were supplied, the food he ate. Natalia played her role brilliantly. She is an accomplished actress. If her father hadn't been killed, she'd probably be a movie star in her country by now.

'On the first anniversary of her arrival, early in July this year, contact via the code commenced. Her mobile phone, the one that you told us is now in the Thames, had been adapted so that when she switched it to selfie mode it transmitted to Viktor. The main element of the code seems to have been whether, at a set time every morning as her train approached Clapham Junction, she applied lipstick or mascara. There were a couple of false starts when Smolnikov was in the hotel but "waitress Arina" wasn't going to be able to get anywhere near him. These were lipstick days.

'But they were patient. This was a long-term project. They could afford to wait, confident that one day the stars would align. That day came on 10 July – mascara day.'

'But why apply her make-up on the train? Surely it would have been better to send the message before leaving home,' Gary said.

'True,' replied Mangan, 'but as you'll have noticed, lots of women these days like to finish making-up as they're travelling to work, so it's not remotely unusual or suspicious, although it might have been when I was young. More importantly, the timing had to be right. Poisons may be easy to administer but they leave a trail and the crucial thing here was to avoid any sign of the stuff coming in or out of the Strand. They wanted this to look as if Smolnikov had poisoned himself by drinking from a cup meant for his victim.

'As soon as he saw mascara being applied rather than lipstick, Viktor knew he had a couple of hours to get to the hotel with the poison. If the mascara message was sent the previous evening or before she left home, they ran the risk of train delays or cancellations interfering with the plan. I think you have some idea of how unreliable the train service can be on that particular line. Viktor could have arrived at the hotel while Natalia was still struggling into work. That's why it was vital that she sent the message as the train reached Clapham Junction with everything running to time.

'So, on 10 July it all went like clockwork. Viktor knew the mascara sign meant he'd find Smolnikov in the bar, restaurant or one of the two reception rooms, holding court at some meeting or other where "Arina Kaplin" was serving teas and coffees. She left a Strand Hotel manager's blazer hanging on the coat stand in reception ready for him to put on before strolling into whichever room Smolnikov was in and passing a phial of polonium-210 to Natalia, which she then emptied into the coffee Smolnikov was drinking, handing the empty phial back to Viktor, who left the room, dumped the jacket and returned to his flat in Battersea.'

'Which is where I saw him with his throat cut,' Gary interrupted.

'You certainly came across the gruesome sight of a man with his throat cut, but it wasn't Viktor Rubchenko.'

Gary had shown no sign of being shocked by any of these revelations until now.

'But Arina thought it was Viktor.'

'I suppose she might have. After all, the only time she'd have actually seen Viktor was at the hotel, fleetingly, as he passed her the phial and retrieved it empty a few minutes later. The story she told you about them being trafficked into the country with a truckload of agricultural equipment was a total fabrication. I wish I could share the charitable view that she genuinely thought the dead guy was Viktor. But I'm pretty sure she knew it wasn't. Viktor had a beard and the dead guy didn't. Granted, he could have shaved it off in the days since Smolnikov's poisoning but all the evidence is that her reaction was a typical example of her nimble thinking, pretending it was Viktor Rubchenko for your benefit. Did you see the mobile phone that she claimed to have taken from the flat?'

Gary confirmed he hadn't.

'And you didn't see her throw anything into the Thames?'

Another confirmation.

'Viktor's mobile phone had not been left behind. After murdering the man who'd come to murder him, Viktor left the flat, not long before you arrived, with two phones, his own and that of his assailant. Natalia knew her phone was secure and that the only person who could track her through it was Viktor. She couldn't tell you the truth about him, so it was best to pretend she no longer had a mobile phone rather than risk you finding out that she could still be contacted by Viktor. It probably ended up in that big make-up pouch of hers, to be checked in the night while you were asleep.'

'So, if the body wasn't Viktor's, whose was it?' Gary asked.

'An unknown Russian FSB agent is all I can tell you. The one bit of the Ukrainian assassination plan that went wrong was Miranchuk's suspicions about Viktor in that manager's jacket. He'd never seen him in the Strand before. He detailed Morozov, who, unknown to him, had infiltrated Krovnyye Bratya on behalf of the FSB, to follow Viktor. Morozov delayed reporting the address back to Miranchuk until he'd informed his FSB masters. They left it a few days before sending one of their agents to take care of Viktor, unaware that he was an SBU agent or how dangerous he was. This agent went to the flat in

Battersea carrying the tape with Krovnyye Bratya written across it as part of a crude plan to finger them for the murder. Viktor killed the would-be assassin and then took the opportunity to fake his own death.

'Although the flat was rented in his name, he'd been careful not to be seen going in and out. We had no reason to doubt that the body was his. Some documents identifying Rubchenko had been planted on the corpse, and Viktor's final flourish was to tape the Krovnyye Bratya label across his victim's mouth, which added to the FSBs belief that their man had succeeded in his mission.

'As I said,' Mangan went on, 'the man known as Viktor Rubchenko is one of Ukraine's elite Alpha team – their top man. Before disposing of the FSB guy, he tortured him in ways you won't want to know about, to discover the code words FSB agents use when contacting one another. He then assumed his victim's identity, taking his phone and texting back to FSB that he'd accomplished his mission but would need to lie low for a bit. He told them that before killing Viktor he'd extracted an important lead about where the missing waitress was, and that they could safely leave her capture to him. They fell for it. Viktor was not only able to tap into some information about what was going on in the Russian secret service, he'd also convinced them that they needn't pursue Natalia because he was on the case.'

Mangan paused before continuing. 'As for Natalia, she'd undertaken this mission knowing that if either agent was identified, captured or killed there would be no rescue operation. She knew that Viktor had the false passports and he alone had devised the escape route. It didn't matter if he was dead or alive, once she saw the body in the flat, she knew she was on her own – except that she had you.'

'But if she thought Viktor might be alive, why stay with me?' Gary asked.

'Because for all she knew Viktor might have been halfway to Kiev, having decided to abort the operation. They were supposed to meet up to plan the next stage of their mission in the days immediately following the poisoning, but after we'd detained her she'd been unable to get back to her flat to get the things she needed. Your meeting on that late train to Gipsy Hill at least meant that she didn't fall into the hands of Krovnyye Bratya but it also messed up the timing of her liaison with Viktor. She needed help and you were pretty insistent, from what you've told us, about providing it. But Viktor hadn't gone back to Ukraine. He was tracking you both every step of the way.

'When Natalia went to her flat in Sutton, it was Viktor who finished off Albert Turner after she'd driven off in the Parcelforce van. He probably hoped that she'd get into the Ukrainian embassy, but as we know, that went slightly awry.'

'Because I messed things up,' Gary interjected. 'But what I can't understand is why they didn't just arrange to meet up so that they could return to Ukraine together.'

'Well, they did eventually. He'd been waiting in Euston station and met up with her on the train to Liverpool. They got off at the next stop and returned to London, but they didn't go back to Ukraine as their mission had yet to be completed. Incidentally, when they were reunited Viktor told the FSB that he'd captured the waitress and was in the process of interrogating her. They believed him, and in turn so did we because that's what the FSB told our spooks. There was no need to continue searching for Arina Kaplin because the Russians had her in custody.'

'But why didn't they go back to Ukraine? What was this other part of their mission? They'd killed Smolnikov. Wasn't that what they came to do?'

'No, that was mission half-accomplished. There was another man involved in Captain Tarasova's murder.'

'Let me guess,' Gary said. 'The guy who tried to kill me on the bridge was the other one they were after?'

'You are a very astute young man. But to explain about Miranchuk I need to rewind a little. The important point to bear in mind is that far from being upset about Denis Smolnikov, as the Russians pretended to be, they were secretly delighted. The man was starting to be an embarrassment, and for him to have apparently poisoned himself by drinking the wrong coffee in a London hotel was the perfect solution to the problem that Smolnikov was becoming. In addition, the FSB in London is under new management. This very clever young man – so much younger than the usual old fogies who the Russians used to promote to these positions – is now in charge, working from the Russian embassy.'

A new photograph appeared on the screen, one taken surreptitiously by the security service, of a slim, well-dressed man. 'This man's name is Ivan Ilkun,' said Mangan. 'He's been more open with our spooks than any of his predecessors, not least because he believes us to be on the same side in wanting to dismantle Krovnyye Bratya.'

'You talk as if you suspect that's not quite true,' Gary said.

'Oh, it's certainly true that we want to destroy KB, but they just want to change the leadership so that the organisation comes back under FSB control. Krovnyye Bratya blundered badly when they killed Sergei Dzyuba, who you'll remember was the other man poisoned at the Strand that morning. We told you all about him during your three days here in July.'

Gary nodded to confirm that he did indeed remember. 'You mean the journalist who they killed by spiking his mineral water?'

'Yes; he had been given a guarantee of safety from the President. His death was the catalyst that forced the FSB to act against the organisation's leadership. Anton Sidrenko, the leader of Krovnyye Bratya, is currently in a Moscow jail facing a sentence of at least twenty years for fraud, corruption and tax evasion. His two immediate subordinates died in what were meant to look like a suicide and a road accident.

'Ilkun convinced Miranchuk to arrange the deaths of those two men, Granat and Podkolzin, on the understanding that Miranchuk would then take control. But, Ilkun had plans for somebody completely different to lead Krovnyye Bratya – a woman called Maria Paseka,

Sidrenko's wife and, apparently, Miranchuk's lover. Once Miranchuk had exceeded his usefulness by clearing a path to the throne he would need to be disposed of. Your rescuer saved Ilkun the trouble.'

'My rescuer being Viktor Rubchenko.'

Mangan nodded.

'He was part of the crowd that ended up at the Strand Hotel,' said Gary. 'I know you had no control over him being there, but what about your lot? You promised to come alone.'

Mangan pressed another photograph into service. A picture of a uniformed police officer appeared on the screen. It was the one taken covertly on Marilyn Kelsey's doorstep. The one that Gary had obtained and passed to Mangan.

'This is Assistant Commissioner Brian Baker, who I've known for a long time and who was the last person I'd have suspected of corruption. He has an impressive police record and was due to retire on a full pension next year. Now, thanks to the information you provided, he'll probably be commencing a substantial prison sentence after his trial early next year. He's admitted everything; was relieved to get it off his chest apparently. Twenty-three years ago, Brian was involved in a fraud case involving a Russian businessman operating in the UK not long after Russia emerged from behind the iron curtain. Brian was offered a wodge of cash by this guy to close down a line of enquiry. Like a fool, he took it. He says his mother was very ill and needed an expensive operation in America.

'The Russian businessman was Anton Sidrenko, who

recorded the entire transaction. Within the past year or so, Sidrenko made contact again. By now he was the leader of Krovnyye Bratya and Brian was an Assistant Commissioner. Brian was blackmailed into becoming an agent for one of the most vicious Russian criminal gangs.

'Sidrenko realised that the fewer people who knew about Brian the better. However, he also knew that he needed someone trustworthy within the organisation to be aware of Brian's identity as a failsafe. Reluctant to let his two senior colleagues in on the secret in case they became rivals, he chose Miranchuk.

'Everyone in KB knew they had a Met officer under their control but only Miranchuk and Sidrenko knew who it was. If you'd shown this photograph to your Arina she'd have recognised the police officer who told her she could leave the Strand Hotel when we were doing the re-enactment. You became involved with her that evening on the late train to Gipsy Hill. Brian knew that Miranchuk would be outside the Strand waiting; and it was Miranchuk who ordered Baker to pay that visit to Marilyn Kelsey. Brian must have thought there was little risk involved. Even if there'd been CCTV outside the house, it wouldn't have been much of a problem. Your Ms Kelsey was hardly likely to contact the police about a visit by the police. Only you knew the significance of that visit and thanks to you and Natalia we have this very clear piece of irrefutable evidence.'

Gary shifted in his seat. 'Is she dead?' he asked softly.

'Let me finish the story; nearly there now,' Mangan replied, pressing the button once more.

The photograph of Brian Baker was replaced by one of somebody in a face mask. Gary only had to see those grey eyes to know who they belonged to.

'Here's Natalia once again, this time in the reception area of the Strand Hotel. So far as I knew, I was coming alone, as promised, but I needed authorisation from the Commissioner to meet you there. I insisted to him that I go alone, and he agreed but unbeknown to me and with the best of intentions, he told his deputy about our meeting and that you were going to pass me information about a police informer. She blabbed to a small group of officers that included Brian Baker. Brian probably contacted Miranchuk immediately. He then picked up his four henchmen before dashing across to the Strand Hotel. You'd texted Arina to tell her that's where you were staying, so Natalia probably went there to make sure you were okay. Meanwhile Viktor Rubchenko was keeping tabs on Miranchuk – when he diverted to the Strand, so did Viktor. He contacted Natalia, who prepared your escape route. That heavy skip just by the back door of the hotel didn't get there by accident.

'After you'd been led through that emergency exit, my guys had enough fire power to corner Morozov and the other three, but Miranchuk must have guessed what was about to happen. He'd left the hotel to head you off. You know what happened next.'

'Viktor saved my life,' said Gary.

'True; and you saved Natalia's. It was incredibly brave of you to throw yourself at Miranchuk the way you did.'

'Please tell me now – is she dead or alive?'

'We don't know, is the honest answer. She was leading you towards a vehicle they'd parked in a side street close to the bridge. Rather than use it to help you escape from Krovnyye Bratya as they'd planned, Viktor must have pressed it into service to get Natalia to the Ukrainian embassy. Viktor would have known that Krovnyye Bratya were unlikely to still be staking it out. All the turmoil caused by the arrest of Sidrenko and the deaths of Granat and Podkolzin diverted their attention. The Ukrainians, helpful as they've been, are saying nothing about Natalia. All we know, because of the stains on the pavement, is that she lost a lot of blood.'

Gary's mood darkened but he composed himself enough to ask, 'But we do know that Viktor is safely back in Kiev?'

'No, we don't. We're unsure about Natalia but we're certain that Viktor stayed here to finish the job.'

'But Miranchuk is dead. You told me he was the one they stayed behind to deal with.'

'No, Gary, you said that. All I said was that you're very astute and you are. You followed our reasoning exactly. Even the Russians believed it. The FSB is so confident that Viktor is no longer around they've just withdrawn the personal protection from all their senior officers. They believe that everything is back to normal.'

'And why do you think they're wrong?' Gary asked.

'Because yesterday we received a piece of intelligence from our guys in Moscow that altered our assumptions. The other man with Smolnikov when Roman Tarasova,

Natalia's father, was killed wasn't Miranchuk – it was Ivan Ilkun.'

At about that time, in Knightsbridge, the head of the London bureau of the FSB was attending his weekly private communion at the Russian Orthodox Cathedral of the Dormition of the Mother of God and All Saints.

Walking solemnly to the altar, he noticed a veiled woman lighting candles down one aisle of the church. Women were often here performing menial tasks, heads covered in accordance with tradition. He noticed nothing unusual about this one apart from a pronounced limp.

The priest emerged from the robing room. Ilkun didn't recognise him, but there again, he mused, one robed and bearded prelate tends to look very much like another.

The dapper spy knelt down ready to receive the body and blood of Christ the Lord. The priest dipped a spoon into the chalice of bread and wine before placing it into the worshipper's mouth. It would take Ivan Ilkun two days to die from the 40 micrograms of polonium-210 he swallowed in prayer that day.

38

Nine months later

On a warm July evening, Gary Nelson and his mother were sharing a bottle of wine after a good dinner. It was the night before Rachel's wedding to Will the Plumber; the last night that mother and son would ever spend at this house on the Mandeville Estate that they'd grown up in, albeit a generation apart. The house was up for sale. When they returned from their honeymoon in Gran Canaria, Rachel would move in with Will in his three-bedroom bungalow in High Wycombe.

Rachel had suggested a 'last supper' because she felt a profound sense of disconnect; not just from all the years she'd spent in this house, but from her freedom as a single woman and her status as a determinedly single mother. Gary had obviously long ceased to be dependent upon her, but it was something that had been hard to accept. Having made such an emotional investment in her son, she'd found it difficult to acknowledge the diminishing returns.

As for Will the Plumber, Rachel didn't love him but, as she'd explained to her friend Louise Mangan, she saw him as a safe haven. Trustworthy, steady and considerate, Will would be a reliable companion and that was more important to Rachel than having a passionate relationship. She wondered if she'd previously avoided marriage because of some subconscious commitment to the man who'd fathered her child; as if knowing the truth about what happened to him had released her from a kind of spiritual constraint.

For she did now know what became of Daniel Martin and in addition to a last supper, this dinner, on the eve of her wedding, was also the perfect opportunity to tell her son. It was Tobias Parnaby who'd discovered a truth that though tragic was ultimately consoling. The indefatigable dentist had gone to Hendon by arrangement to meet a Mr Faraday, the long-serving police tutor. Using the dates that Parnaby had given him, Faraday had searched through the files of official photographs taken of every intake since the college opened. When he saw the photograph from the summer of 1992, he remembered Daniel Martin (or 'Martin Daniels' as the official record still mistakenly named him). Daniel was in the back row, tall and handsome, the regulation helmet covering his shock of dark curly hair.

Mr Parnaby had explained why it was important to find Daniel, and Faraday was able to ascertain that he was no longer with the Met. Neither was he with any of the other forty-two police forces in the country. Intrigued by Parnaby's quest, the tutor asked if he could work with him to try to find his former pupil. Eventually, after a few months, they tracked down Daniel's sister, Sandra. It was through her that they uncovered the facts.

Daniel Martin hadn't remained with the police for long. His sister described him as a restless individual forever seeking new experiences. He'd resigned from the Met two weeks after finishing the course at Hendon (and six weeks after the dance at Aylesbury College) to take what he told his sister would be a gap-year working his way around the globe. Sandra had kept the postcards he'd sent to his parents – from Paris, Athens, Istanbul – in the early days, and ever more remote locations thereafter.

Six months after leaving, he'd reached Malaysia where, relaxing on a beach, he heard a cry for help. A woman and her child had swum out too far and were struggling against high waves and a strong current. Daniel went to their rescue, bringing the child ashore before going back for the mother. He succeeded in getting her into shallow water but was sucked back out by the drag on a freak wave that broke just as Daniel had ushered the woman to safety. His body was washed ashore on a Malaysian island three days later.

The authorities were slow in identifying Daniel and even slower conveying the news to his family. The remoteness of the location, Daniel's peripatetic lifestyle and the long delay combined to suppress the story's news value. Sandra said she'd been dismayed by the lack of publicity given her brother's heroics; only one small paragraph had eventually appeared in their local north London paper.

Rachel Nelson conveyed all this to her son over dinner, showing him a copy of the class photograph from Hendon Police College, the first time Gary had ever seen his father. Content as he was with his fatherless upbringing, Gary was naturally interested in the life (and death) of Daniel Martin. However, he didn't realise the significance of the timeline until Rachel pointed it out to him.

'Daniel died while you were still in the womb,' she explained quietly. 'Which means that my selfishness didn't deprive you of a father, the ocean did.'

'And he died saving two lives,' Gary added, 'having already created mine. The man's a legend.'

Having got this weight off her mind, Rachel turned to the more frivolous issue of her wedding. She ran through the reception guest list for Gary's benefit.

'Your grandmother will be there with her husband, of course, and Mr Parnaby, who you must remember to thank for all his efforts on your behalf.'

'On your behalf, Mum. The guy adores you.'

'No, he doesn't. He adores Mrs Parnaby and she'll be there as well,' Rachel said, pithily disposing of what she regarded as one of her son's mischievous fantasies.

Louise Mangan, now an Assistant Commissioner, would be coming with one of her daughters, and two of Gary's former housemates would be there, Jason having declined the invitation.

Knuckles was coming with his boyfriend, Calvin. Gary had already heard the story of how they'd met. Knuckles had been a gofer on a show called *Love Estuary*, which involved twelve tanned and lovely young people – an equal number of men and women – being marooned on a fort in the Thames Estuary to see who paired with whom. Unbeknown to the producers, one of the contestants, Calvin, had already paired with Knuckles off-screen during preparations for the programme. After Calvin had been one of the first to be evicted from the show, the relationship had developed and Calvin moved into 27 Mount Street, taking one of the vacancies created when Gary and Melissa moved out to live together in a flat close to Gipsy Hill station.

'Remind me when Mel is arriving?' asked Rachel. Gary's girlfriend had been visiting her parents in Swansea and would be arriving the next day.

'Duncan's picking her up from the station at 10.30 to bring her straight here so she can get ready,' Gary said.

'That's a bit tight. The ceremony at the register office is at one o'clock.'

Gary filled their glasses with the last of the wine and said, 'Don't worry, she'll have done her make-up on the train.'

Rachel was about to say 'just like that Ukrainian girl used to do', but stopped herself in time. She was fond of Melissa but knew that fondness was about the extent of Gary's feelings towards her. Just as her son knew that she was marrying Will the Plumber more from convenience than love, so she knew that Gary's heart remained firmly fixed elsewhere.

Some time ago, Louise Mangan had given Gary a supplementary briefing on the assassination of Ivan Ilkun. The three Russian Orthodox priests who'd been found bound and gagged in a back room of the cathedral in Knightsbridge had testified that two people were involved, one of them a woman. Arina was alive. It was a piece of information that filled Gary with joy and hope in equal measure. Having asked if she might still be in the country, Mangan had told him that the spooks were certain that Viktor Rubchenko and Natalia Tarasova were both now back in Kiev.

Rachel had hoped that Gary's fascination with the Ukrainian woman would gradually fade, allowing his relationship with Melissa to develop further. Gary must have had enough of adventure. Mel was the kind of girl that a man could settle down with, but Rachel couldn't tell him that. She and her son could discuss most things, but Gary's relationships were off limits.

A letter had arrived at the house in Aylesbury a while ago with a Ukrainian stamp, addressed to 'Gary Nelson, in the care of'. Rachel knew it was from Arina (as Gary continued to call her), who'd know the address having lived there for four days last summer. Rachel hadn't mentioned it to Gary and she'd contemplated destroying it in her son's best interests. Unable to do anything so drastic and underhand, she'd placed it in a drawer hoping that time would dim the flame of his passion. But on this special evening, when past evasions were being confronted, she felt unable to continue with this one any longer.

'Oh, this letter came last week,' she said, retrieving it from the kitchen drawer.

The date stamp was illegible, allowing Rachel's white lie to go unchallenged. In truth, the letter had been in the drawer for at least two months.

'I usually forward them to you in London, but as you were coming over . . .'

Gary was loading the dishwasher and showed no inclination to open the letter. They finished the evening with the unopened envelope still lying where Rachel had placed it on the kitchen table.

Gary took it with him when he went to bed and later, alone in his room, the room that still held delicious memories of Arina, the room he would never sleep in again, Gary carefully opened the envelope. The only thing it contained was a playing card – the King of Hearts.

ACKNOWLEDGEMENTS

After four memoirs this is my first work of fiction. The two forms are very different, not least because the memoirist relies heavily on the memory whilst the writer of fiction relies mainly on imagination.

I formulated the basic idea behind this novel some years ago, but imagination alone couldn't provide the background knowledge I needed to turn the idea into a proper story. Luke Harding's *A Very Expensive Poison* taught me a great deal about the use of polonium as a murder weapon and the superlative *Putin's People* by Catherine Belton provided the reassurance that, however far my imagination roamed, nothing I wrote would seem far-fetched against the reality of Russia today.

I've never needed the advice and talent of my wonderful agent, Clare Alexander, more than with this book – and I received it, in spades, along with her expertise and encouragement. Alex Clarke, Ella Gordon and Serena Arthur at Wildfire have also been super-committed from the off and through them I received the expert help of editor Martin Fletcher and copy editor Jill Cole. On a personal level, my wife Carolyn was a constant source of encouragement. She read the first drafts, made sensible suggestions and, above all, convinced me that it was worth carrying on.

Finally, my thanks to Reece Hanson from Language is Everything for providing me with the Russian translations I needed.

Sign up to the brand-new Alan Johnson newsletter for book updates, extracts, and exclusive year-round content from Alan Johnson himself:

https://www.headline.co.uk/landing-page/
alan-johnson-newsletter/